MARCHE'S MADNESS

The Week From Hell

Susan Ronayne

P.O. Box 195
Paola, Kansas 66071
www.bullybookspublishing.com

Marche's Madness © 2009 by Susan Ronayne

Published by Bully Books
P.O. Box 195
Paola, Kansas, 66071
www.bullybookspublishing.com

Printed and bound in the United States of America
First edition

Cover design by Tara Houston-Sawyers

Professional printing by
Technical Communication Services
North Kansas City, Missouri

ISBN: 978-0-615-29896-2

Thanks and Dedication

As an aspiring writer and paranormal enthusiast, I extend my sincere gratitude to those individuals who have encouraged and inspired me along the way. Whether you were willing to read a chapter, listen to an idea, join me on a ghost tour, or simply show a little interest in what I was up to...you have no idea how much your support and companionship have meant. Special thanks to my son, Dennis, whose supportive imagination knows no bounds and whose own writing abilities never cease to amaze me. Also, to my daughter Erin who was always willing to read a chapter or listen to a new idea. To my husband Dave, who provided both technological and moral support, as well as the liberty to pursue my own dreams. My appreciation is also extended to Tara for her amazing artistic abilities; in addition to Liz, Mart and Jon, for their project review and suggestions.

Although writing is largely a solitary endeavor, I was assuredly never alone on the course of this venture. I dedicate this book and my deepest affections to my most devoted supporters, Budwizer and Dexter. Over the years my bully boys have serenaded me with their snores as I wrote. They've provided comic relief, and reminded me when it was time for a much needed break. Holding vigil near my chair on late nights and over long weekends; they were the utmost loyal companions as I typed or edited the hours away. Budwizer, I know that you are drooling upon me from heaven with that rascally bulldog grin on your handsome face. I still miss you everyday. And, my darling, darling Dexter, who is presently by my side...wake up! We can take our walk now!

Susan – August 2009

"...because our world is comprised of more than the human mind can possibly conceive."

Prologue

It Would Begin

1647

I stood up and watched him over the edge of the table, chewing on my lip, enthralled by what I had just done and searching my conscience for a hint of guilt. Richard was writhing on the floor, dangerously close to the sooty hearth and the flickering fire, which provided the only light in the cold room because we had run out of lamp oil and could not afford more.

He kicked and clawed and spun in the dirt. Perspiring, convulsing, face red, veins straining, eyes bulging at me in disbelief until his stare grew vacant and his body stilled. It seemed to last forever. Not because it was hard for me to watch, but because I was afraid the children might awake and see. I didn't need any witnesses.

Then, out into the night we went. I drug him by the heels of his boots, trying not to trip over the muddy, frayed hem of my dress as I tugged him inch by inch from the house, through the tiny grass-bare yard, and down the slope into the denser woods.

In spite of the chilly spring night, I could not take my shawl, or a torch. My hands were too full of my task. No matter. I was soon sweating profusely from exertion, and handily relying on the bright moon, which winked between budding branches, to guide me to the spot I had already chosen.

Deep into the forest, but not far from the road, beneath a large cedar, where the ground was already soft, I beat Richard's head with a stone, just in case there was any question. Then, I threw the rock away, down the hillside. This would be my husband's final resting place. This would be the spot where Richard would rot away into forever, hopefully unbeknownst to the rest of the village, if I were to be successful.

Wild dogs howled in the distance. Yipping and yapping, as I rolled him into the shallow hole I had dug the night before. Then I began to fill it up, first working with the small shovel from our barn that I had left hidden behind the tree trunk, and then on my hands and knees because the scooping was faster and more effective.

Within the hour it was done, and within two my raggedy dress was clean and hanging up to dry as I lay alone on our bed of straw and down. Alone. For the first time in eight years. Alone, and glad of it. My secret safe within me.

* * *

"Mistress Powell, what say you?"

"I am not guilty, sir," Rachel Powell stared the magistrate square in the eye. "I swear it. T'was a band of robbers, to be sure. I swear that I thought Richard had gone away for good. Leav'n me and the babies to fend for ourselves."

"My son would not!" The elder Mistress Powell jumped to her feet, her face red with indignation. "She lies!"

Rachel scowled over her shoulder at her mother-in-law then swiftly turned back to the man serving as judge. She wielded wide, guiltless eyes. If she were convincing, he would be her savoir, and only he. She must concentrate on him. "Sir, with no disrespect to my husband's family, the town knows Richard to have been a wayward drunk, though he'd also been a church going man. Too often he would stay out late…spending all our money and coming home full of ale, frightening me and the children. *We* lived this life with him...not her. I cannot deny that a mother would not wish to believe it…but it is true. I am no murderess, sir. I beg you to spare me from these accusations and allow me to raise my children in peace."

"She lies!" Maggie Powell bellowed again, as fellow churchwomen sought to comfort her. A murmur rose throughout the crowd then fell as Magistrate Bishop's brow furrowed and he began to rap his gavel sharply.

"Quiet! Quiet or you shall all be removed!"

He waited for the tiny meeting hall to settle down then began to review the facts. "All I have here is a man, missing for weeks, found deceased from apparent blows to the head, beneath a tree, in a shallow grave, near a well traveled road. I have no witnesses. I have no reason to believe that Rachel Powell murdered your son as you accuse, Mistress Powell. For a woman to kill and bury her husband in such a manner, leaving her small children alone to fend for themselves while she carried out this deed, a mile from her home…I find it unthinkable, and unbelievable."

The elderly Mistress Powell swooned in her seat, while her red faced husband twisted his hat with his hands in angry disbelief. "There has been mischief on that road before," the judge continued. "Poor old Richard was also known to imbibe a bit too much…that much is true. I cannot condemn this young woman, leaving three orphans, without sufficient evidence. Rachel Rebekah Powell, I find you…not guilty." As the assemblage gasped and a roar of talk began, the magistrate issued his verdict with a brisk crack of his gavel and hurried from the room to the chamber beyond. His decision had not been a popular one, he knew, but the fact remained that there was no evidence, and the law must be his guide.

Rachel ran out the side door leaving the shouts of "murderer", "whore", "devil" and "liar" behind her. There, Sarah, her only friend in the world, waited with Rachel's three small children. They all ducked behind the meeting building that served as the village's church, school and court and slipped between two sheds as the front doors burst open and an outraged mob exited onto the street.

"You are free!" Sarah cried. The children clung to Rachel's skirt.

"I am for now," Rachel smiled, then sobered. "For now. But we must go, Sarah. We cannot stay here. Richard's parents were never friends to me and I truly fear for my life…no matter the verdict."

"Where will you go? You have no family. You have no one to support you and the children."

"Nor did I before, now did I Sarah? Worthless husband that Richard was!" Rachel felt intense hatred for her late husband well up within her and she took a deep breath to calm herself. "We will walk a few villages away and I'll find work, sewing or cooking. The church will take pity on us there and we will start a new life. It will be hard, but I will be free. Perhaps, someday, there will be a good man in my future. I cannot stay here. You know I cannot."

Sarah brushed a tear from her eye, nodding sadly. The two friends hugged briskly.

"I shall miss you Sarah, and I thank you for your friendship. Now go, before the entire town turns against you over me."

Suppressing a sob, Sarah checked the street for passersby, then slipped out from behind the building and made her way toward the center of town alone. Rachel shushed her children and waited a fair amount of time before she did the same, instead heading hurriedly away from town, for the long walk toward their ramshackle home in the woods.

* * *

Violet. It was the nicest dress I had, and it had stayed nice too, because I never wore it around here. Not to feed pigs, chase down scrawny chickens and wring their necks, or dig trenches to keep the rainwater from running down the hillside into my kitchen. Not to scrub floors, pull potatoes and carrots, wipe noses, or rinse laundry in the spring. I was a different person in this dress, a different woman. A woman with hope. This dress was who I deserved to be, before I came to this Godforsaken village, a desperate bride with a stranger for a husband, because I had no family of my own.

I spun around the room. The bodice was a little tight from carrying the babies, but still fit well for the most part, due to hard labor and my hunger since the birth of my youngest. I fastened my dead mother's locket pin to my breast. Void of any photo, it was the only piece of jewelry that I owned, and the only remnant of my people that I had left. I covered it with my palm for a moment and thought of my mother and father, and how horrified they would have been over what I had done. Then, hastily I chased such thoughts from my mind, pulling my long dark hair up with one hand and humming to myself, twirling carelessly again.

There was no mirror to inspect my image, but in my mind I knew that I looked and felt better than I had in eight years. Too bad Richard had been found. Thank God I had thought to strike him with the stone before I threw him in his grave. With a cracked skull they never thought of poison. Not that it could have been proven anyway. The trial was over and happily these parts would soon see the last of me.

I had sent the children to play down by the spring and watch over each other in the moonlight while I prepared to go. Take them or not? I could not decide. My heart tugged uncomfortably and I was annoyed by it. They were a part of me, but they were also a part of Richard. So jaded by his abuse, I realized I was often a poor mother and I resented the young ones that bound me to him. His family could care for them and I could go unencumbered. It was tempting to be sure. I vowed I would decide at the last moment, unwilling to spoil my current pleasure. Perhaps I would simply tuck them into bed tonight and then be on my way. The eldest was seven and could easily guide her younger brother and sister to their grandparent's house on the edge of town in the morning.

There was not much to pack, especially if I left the children behind. I was surveying the room by the dying firelight one last time when I heard the commotion coming up the hill and ran to the window. A lynch mob! Nearly the entire village giddy and shouting curses in my name. In a split second I determined that I must go alone and grabbed only a tiny purse of coins that I had kept hidden from Richard off of the rough-hewn table. The crowd approached from the front so I made a dash for the back door, only to be nabbed by two strong men, drunk and surly, who waited outside.

"Yeah," one of Richard's drinking companions pulled my hair and snarled into my face. My eyes watered from the sting of his stinking breath. "We been watch'n ya. We seen ya' through the window, twirl'n round the room in your fancy dress while Richard is rot'n away and his mama's heart is broken. Com'on!"

I struggled futilely as they drug me roughly through the hovel, kicked open the front door, and tossed me like a rag doll onto the dilapidated front porch. The people had gathered a safe distance in the yard, but before I could find my feet to flee two more scoundrels had me by the arms. In the torch light Richard's mother stepped forward. She slapped me hard and spat in my face.

"Rachel, you are a murdering whore." The village people cheered and she slapped me again. My cheek stung. I could taste blood in my mouth and my lip throbbed as it began to swell.

"Devil's slut! Devil's slut!" The mob began to chant.

"I have been freed! I have been found 'not guilty'! Unhand me at once and let me go to my children!" I was shouting and shaking with fear like I had never known before, not even in anticipation of Richard's severest beatings. "Justice has spoken! You cannot speak otherwise!"

"Justice has not spoken…but it is about to." My father-in-law leered from the front of the circle and to my horror I realized he held a noose in his hands. "It'll be the rope for you little missy, and you shall swing tonight!" The assemblage cheered anew.

"But, the children….Sir…Mistress…I beseech you. I did *not* kill your son! You have *no* authority!" I tried to appeal to my mother-in-law with thoughts of her grandchildren, but she only laughed and the men tightened their grips upon me as several others perused the trees, throwing the rope over one low hanging branch or another, and testing its strength with their own weight.

"See what you have done with your wickedness, Rachel? See what you have driven God-fearing people to do? Do not worry about your children…I will care for your children. Worry now about your soul." My mother-in-law was cackling with mad glee as they drug me to the ring of trees around the shack. The torches followed and I could see that the noose now swung from a sturdy branch of the largest oak.

I continued to struggle as several men raised me onto a panicked horse that whinnied and stamped nervously. Once the noose was tightened around my throat; however, I grew still, praying for the horse to do the same.

"What say you now, Mistress Powell?" Several women taunted, imitating the magistrate, as the men whooped and hollered. I could see Sarah in the shadows, near the back of the crowd. My children, who had run up from the spring, gathered around her. She was crying and tried to hide their little faces in the folds of her gown. "What say you now?" The people continued to call.

It was clear I would find no escape and in an instant I felt my fear turn into a frustrated anger I could not contain. It bubbled forward and I howled from atop the horse, twisting my head and gnashing my teeth, more to frighten the people than anything else. If they were to kill me I did not want to leave them wholly satisfied with their handiwork.

"What say I? What will you say when you meet fates worse than mine?" Most of the crowd laughed, but those closest to me began to sober and regard me warily. The horse snorted and his sides heaved between my legs. He leaned forward a bit; cutting off my wind momentarily and making me gag. My hands were tied behind me now and I was completely helpless, yet when I managed to speak again I addressed my in-laws belligerently.

"What will make you happy Mistress? What will spare my life? That I admit to murdering your son? Your beloved, worthless, drunken Richard?"

Maggie Powell sneered and trumpeted, "I will be happy when your face is the color of your fancy gown, *witch*!" She emphasized the last word and the gathering roared. I surveyed the mob of them in their customarily plain black garb and my blood ran cold. To me, in the torch light, they appeared a gaggle of ugly, devilish crows, scratching and cawing excitedly at the prospect of my demise. The horse danced and for a moment I could not breathe again. My eyes bulged and I thankfully gasped for air when he stilled.

There was no way out and I had no idea when the stallion might bolt, so, impulsively, I left them with this. "Witch? Devil's slut? You think I have the power of a witch as well? I am not merely a murderess? So be it!" I spit toward the ground and they all stepped back a pace. "May your offspring, like a doomed harvest, wither on the vine; and may this hellish little hamlet become the breeding ground of disaster. Bloody disaster! I curse you Powells one and all! I curse you to hell! For each of you that dies, my strength will gather. I shall not perish, but will haunt you with a vengeance! I hex you Powells for centuries to come!" When I had finished speaking the revelers were wide-eyed and silent, only my ragged breathing, the crackling of the torch fire and the snort of the animal beneath me could be heard.

I felt a sense of useless satisfaction in their idiotic fear. Then, perhaps by sheer coincidence, or perhaps because the stain of murder upon my soul had already bestowed me with an evil power of which I was not aware, a lightening bolt suddenly lit up the clear night sky. It struck close and no one was more surprised than I…except perhaps the horse.

As the startled beast beneath me slipped from between my trembling thighs the sound of my neck snapping echoed in my ears. I caught one last glimpse of my horrified children, then, indeed, soon my face was violet, the color of my gown, just as Maggie Powell had desired. And so, it would begin.

Chapter 1

Present Day

Tangy pureed tomatoes, blended with olive oil, oregano, garlic and onions. I knew how to make a sauce, but for the life of me I could not replicate the wondrous concoction that currently beckoned from the backseat of my secondhand sedan.

What was the consistency of that intoxicating mixture that had Cassie and me staying up late at night experimenting to no avail? Sal wasn't telling, and that kept us coming over for lunch at least once a week since he had opened his sandwich shop a couple of years ago.

Right now, fat, spicy meatballs, beyond my reach, were wedged between buttery, toasted Italian rolls, bathing in Sal's signature marinara, beneath a gooey blanket of mozzarella. Yes, I, Al Marche, in spite of my incredible culinary capabilities, was a serious Sal's Subs junky...and I was not ashamed to admit it.

Mmmm...I was pushing the speed limit, thinking grimly of afternoons past when I had returned from the lunch run covered in sauce, having ruined another of my uniform blouses from trying to manage one bite...just one...while operating a moving vehicle. That is why the savory, warm subs were sacked up safely in the far rear passenger corner of my car, as mandated by my partner, Cassie, who was also the chief laundress of our co-owned business.

On this particular autumn Saturday I whipped into the driveway of our catering company, The Delectable Dish, none to soon. I had been up since the crack of dawn meeting with brides at their respective venues and finalizing banquet plans for next weekend's weddings. All that talk of food had me nearly beside myself with hunger.

My best friend Cassie and I worked out of a small, one bedroom house with a detached garage, wedged between Chantilly Lace Antiques and Bernie's Laundromat on Central Avenue in the older district of Crescentville, an area that was slowly changing from residential to commercial. Financially the house was a steal and in a very strategic location. We were extremely lucky to land the deal when old Mrs. Phillips passed away. Her children had long since moved to greener pastures and were eager to unload the property.

Cassie and I had merged the kitchen and dining area into one huge work space, and the much smaller living room served as our reception and event planning area. Two individual desks were in the single bedroom next to the only bathroom. The basement was still in great shape and was perfect for storage and laundering. We had put a lot of time and money into renovating and making the cooking area state of the art and our investment was really starting to pay off.

I entered through the back door into the kitchen and found my mom peeling eggs and humming to herself. She was awash in the afternoon sunlight pouring through the little window above the sink and I stopped for a moment to admire her simple loveliness. My chest panged and I took a mental snapshot of the moment. She really was lovely;

inside and out. Soft hearted and soft spoken, with kind, crinkly blue eyes and steel gray hair bluntly cut above her shoulders, but left long enough to pull back if she desired.

Her careworn hands worked deftly, peeling and rinsing. Those hands had molded my life and I felt my eyes well with tears; something that seemed to happen more and more often of late. The anxiety of our situation would sometimes overcome me unexpectedly.

Dad died suddenly when I was thirteen so Mom and I were close and it was hard to witness the recent changes in her. She was drawing more and more into herself, afraid to say or do the wrong thing; afraid of making the very obvious even more apparent. Oddly, as close as we were, since her official diagnosis several months ago, we never spoke of her disease except to mark her doctor's appointments on the calendar, or to note a reminder to pick up a prescription.

Something huge was happening. Important, slow, and cruel. But, we tiptoed around it daily. There was this big, loud, smelly dinosaur in the room called Alzheimer's, and we intently tried to ignore him. No talking about the labels on the kitchen drawers or the bathroom cabinets, no discussion of the lists and notes Mom often made but couldn't remember why. We concerned ourselves with the mundane. Dinner plans, television programming, the daily weather forecast. Things we could directly control...things not too far in the future...or too far in the past.

Perhaps my mom felt she was teaching me patience or faith with her silence. Or, maybe she was simply protecting me as long as she could from the weight of the unavoidable issue that confronted us. I didn't know what to say anyway. I tried to give her as much independence as possible, but our relationship was changing, our roles were switching, and it was awkward for us both. Mom was becoming my responsibility and I was terrified I would someday make a poor decision about her care.

So, for now, I gave Mom her quiet dignity and she allowed me my denial. Since I had been brought up with the notion that you could do, or be, anything if you worked hard enough, this excruciating concept of waiting helplessly for the inevitable was completely unacceptable to me. I had developed a love hate relationship with time, which I had come to consider both a precious commodity and a filthy thief.

Choking back my emotions I tried desperately to swallow the lump in my throat before she caught me crying, but the stench of boiled yolks seeped up my nostrils and settled in the back of my mouth and I gagged before I had a chance to say hello. "Accckkkkk!" My sack of sandwiches dropped heavily on the small utility table we reserved for our own dining, waking our Pug dog, Petey, who had been snoring contentedly beneath it.

My mother didn't even jump; she merely turned her frail frame calmly toward me. I hastily wiped my eyes and smiled, pointing at the eggs in the bowl by the sink and gagged again for effect.

Dressed in pale blue cotton jeans and a red gingham blouse, Flora Stanley was still a slender, handsome woman and I hoped my genes would continue to lean toward her side of the family, rather than the rotund Marche frame of my father's...the very frame that I had sported as a child but luckily outgrew. I was a little taller than Mom, and though my hair was apparently the same dark brown that hers had been in her youth, I had inherited my dad's green eyes and strong chin.

Now, Mom shook her head, rolled her eyes heavenward and laughed softly before returning to her chore. I leaned close and caught the comforting scent of her familiar perfume, before brushing a kiss across her cool cheek and darting across the room to grab an apron. "Sorry," I said lightly. "Boiled eggs tend to trigger my overactive gag reflex." I went dutifully back to the sink to wash my hands and help her peel.

Cassie trudged up the basement steps with a clean stack of towels and dish cloths. "Well," she panted, "the profit on two hundred and fifty deviled eggs remains enormous whether you like how they smell or not." Cassie was a straight shooter, and right now she shot me a straight out 'deal with it' smirk, wrinkled her pert nose and wiped a trickle of sweat from the back of her neck, beneath her black bobbed hair.

The basement steps were Cassie's chief nemesis. Constantly on a diet, she had been threatening to lose the same fifty pounds for about as long as I had known her…which had been quite a while. We met our freshman year of high school when the two middle schools in Crescentville merged. Cass and I had been nearly inseparable ever since, having gone away to the culinary academy together, and coming home to start our own business. Cassie was the sister I never really had, in spite of the fact that I technically had three…and a brother.

I was a love-child…a change of life baby. My parents never married but were together for over sixteen years before dad's death, their older children from first marriages long grown and moved away by the time I was born. Now, at twenty-seven Cassie and I were still joined at the hip and, by working hard side by side, were managing to do rather well for ourselves.

Last month Cassie began a new diet program in anticipation of our friend Gretchen's wedding.

Unfortunately, this strategy had added another three or four pounds to her ample waistline, making the formidable basement steps all the more difficult to climb.

Cassie was cranky today. I could already tell. Probably ready for lunch. I could read her like a book, but never took her grumblings personally. Right now, I simply smiled and tried to breath as shallow as possible, tilting my head away from the odor wafting up from the shells being caught in the colander in the sink.

"Did you call your Aunt Rose about Petey?" Cassie inquired, with a frown.

"Oh, shoot!" Mom would have called her sister Rose, but the success rate for favors granted was usually higher when I was doing the asking. The fact that I was Rose's favorite niece had always been obvious, and though I was not looking forward to making this particular call, my favored relative status made me the best candidate for the job.

Thankfully, I abandoned the eggs and Cassie took over at the sink while I dialed Rose's number by heart from the kitchen phone. As I waited for her to pick up I imagined my aunt out on her back porch in a stretchy shorts set lighting up a smoke and cracking open a frosty beer, or, heatedly scratching lottery tickets at her kitchen table, surrounded by dusty ceramic projects in various stages of incompletion.

Rose was my mother's only sister, younger by four years, and they were complete polar opposites. At seventy-three my mom was bookish, serene and kindly reserved. Aunt Rose, on the other hand, was loud, obnoxious and brutally honest. Just about every ring she owned adorned her ten fingers. Glints of tiny diamond chips competed with whatever gaudy polish or nail stencil she sported that week. Mom's voice was melodious and gentle, while Rose's was gravelly from years of cigarettes. Mom practiced piano and yoga, while Rose practiced blowing fabulous smoke rings that grew to amazing circumference before floating aloft, further staining her yellowed trailer ceiling. Once, I saw her stand up into several and before they dispersed, the bluish smoke circled her grey bouffant hair perfectly, like the rings of Saturn. You had to be there to appreciate it fully, but believe me when I tell you, as a seven year old I remember finding the sight quite mesmerizing.

Rose and her husband Chuck owned a trucking company, which they ran together until his death. Rose managed the business herself for several years until she sold it and moved into a retirement trailer court about two hours away from us, close to the casinos. Her park had a pool where she worshiped the sun at every opportunity, and Rose had a complexion to be envied, if you aspired to be a leather handbag. Sometimes Rose's boyfriend Barney stayed over…sometimes he didn't. After forty-three years of marriage, she said she liked her freedom and intended to keep it that way.

When Rose wasn't poolside, playing the slots, lost between the pages of a trashy novel, or engrossed in one of her many, unfinished craft projects, she was touring the countryside with her motorcycle group; a troop of fellow grannies who referred to themselves as the Motor'n Mamas.

Yup…my mom took life by the hand, while Aunt Rose took it by the horns and wrestled it kicking and screaming to the ground.

I listened to the phone ring eight times, and was just about to hang up when I heard Rose fumbling for the receiver, cussing rampantly.

"What? Goddamn it!" she snapped. I must have interrupted something important.

"Aunt Rose? It's Al. Is everything okay?"

"Oh, Al," her voice softened. "Sorry, honey. I was cleaning Betty's cage and she got away from me. It's alright now. I caught her. Hang on a minute." I could hear Betty Jane, Rose's parrot, squawking in the background. "Awwwkkkk! Goddamn it! Awwwkkkk!" Although Rose sounded pretty winded, I sensed she was pausing to light up, rather than catch her breath. She returned to the phone, exhaling as she spoke. I imagined the magic smoke rings swirling about her puffy hair and forgot why I was calling for a moment.

"What's up kid?" Rose's dangly earrings jangled against the receiver's mouthpiece as she turned her head to emit a croupy cough.

"Oh, well, I was calling to ask a favor of you." I said tentatively.

"Mmmhmm?" She grunted suspiciously.

"Remember my friend Gretchen? She lived here in Crescentville."

I endured the silence as Rose thought a moment, coughed again, and thought a little more. "Oh yeah, Gretchen. I remember her. Her daddy was the trash man, ran off with that waitress from Smithy's, her mom went off the deep end and her grandpa raised her after that. I remember Gretchen." Rose declared.

"That would be Gretchen." Aunt Rose associated by gossip. Her brain was a web of who did what; forget the validity of the source, or the information. Actually, Gretchen's daddy was a mechanic and he ran off with a hairdresser, and her *grandma* raised her after that, but it wasn't worth getting into. Although, the girlfriend's beauty shop had been called Smithy's and I had to give Rose credit there. "Anyway, she's getting married in a couple of weeks and Mom's gonna go, and Cass and I are going down a week early to help Gretchen out, do some cooking and decorating, throw a little engagement party…" I was starting to ramble, picking up momentum as I nervously broached the subject of my call.

"You're gonna ask me to watch that miserable little excuse of a dog, aren't you?" Rose interrupted.

"Well, I…"

"You are! Hell no! Last time I kept that little bastard he humped a skunk, ran in my trailer and I had to replace my sofa. Couldn't get the stink out of it."

"I offered to buy you a new couch, Aunt Rose." I countered defensively and glanced down at Petey, who peeked out from under the table with wide eyes and a guilty expression on his wrinkled little mug.

"Doesn't matter, I was thinking of getting a new one anyway."

"Then what's the problem?" My left eye started to twitch.

"The problem is," she paused for dramatic effect. "The problem *is*…," she repeated with emphasis, "that dog is demented. He has some sort of disorder." Likely true. "He doesn't listen." Agreed. "He humps everything that moves." Sometimes. "And, he stinks to high heaven after he eats." Amen, sister! "Doesn't matter what you feed him either. I don't know how Flora can stand to live with him. She was always the prissy one. Not me. And that fainting thing he does…freaks me out. Hell no! I can't take 'em. Betty Jane doesn't like 'em either." There was a squawk of agreement in the background. As if on cue, I could hear Betty Jane's "Awwwk. Hell no!" quite clearly.

"Sorry, Hon." Rose croaked with finality, nearly out of breath. I heard her inhale and exhale slowly. "He's a humpicidal maniac."

Mentally, I heaved a heavy sigh. I couldn't really blame her. Arguing would be pointless so I chatted politely for a couple more minutes about her Bingo winnings, her achy hip and how my cousin Lenny might have caught a staph infection from wearing a dead guy's pants.

"Well?" Cassie and Mom had finished peeling the eggs by the time I hung up and Mom was breaking open the sack from Sal's.

"No deal."

"Why not?" Mom inquired, crestfallen. "Oh, dear. He hates the kennel." Actually, she sort of had the situation backwards. When Petey visited the kennel he was in solitary confinement the entire time, for a variety of reasons. Mom gazed sadly down at the dog, which was now eyeballing the sandwich in her hands and sitting prettily, hopefully, at her feet. "I'll really miss being at Gretchen's wedding, but I guess I'll have to stay home and watch him."

"No!" Cassie and I exclaimed at the same time. Mom jumped and nearly dropped her lunch on the floor. "No." We repeated more sedately, still in unison, and sat down to the table.

While Mom's memory condition was pretty stable as long as she took her meds regularly and was in familiar territory, she still had her moments, and they were unexpected. Sometimes she couldn't remember what simple objects were...or how to pronounce what they were called. Months ago, I left her alone for a couple of days to go to a cooking convention in St. Louis and she put the car into drive instead of reverse and ended up in the pond behind our house. She might have drowned if my boyfriend Alex hadn't stopped by to check on her and seen the tail lights disappear down the hillside. That had been the final straw in an increasing series of mildly disturbing issues that sent us for a definitive diagnosis. Leaving her alone was too risky and out of the question.

I took a big bite of my messy, delicious meatball sub and thought a moment. We all chewed silently, wracking our brains, trying to think of who a potential Petey sitter might be. I honestly couldn't think of anyone I disliked that much. Suddenly, a brilliant idea occurred to me. "We'll take him with us!" I exclaimed, then quickly covered my mouth. Did I say that out loud? Without consulting Cassie? I snuck a peek and noted that her eyes had dilated and her round face was reddening. For a second I thought she was choking to death. She looked at me like I'd lost my mind. I knew she was already angry about gagging down a vegetarian sandwich while Mom and I had meatball sauce all over our faces. Maybe I should have approached her separately, after lunch.

Mom, however, considered my idea momentarily and clapped her hands excitedly. "That's a wonderful idea! A vacation for *all* of us!"

Petey was shaking his little Pug butt and running in elated circles while Cassie, seated next to my mother, made violent gestures at me from behind Mom's head. What else could I do?

"It'll be great." I insisted lamely. Cass looked pained and merely nodded when my mother beamed her way.

"Yeah, great," Cass echoed, making a slicing motion across her throat and stabbing her finger in my direction as Mom turned back toward me. "You … are … a … dead …woman," Cassie mouthed viciously, shooting me a glare that almost made me swallow my tongue.

"Yea!" Mom squealed in elation and waved her fists in the air, her eyes glimmering with excitement. This was the happiest I'd seen her in a long time.

"Yea!" I forced a saucy grin, waving my fists as well, and managing to avoid eye contact with Cassie, who was actually starting to scare me.

As I watched a glob of Sal's secret tomato sauce dribble down the front of my new white blouse, visions of Petey molesting the minister during Gretchen's wedding ceremony skidded across my mind. "Good gravy!" I sighed inwardly.

Chapter 2

Sunday – One Week Later

Late the next Sunday morning my boyfriend Alex came by my house to say goodbye. He spied me through the window of the kitchen door in the throes of last minute packing. I was by the counter, having finally found a lint roller, the sticky tape kind, in our junk drawer. In the process of trying to pick old petrified tape from wads of grocery receipts, twine, a battery, a couple of crayons, and a tack, I had somehow ensnarled my hands with the roller. Clearly, I was not good with tape, and Petey, never missing an opportunity to be helpful, had attached himself to my left leg and was going to town. When the doorbell rang, I squealed, lost my balance and, hands useless, hit the hardwood floor like a ton of bricks. Alex was twisting the door handle as Petey, snorting deliriously over his good fortune, mounted my head.

"Whoa, big guy," Alex chuckled and bent to retrieve Petey, whose claws were caught in my long, tangled, brown hair.

"Owww! Get him off me! Get him off me!" I was kicking in circles on the floor; my tape entangled hands now stuck to my head in an effort to protect my face from what I was pretty sure could *not* be Petey's hind leg. "I think he got my ear!" I squealed.

"Hold still, Al." Alex, soon frustrated with both of us, wasn't laughing anymore. "Damn it Petey! Let loose!"

"What on Earth is going on in here?" At the sound of my mother's voice Petey dismounted and retreated quickly. His little toe nails clicked innocently across the kitchen floor as he crossed to my mom, with a wad of tape stuck to his behind.

Physically, Petey had been the pick of the litter; muscular, stocky, with soft fawn fur and the roundest little wrinkled face and bright eyes. One little ear bent slightly more than the other perked, giving him a jaunty, playful expression. He was Flora's little angel. Ha! The mentally demented devil! She bent and scooped him into her arms. Petey's eyes were wide and he stared accusingly at me now.

"Oh, Petey," Mom crooned and cradled him, running her fingers gently through the folds of his plush coat. "What were they doing to my precious Petey Pie Puggy Wuggy?" He licked her face gently, and then haughtily glanced back at me.

Two years ago I bought Petey to keep my mom company because I was spending more and more time at the catering business, often I rued the day. To me, he had become more of an annoying little sibling than a treasured pet. His one redeeming quality was that he was usually in more trouble than I was…a pleasant distraction.

"Us? Jeeez, Mom!" Alex helped me to my feet and ripped the tape to free my hands. The roller hung from my hair…complete with receipts, battery and crayons. As Alex peeled pieces of tape from my arm hair as tenderly as possible, I tackled my head and felt the lone tack sink into my bare foot. "Ouch! Damn it!"

"Deloris. Language." Mom admonished quietly and headed back toward her room. I swear to God, Petey stuck his tongue out at me over her shoulder as they disappeared down the hall. I was happy to return the favor.

Although I was a grown woman, and had gone by "Al" for many years, Mom still called me "Deloris" when I was in trouble. And, it still made me cringe. My given name remained Deloris Eugenia Gladiola Marche. What were my parents thinking? Excellent question. Apparently, I am the namesake of select dead aunts and a great grandmother.

At any rate, it was the relentless creativity of a little red haired bully named Johnny Franklin who preempted my name change in fifth grade. Then I was a chunky, quirky kid; clumsy, with thick glasses and unruly hair that was forever lamenting its lost barrette. The fat girl with few friends. I remembered Johnny quite clearly. He was your stereotypical bully, with mean, squinty little eyes and abundant freckles. Numerous cowlicks kept his orange mop of hair hopelessly awry, unless he was sporting a buzz cut, as he did at the beginning of each school year.

Johnny was the kind of kid who always seemed to be a step ahead of everybody else, whether it was the latest cuss word or cutting barb that nobody seemed to understand, he was brilliant at making you feel inadequate and immature. He could have bottled his own brand of mean, and nobody went unscathed. Oddly enough, the other kids craved his acceptance no matter how much they hated him. Probably just to keep out of his line of fire…someplace which I, unfortunately, appeared to find myself all too frequently.

Johnny had a variety of clever slams that centered on my generous weight. Delori-saurus. Delori-ginormous. And, the ever popular, Delori-Me-From-My-House-With-A-Crane. Yes, Johnny was pretty creative, yet fairly innocuous, until one day during morning recess, after smacking me in the face with a kick ball and breaking my glasses, his inventiveness went a little too far. I was forced to take matters into my own hands; hence, the name change.

Long story short, Johnny was pretty adept at rhyming heinous things with my name, as previously mentioned, so the day he rhymed my name with a particular portion of the female anatomy which also ended in the letters O...R...I...S I was completely confounded. After lunch I asked to go to the library, where, with the help of a medical dictionary and an uncomfortable librarian, I sorted it all out and decided I didn't like where things were heading.

Later, in a fit of fury, in front of about thirty other kids, I gave Johnny Franklin a bloody nose in gym class and proclaimed to a good chunk of my peers that I had officially changed my name to Alice. Our neighbor had a Siamese cat called Alice and she didn't take business off of anybody...not even our English bulldog, Buddy. Plus, in the short amount of time I had, I couldn't find anything dreadful in that medical dictionary that rhymed with Alice.

So, that Tuesday after Mrs. Proctor blew her whistle in my ear and pulled me off of Johnny...who, by the way, was screaming like a little girl...I was reborn. By the time I landed in the principal's office I had a new name and the benefit of two priceless tidbits of information. Number One: Nobody gives you trouble when you have a solid right hook. Number Two: Sometimes, detention is totally worth it. Ah, memories.

"What is this stuff made of?" I grumbled presently, pulling at the lint roller in my hair with little success.

Alex continued to pick gently at my arm and ignored my question. "That Petey's something else. I thought getting him fixed would cure some of that….uh," he wrinkled his brow, searching for the right word, "desire."

"So did I," I sighed, having a brief flashback to when I had gotten Petey neutered. With the plastic cone on his head, still woozy from anesthesia, I caught Petey firmly attached to a stereo speaker in the living room…the very day I brought him home from the vet. Within a week we'd taken him back twice to have his stitches repaired. Apparently Petey's issues transcended the realm of the physical. Mom and I had considered a doggy psychiatrist on more than one occasion.

"Are you sure you want to take him with you for the entire week? I'll be down in a few days. I could keep him and bring him with me." Alex offered generously.

"Who would let him out when you're on duty? Besides, I got myself into this and I'm going to see it through. I've already bought a little travel kennel and some new toys for him. Mom's excited. And, now I have something to prove to Cassie." I frowned and wrenched the roller from my hair with a grunt. Alex took it from me, easily pulling the old tape off into a sticky ball; hair, paper, crayons and all.

"Will you be needing any of this?" he inquired with a smile, already heading toward the trash can.

"No." I frowned. He returned and handed the tape roller back to me. "My hero," I groaned. Alex encircled me in his arms and nuzzled my neck. My toes involuntarily curled and I nestled against his chest sighing contentedly. I lost all sense when it came to Alex. He was what you might consider "the entire package." Sandy blonde hair, baby blue eyes, an easy grin, hunky fireman arms, sweet, funny, attentive as the day is long…and did I mention hunky fireman arms?

Alex was also a local of Crescentville and though he was only three years older than me we didn't really know each other in high school. He had lived in a run down apartment complex on the far side of town, while I grew up in the country in the beautiful old farmhouse that had been in my father's family for generations. Both of my parents were professors at the local junior college and, being older and tempered, they doted on their only child together with unending love and patience.

Alex, unfortunately, had a rough home life, with a drunken father absent more often than not and a work wearied mother stressed from trying to make ends meet for five kids. He graduated from high school early, and left for the Marines as soon as he could, but after one tour of duty he returned home to help care for his younger siblings. He worked odd jobs and studied hard to become a paramedic and currently worked as a firefighter.

We officially met at his little sister's wedding almost two years ago. It was one of the first larger events that Cassie and I catered. As he continually drifted in and out of the kitchen, Alex and I quickly discovered that we had a lot in common. Besides a strong attraction to one another, there was the deep love for cold, day old Hawaiian pizza, classic Western movies, and more than a minor curiosity in the realm of the paranormal. By the end of the night he had my home number and I was pleasantly surprised when he actually called the next day. Gradually our comfortable relationship developed.

I didn't mind his odd schedule or his being on call for his job, and Alex didn't seem to mind my devotion to my aging mom, my countless hours spent building my business with Cassie, or my many personality quirks. I felt that Alex was the first person, other than Cassie or my parents, who accepted me as I was. This said a lot for Alex.

Though I had far outgrown chunky by junior high, and contacts had replaced my thick glasses, my innate clumsiness as a kid remained. In addition, as an adolescent who watched her father die unexpectedly before her very eyes from cardiac arrest, I had developed a mild case of hypochondria and random bouts of panic attacks. My feelings of helplessness had transformed into a hyper vigilant sense of dread. I was ever wary of bad news, and waited for the other shoe to fall when things seemed to be going a little too smoothly in my life. Vowing that nothing like dad's death would ever catch me by surprise again, I was haunted by an underlying sense of anxiousness at all times and became a chronic worrier...rarely able to shake my unease. It was emotionally exhausting.

In addition, I possessed a slight sensitivity to the spiritual world. So, it is no small wonder why I always felt different from the other kids. My ardent interest in the paranormal and the afterlife intensified as I grew older. Before long I was spending a lot of time with my nose in a book about the subject and I was dragging a reluctant Cassie on cemetery vigils, or to purportedly haunted locations.

I was amazed at the interest Alex took in my little hobby. Though I had never seen an outright apparition, I had experienced shadows and sensations. He found that intriguing rather than weird, and as we became closer the ghost hunting aspired to a whole new level. We obviously couldn't afford to quit our day jobs and become full blown professional investigators, but Alex, somewhat of a techie, acquired more sophisticated equipment. Now our catalog of findings contained a couple of impressive audio recordings and a lot of questionable photographs.

Compatible as we were it seemed a foregone conclusion that marriage loomed in the future, though neither of us brought the subject up. Superstitious to the bone, I didn't want to jinx things and was happy to carry on as we were for now.

"Stay away from handsome groomsmen while you're gone," Alex cautioned with a whisper, drawing my thoughts back to the present as he playfully bit my ear.

"Whaaaa?" I shivered and broke out in goose bumps, catching a drop of drool on my lip with my tongue before it slid down my chin onto his t-shirt. Sometimes I wished I could just freeze time.

"Get a room." Cassie burst through the door, huffing and puffing from climbing the porch steps. She grimaced as Petey re-entered the kitchen. "Are we ready?"

"Ready as we'll ever be." I kissed Alex soundly on the lips and he released me with stars in his eyes and a silly grin on his face. I still could not fathom what this gorgeous guy thought he saw in me, but whatever it was, he was obviously hooked. Yea me!

"Mom, let's go!" I hollered, having already checked her luggage to make sure she hadn't forgotten anything super important. Her medications were in a zippered pouch strapped around my waist. When she appeared she wore two different colored shoes and only one earring. None of us said a word. She seemed so darn happy I wanted to cry.

Alex helped us carry our luggage to the catering van, and then we were on our way to what should have been a very relaxing respite, but unfortunately, was not.

Chapter 3

Spring Valley, a five hour drive from Crescentville, was an area noted in the late nineteenth century for its healing spring waters. It was now a small tourist town close to a popular state lake where trendy restaurants and quaint shops thrived.

We had never been to Spring Valley, but from Gretchen's e-mails and photos we couldn't wait to see the bed and breakfast she and her fiancé, Roger, had purchased outside of the village proper.

Apparently their place was pretty secluded, surrounded by someone else's farmland. Their sixty acres included a large, old house, the remnants of a building that had once served as some sort of care facility, and the bulk of famed spring waters that so many had sought for physical treatment decades before. There were also a handful of cottages on the property where additional guests could stay.

Roger, an attorney, had recently left a big city firm back east so that he and Gretchen could pursue her dream of running their own business. He had joined a small local law practice where he worked part time while he and Gretchen renovated their Victorian home. They planned to be wed there and open for business soon after.

Intent on making our own company a success, Cassie and I had not had a real vacation in years. Though we had offered to put on a small engagement dinner for the guests and wedding party in a few days, and cook some of the reception food, otherwise we would not be working at all. So, as our catering van wound its way through the fall countryside, we were cheerful and relaxed.

It was unseasonably warm for mid-October. Cassie and I were in front with the windows down, she driving and me lounging on the passenger side with one bare foot out the window, commenting over the changing leaves and passing her carrot sticks upon request. I sipped a soda and snacked on red licorice and snack sticks of spicy meat while Mom and Petey snored gently from the bench seat directly behind us. Chafing dishes clattered softly against luggage in the very back of our van as we rounded curves and crested knolls.

It was an uneventful drive and as we approached our destination I had asked Cassie a question she had entertained many times in our long relationship, and, true blue best friend that she was, Cassie considered my inquiry as seriously as if it were the first time we had discussed the matter. If you could have a super power what would it be?

Cassie always chose starting fire with her eyes. She had a pretty severe case of road rage and admitted it would be fun to ignite the hair of annoying drivers in front of her. Impressive, but I selected rubber band arms this time…delightfully freakish, yet highly functional. We discussed the merits of x-ray vision and super strength just the same, and it wasn't long (after only one wrong turn, due to my phenomenal lack of direction and map reading skills) before we had reached the outskirts of the happy hamlet of Spring Valley.

"Mom, wake up. We're at Spring Valley! We're at Spring Valley!" I chanted enthusiastically at the five mile sign.

Mom stirred in the back seat. Cassie shot me a look and frowned as if she wanted to set *my* head on fire. "You sound like a nine year old."

"Do not."

"Do too."

"Do not."

"Girls!" Mom exclaimed in her sternest professor voice. "What time is it?"

"A little after four."

"Oh, no wonder I'm starving. Are we eating at Gretchen's or in town?"

"I think Gretchen was going to grill or something. But, we could stop and get a treat before dinner and check out Spring Valley. Petey probably needs a potty break anyway." At mention of his name, Petey stretched his front legs and arched his little Pug butt into the air. So far he had been sleeping like an angel nestled close to Mom.

We left the state highway where indicated and wound between the golden remains of harvested cornfields before coming across a wooded area bisected by a stream and a lovely old covered bridge. Since it had been a warmer than usual fall, the leaves were in full brilliance; still clinging onto the trees. The sun was just beginning to set and was washing the countryside in yellow, syrupy light.

"Take my picture!" Mom was already unzipping her camera case as Cassie pulled off to the side of the road.

"Is it okay to stop here?" Cassie, ever cautious and safety minded, rolled down her window and looked up and down the empty road.

"It's practically deserted," I observed and joined Mom and Petey on the dusty shoulder. Petey ventured about four feet from Mom, down a steep slope near a small stream, where he watered a clump of dried wild flowers, and then scampered back. Mom slipped him a treat from her pocket and scooped him up.

"Don't venture so far, Petey Pie," she crooned into his little bent ear. Mom handed me the camera which hung from a strap around her shoulder and crossed the road toward the bridge with Petey still in her arms. "Al, take my picture…then, Cassie…take me and Al and Petey's picture."

She stood on the wooden planks at the rail just outside the entrance of the redwood painted covering, her back to the woods and stream below. The evening light was perfect for photos and since the sun was no longer directly overhead, a cool breeze mingled with the woodsy scent of leaves, dirt and water. The trees were a riot of color and the bridge was completely void of traffic, so Cassie took several shots of Mom with Petey…then the three of us together…and Mom shot a couple of photos of me and Cassie.

Mom loved photography but refused to go digital. As a result she always took a ton of extra shots and we spent a fortune on film but I didn't care, so little seemed to make her happy these days. Next, Cass and I waited patiently and watched Petey as the bridge itself became Mom's subject of interest.

"Look at this, girls." Mom had discovered a brass plaque affixed to the entrance of the bridge. She stepped closer to take a picture of it then read aloud.

"Spring Valley, established in 1635." Ever the teacher and student, her blue eyes lit with intrigue. She had been a literature instructor, but my father had taught history, an area of study that was also a love of hers. "I had no idea this township was so old. Did you?"

"Gretchen mentioned something about it being a settlement. I don't think the area really became popular until the springs were rumored to have healing powers in the 1800s." Cassie stated.

"Hmm, just imagine how many people have crossed this bridge," Mom said thoughtfully. "From different eras, with different stories. Fascinating. I wonder if they have a museum in town."

"Well, let's go check it out."

Merrily, we packed back into the van but halfway through the picturesque covered bridge the prospect of venturing on to Spring Valley became a lot less charming and a lot more gloomy and dank. The bridge was longer than it first appeared and it didn't seem as sound as it had looked from the road.

Cassie tapped the brakes with every creak and groan. "I'd hate to get stuck in here at night," she murmured. Suddenly it seemed too quiet and close in the vehicle. A sense of dread began to throb in the pit of my stomach for no apparent reason.

"Just go." I urged; more to disrupt the silence than anything else. My throat felt tight and I was a little lightheaded. I tried to rationalize with myself; maybe I was allergic to some wildflower back on the side of the road.

"I'm sure it's sturdier than it sounds." Cass grimaced and gave the van a little more gas.

We all heaved a sigh of relief upon emerging on the other side, back into the sunny countryside. I hadn't realized that Mom had practically been holding her breath as well and I wondered why I felt so uneasy. Maybe we had been in the car too long. Maybe I was hungry. As my heart raced I hoped I wasn't about to have an anxiety attack. My chest tightened at the prospect. Sometimes I could talk myself into one, particularly when I was out of familiar territory. I tried to breathe deeply and patted the pack attached to my waist with a sweaty palm to reassure myself that medication was close by. It was ridiculous the comfort that little ritual of checking my hip had often given me throughout the years. I hadn't had a full fledge attack in many, many months, and the pills in my pouch were outdated, but I still carried them, especially when I was far away from home. Just in case. I hated depending on medicine, but its mere existence calmed me, and often helped me feel the control necessary to ward off an episode of panic by myself, without actually having to swallow the pills.

One more twist and turn, up a little grade, and Spring Valley lay before us. Tourists excluded…population just over three thousand. We were used to small town living, and Crescentville was plenty cute, but Spring Valley was just short of magical. The main street's brick countenance could not have changed in a century or more and it was easy to imagine horse drawn buggies, gentlemen tipping their hats to women in long gowns with high collars, and Victorian children purchasing sweets, three for a penny, at the General Store. The air of gentleness soothed my palpitating heart as nostalgia took hold. It was a pleasant distraction, and soon we had all but forgotten the creepy covered bridge as we pointed one novelty after another out to each other.

I thought back across the centuries to the pilgrimage of ill individuals who sought Spring Valley. What better place to convalesce, I dreamt. The buildings were two or three story store fronts of brick and stone. Each had its own unique flair, and most bore a plaque similar to the one on the bridge, stating the year it was built and for what original purpose. The town was proud of its history.

Right now, the town was decorated for Halloween. Pumpkins and cornstalks adorned stoops. Cardboard witches and skeletons were plastered to windows. We cruised to the end of Main Street and parked, slipped a few coins into the ancient meter, and took off on foot. We blended in with families and honeymooners on vacation, exploring the town up close on our own.

Hustling up one side of Main and then down the other, with Petey on a leash and in lead, we noted that many of the businesses were closing early for Sunday evening church services, but still we stopped to examine each one. We encountered stores of antiquity, cafés, a grocery, and a beautiful old movie theatre, which had first been a tea room and dance hall. There was the museum that Mom had been seeking, though right now it was closed. There was also a rather large law office which took up two building fronts. The sign hanging from a cast iron hinge boasted the name of "Douglas Dockings, Attorney at Law", and underneath in smaller print and newer paint, Brewster Thistle, Esquire, and, Roger Richardson, Esquire.

"Look! Here's Roger's name. This is the firm he's been working with part time."

Cassie and Mom stopped to consider the handsome building and we peered into the darkened interior before moving on. We headed past a dance studio, where cherubic kindergartners in pink tutu's could be seen pirouetting from the street. Then, past an herbal remedies store, which boasted natural cures for common ailments. We drifted past the front window of Flavell's Bridal Boutique, where an elderly woman with thick hips and thighs draped an emaciated mannequin in champagne colored tulle.

At last, we happened upon a pharmacy with an honest to goodness soda fountain. Tying Petey to a park bench next to a little tree by the curb where we could see him from inside, we entered and soon emerged with malts and cones. We retrieved Petey and walked to a small park area where we sat on the steps of a gazebo and contemplated a large running fountain and children playing on playground equipment beyond. Through the fringe of trees and more modern business structures, such as a hardware store and grain co-op, we caught glimpses of colorful Victorian homes. An American flag unfurled in the soft breeze before the enormous clock of the city hall. And, gleaming above it all, some distance away, was a stately church steeple. As if on cue the ringing of bells signified six o'clock.

"We've lost track of time," I stated.

"This place is so cute it's sickening." Cassie decreed, placing the remainder of her vanilla cone in the grass for Petey, who eagerly lapped it up.

"Uh, I don't think that's such a good idea." I was checking my arms and elbows for chocolate. So far so good. I had been careful not to drip any that Petey could get a hold of since chocolate wasn't good for dogs.

"Why? The chocolate is on your nose, Al."

"You don't have to sleep with him later." I retorted and swiped at my nose.

"Well, neither do you, so what are you complaining about?" Mom ran her fingers lightly over Petey's furrowed brow. "You're so misunderstood, aren't you little Petey Pie." She poured a bit of her vanilla malt on the ground for him to lick up. His moist, buggy eyes were thankful.

"Humph," I grunted and considered the growing shadows. "We'd better get going. Gretchen and Roger are outside of town a little bit."

Mom stretched her stiff frame and yawned. "It's so beautiful and peaceful. I could just sit here all night."

We drifted back to the van, lulled by the dusky onset of evening, our bellies full of milk and malt. As Cassie drove on through town, the rest of Main Street was a blur of additionally quaint edifices, set further apart. The Elderberry Inn and Restaurant. A stone library, complete with lion statues guarding the double doors at the head of wide steps. A Post Office erected in the same architectural style and a fire station where a fat old Dalmatian dog slept on the concrete in front of the open bay doors next to an outdated, yet functional to be sure, fire truck. Alex would love it. I missed him already.

Several older homes drifted by my window, interior lights popping on here and there, and before long we were in the countryside again.

About three miles outside of town we passed a fenced in area that appeared to be a park; however, little rustic buildings were clustered within. It had darkened considerably, but our interest was piqued. Cassie slowed so we could read the sign posted on the locked gates by headlight. I rolled down my window to lean a little closer and when I did a butterscotch scrap of fur hissed from the weeds on the roadside and slipped between the gate posts. Petey growled and hit the sliding door's window as we all watched a fluffy cat bound across a gravel parking lot and disappear between two of the structures. The sign indicated that this was what was left of what had been the site of the original settlement of Spring Valley, but unfortunately, the structures were closed for the season and would not reopen again until spring.

"Too bad," Mom muttered and Cassie started to pull away. Just as I rolled up the window I thought I glimpsed a form stepping from between what appeared to be a small shed and a larger building which looked like a church or meeting house. It was no more than a dark outline and when I blinked it was gone; however, I did catch a glimpse of tan fluff scamper across the settlement's dirt alley before our headlights swept away. Again, my chest felt tight and I forced myself to take a deep breath. Cassie shot me a curious sideways glance and I stared ahead, ignoring the question in her eyes.

I was just tired. I was just stressed out. I was always stressed out. As nice as it would be to be away from home I still had Mom and Petey to care for. I was looking forward to the fun of Gretchen's wedding, but could not deny that it might potentially be a very long week.

Chapter 4

We were searching for Gallows Road, supposedly seven or eight miles outside of the main village. After waiting for a train at a railroad crossing, we passed between harvested fields where cows grazed in the shadows cleaning up spilled corn. Before long the road turned to gravel and led into a densely treed area. We crossed an uncovered bridge of smaller scale than the one leading into town from the highway. The countryside was consumed in pitch blackness and if there were rural houses in the murk beyond the trees, they were not evident.

Once the four-way stop on our map was found we hung a right and the road led back into an even denser canopy of trees. This was Gallows Road and now I truly felt like the forest had swallowed us whole. None to soon the headlights illuminated a wooden sign, affixed to an elm along a curve. 'Spring Valley Resort 1/2 Mile'. A large red arrow pointed ahead and before long another sign directed us right into a long, winding driveway lined with electric lamp posts, and then up a curving tree lined paved path. We were still in the woods though the cover was not quite as thick.

I had just pulled out my cell phone to send Alex a text message, letting him know we had basically reached our destination and I would call him later, when lights began to wink from between the trees. We wound toward an enormous home with a wrap around front porch. The silhouette of Gretchen's slender form waited impatiently on the steps. The house had presence, even in the darkness.

"It's beautiful," Mom gasped.

I wanted to agree but for some reason a chill was running down my spine and I couldn't find my tongue. I rubbed my neck reflexively. That tight feeling had subtly returned again and I breathed deeply through my nose to calm myself down. 'Get it together, Al.' I chastised myself.

Cassie and I had gone to high school with Gretchen. We ran around together for years until Gretchen went out of state for college and Cassie and I left Crescentville briefly for trade school. We made quite a threesome.

Upon graduation I was voted most likely to break every bone in my body. Ever the paranoid dreamer, I was always dragging the other two into some hair brained scheme...to which I might add in my defense, they followed quite readily.

Even as a teenager, Cassie was sensibly minded, the voice of reason, incredibly bossy. She mothered Gretchen and I within an inch or our lives and largely trailed along to clean up my messes.

And Gretchen? Well, she was practically perfect. Good natured, good looking, smart and athletic. The kind of girl you'd hate if she wasn't so damned sweet. Gretchen worked hard at everything she did and her school life was a success, in stark contrast to the miserable cards she had been dealt at home. Her grandmother had done her level best to fill the gaps left by Gretchen's inattentive, unsupportive parents. They were mostly concerned with the drama in their own lives rather than caring for their only daughter, who by all measures was pretty awesome and didn't deserve either one of them.

Cassie pulled the van to a stop beneath a massive tree on the circle drive and we all piled out as Gretchen ran to greet us.

"Oh, you're here! You're finally here! It's so good to see you guys." Gretchen's chestnut pony tail slapped us each in the face respectively as she jumped up and down and spun to hug us all in turn. She finally stooped to pat Petey. "And Petey too, I see." I couldn't read the expression on her wholesome, freckled face in the darkness. Petey's reputation was world renown.

"Is that okay?" I asked hesitantly, not really having a choice in the matter I hadn't thought to call in advance.

"Of course." Gretchen straightened and assured me with a smile. "We're going to be a pet friendly bed and breakfast. We're even planning to construct some kennels out back for guests to leave their animals in while they sight see in town or go to the lake. He doesn't mind cats does he? We have a stray that hangs around. She gets in the house sometimes. I haven't figured out how. Roger appears to be allergic…he sneezes like crazy, but I've named her Caramel and I've started leaving food out back by the garage. She's really loveable towards me."

"I'm not sure if Petey's ever really been around a cat." I looked questioningly at Mom who only shrugged. "I don't think it'll be a problem."

"We only see her sporadically anyway. In fact, she hasn't been around in a couple of days." Gretchen wrinkled her brow and glanced around the darkened yard.

"Wow, Gretch. This house is monstrous. I can't wait to see inside. I bet it's gorgeous." Cassie was pulling our luggage from the back of the van.

"I hope it's gorgeous…and successful," Gretchen said, glancing thoughtfully back at her home. "Roger and I sunk what little we each had into it, and we've taken out enormous loans, of course. It's been quite an undertaking, to say the least."

We left our luggage on the veranda and Gretchen gave us a quick tour of the inside of the house. A heavy mahogany, etched glass door opened into a small foyer. In front of us was a wide staircase to the left of a narrow hall. Beautiful, glossy wood was everywhere and the scent of lemon polish lingered in the air. The stairs led up to three newly renovated bedrooms, each with adjoining baths. Gretchen indicated an area beneath the stairs where a storage closet had been cut open in the wall and converted into a counter which served as an old fashioned hotel desk.

At the foot of the staircase, on the left, a sitting room with divans and game tables could be glimpsed through an archway. Large bookcases consumed one wall and corner near the windows, and two more flanked a huge open fireplace, were big cozy chairs graced the hearth rug. The dining room was through an arch to the right of the stairs and hall. Both rooms had been meticulously restored true to late nineteenth century style, in the blues and greens and reds of the period. European rugs enhanced the glow of shiny hardwood floors and velvet and lace curtains adorned the floor to ceiling windows. Gretchen had thoughtfully placed lush plants here and there, and a beautiful upright piano occupied the dining room. Eventually, they planned to have live music during lunch and dinner hours, she explained.

At the rear of the dining room, around the corner, a little nook revealed a small, cramped staircase. Adjacent was a door leading to the other end of the hall we'd glimpsed in the foyer. Gretchen explained that these stairs had formerly led to maid's quarters, a room that now served as storage. Back out in the hall, on the way to the rear of the house, we passed a small public restroom with period wallpaper and a pedestal sink. Swinging doors led to the butler's pantry, master quarters and adjoining kitchen.

In the butler's pantry the door to the right led to the master bedroom suite that belonged to Gretchen and Roger. The suite was large enough for a small office area, an expansive bedroom with its own fireplace and television area, and an added on bath. Apparently, these quarters had also housed the Powell relative who served as the administrator when the home had been a business for a period of time. The kitchen was on the other side of the butler's pantry.

Upon entering the kitchen Cassie and I were immediately entranced. The old iron stove still functioned and had been kept around for the sake of atmosphere, but next to it also sat a state of the art oven and an enormous grill with six electric burners. A row of sinks and preparation tables lined one wall, while professional refrigeration and freezer units graced the next. In spite of all the modern accoutrements, Gretchen and Roger had managed to maintain an antiquated air during restoration. Booth seating for casual employee dining occupied a window area.

Cassie ran her hand enviously over the bronze cookware hanging over a butcher block island. "Girl, I am so jealous of you."

"How many cubic feet is this freezer?" I groaned, stroking it like a long lost love, on the verge of melting into a puddle on the red tile floor.

Gretchen flashed a brilliant smile and rolled her big blue eyes. "You guys! Come on. Roger's outside making dinner." Though Cassie and I were hesitant to leave the cooking area we tore ourselves away and exited through the rear door of the kitchen which opened into a screened in section of the wrap around porch. Down the steps a fire was visible in a huge brick barbeque pit. The smell of grilling meat wafted to us as the silhouette of a man with a spatula approached.

Gretchen flicked on the back porch lights. "Roger, you met Al and Cassie briefly, last year at Gram's funeral service. I think you met Flora too, Al's mom." Roger nodded his confirmation as Gretchen continued. "And, this little guy is Petey." Petey was sitting obediently by Mom's side, but his black, marble eyes were unmistakably sizing up Roger's leg so I quickly scooped him into my arms.

Though Gretchen had been dating Roger for almost three years while he finished law school and sought employment as an attorney, I had only met him once…a year ago at Gretchen's grandmother's funeral in Crescentville. Gretchen and Roger had attended the same college in Connecticut and that is where they had both been settled before deciding to purchase the Spring Valley property.

Roger had not changed in a year. He was tall and gangly, freckles sprinkled his nose, just like Gretchen, but his brilliant orange hair contrasted with his fair skin. Though he was the least attractive man pretty, peppy Gretchen had ever dated, he seemed friendly and intelligent. They shared similar interests and Roger appeared a stable, loyal mate for Gretchen, whose life had proven to be less than steady in the past. With her grandmother gone, and no contact with her parents, we were the closest thing to family she had. Gretchen deserved to build a solid home of her own with someone she could depend upon, and apparently, she had found just those qualities in Roger. I was happy for her.

It was still fairly warm and comfortable outside so we elected to eat at a picnic table near the grill. This area would be landscaped with flowers in the spring, and now I could vaguely make out small animal statuary in the shadows of the empty flowerbeds. The trees hung with lanterns to illuminate our food, and a large candle, protected by a hurricane globe, was the centerpiece of the table.

Over the course of a meal of grilled pork chops, potatoes and squash, Roger explained how he had coincidentally spent a small amount of time in Spring Valley when he was a young boy. His mother had even been a maid at the Elderberry Inn in town years and years ago and they had briefly lived with some distant relatives before she found work in Connecticut and they moved. Connecticut was where Roger had primarily grown up and elected to remain throughout his college years and his first position as an attorney.

In an odd twist of events, a fellow lawyer from the Connecticut law firm was the means by which Roger came to know about the Spring Valley property. Buck Thistle had moved to Spring Valley some months before but kept in touch with Roger. Having met Gretchen, and knowing of the couple's dream to eventually run their own business, Buck informed Roger of the death of the property's former owner, Lillian Powell, and of the available real estate. Roger made a quick visit and felt drawn to the house almost immediately. It was perfect for what Gretchen had in mind. Although he hated to leave his mother behind in Connecticut, it did not take much to convince Gretchen that they should make a go of it in Spring Valley.

Gretchen and Roger explained what little they knew of the tragic family history that surrounded the Powells, the family who had owned the land for as long as anyone could remember. Many, mainly the men, met with untimely deaths at a young age, and as far as anyone knew Lillian was the last of the family line. She had never married and had no children. With no known living relatives and no will, the land and house were auctioned off upon her death. Gretchen and Roger pooled everything they had to acquire it and took out more loans to fund the restoration process.

The once famous spring pooled into a small lagoon in the forest on the property. For many decades guests had traveled great distances to convalesce and bathe in the waters which were purported to have healing powers.

The main part of the present house had been built in the 1840s when the property had functioned as a rather large and successful farm. An addition had been added to the back of the home toward the turn of the twentieth century and the family had kept the residence well maintained ever since, adding upgrades such as plumbing and central air conditioning over time.

Roger revealed that the home and grounds had been private property until after the Civil War when several of the Powell women were left widowed. Alone and nearly penniless, with their children to support, the women banded together, determined to scrimp and survive as a group. Unfortunately, having few funds between them and a large farm to care for, it wasn't long before the women faced the prospect of losing their home. Unable to pay for taxes and upkeep they sought help from their local parish and eventually struck a deal with the church, offering their home as a treatment facility for sick and wounded soldiers. The church was anxious to acquire the property and supported the cause. The house was protected as the parish allowed the family to stay with the nuns who moved in to care for the ill and maimed men who had no where else to go.

The Powell ladies worked for the church but also bolstered their own income by selling off acreage here and there, and raising dairy cattle. With the help of their growing children, the ladies grew food on the land to feed themselves, the charitable nurses they resided with, and their patients.

By the turn of the century only sixty acres of the original property remained, but word of the retreat's good reputation and the soothing spring waters on the grounds had spread. The home eventually became a hospice for individuals who suffered from consumption, also known as tuberculosis. The spring waters and relaxing atmosphere were considered a last resort for many people who suffered symptoms of the disease that was so prominent during that period of history. The Powell women worked side by side next to the nuns for decades. Eventually there became such demand for patient care that the construction of a sanatorium was funded by the church. The new building was situated behind the house and was created to care for the gravely ill who must be isolated.

By the 1920s, as medical science and the local economy evolved, a legitimate hospital was constructed in the neighboring county and the church awarded the home back to the family. The enterprising ladies, their grown offspring, and extended family, revamped the facility into a resort and spa, continuing to boast the natural curative properties of the spring waters on the grounds. The sanatorium was converted into a luxurious guesthouse with several sleeping rooms. A handful of cottages were built on the grounds as well.

This expansion afforded the Powell family more privacy as the main house became a private residence again. The business met with success, even in spite of the depression of the 1930s. It was operated through the early 70s when younger Powell descendents decided to pursue ventures in town or outside of Spring Valley. Now Gretchen and Roger intended to open the home to the public again as a bed and breakfast.

Remnants of prior enterprises remained, the burnt out structure that had once been the sanatorium, and later more guest housing, still lay beyond the back yard of the primary residence. Roger gestured out into the darkness and explained that the ruined building beyond had been set on fire decades ago by a colorful Powell relative who had spent some time in a mental institution following the death of her husband, whom she had been accused of killing.

Five cottages, some distance apart, dotted the eastern grounds. Gretchen and Roger had not begun to update the cottages, but claimed they were still suitable for guests, as long as they didn't mind the outdated furnishings and plumbing fixtures.

Roger did most of the talking during the meal, and it seemed to me that Gretchen had grown unusually quiet. She was animated when we toured the house, but was now somewhat sullen. I started to notice that Roger and she spoke directly to each other only when necessary and I sensed that there was a bit of tension between them.

Maybe she was tired. Maybe I was paranoid. I kept having that creepy "somebody standing too close" feeling, and turned more than once from my food to glance back at the house. About halfway through the meal I started having trouble swallowing…which was odd. Maybe it was the dark, and the sad history of the property. We'd had a long day. I continued to justify away my symptoms, as I had in the van, a little angry at myself and afraid that I was letting my anxiety get the best of me.

Cassie began to yawn and noted that it was well after ten o'clock. The night was finally taking on that fall chill and Mom was nodding off over her tea, while Petey snored against my feet beneath the table. His warm little body felt good against my cold ankles.

We had a quick discussion about sleeping arrangements and Cassie and I agreed to take cottages since Roger's mother and his aunt and uncle would be arriving in a couple of days and they would be staying in the main house. That way we wouldn't have to move our stuff and Gretchen wouldn't have to change sheets and worry about doing laundry for two bedrooms.

"Flora, why don't you stay in the main house too? Upstairs. You can pick your favorite room." Gretchen invited with a wink toward me. "We alarm the house at night," she whispered.

I felt a bit apprehensive at leaving my mother alone in a strange place at night, but Gretchen was aware of her condition and Mom seemed thrilled at the prospect of staying in one of the newly decorated rooms. Mom never woke up confused at home, but if that happened while we were here, I'd rather she wander around inside the main house setting off alarms than end up in the woods outside the cottages.

After settling Mom and making sure she had everything she needed for the night, Gretchen retrieved keys from the front desk and stepped outside to direct me and Cassie toward our quarters. I had volunteered to take Petey after all so Mom wouldn't have to worry about letting him out during the night.

Cassie hugged Gretchen beneath the monstrous tree in the front yard and headed down the knoll. Gretchen hugged me as well but just before I turned away her grip tightened and she whispered into my ear, "I need to talk to you tomorrow…alone." She released me with a frown but before I could respond she was bolting back toward the house where I saw Roger waiting quietly on the porch. They hurried into the house together and I hesitated for a moment, trying to shake the heavy mantle of unease from my shoulders, before I followed Cassie down the hill.

I took cabin number one and watched Cassie in the moonlight, cursing all the way to cabin number two, her rolling luggage bouncing and catching on every tree root between the cottages. Each of the little buildings had a yellow porch light burning. I waited until I heard her key jangle in the lock and her sleepy "goodnight" wafted to me over the hum of window air conditioning units. Petey relieved himself one more time and we approached our own room.

The door stuck at first, but with a couple of hearty shoves it flew open, and out fled a hunk of fluff who I assumed to be Caramel, the missing cat. With a shriek she streaked between my legs and ran off into the night, scaring Petey and I half to death. She must have gotten in while Gretchen cleaned the cottage. Whew, now my heart was really racing in my chest. I habitually touched my waist pack for comfort, took a deep breath, looked back at the large house on the hill and gathered my bags. Petey ventured forth first.

Chapter 5

She was a problem...this one was. Curious, willful, too stupid to mind her own business, and slightly touched as well. A dangerous combination.

The spirit standing beneath the old oak tree in front of Gretchen's house had sensed the girl's energy approaching all day. Now the ghost observed the little idiot hesitating, looking back up the hill before tentatively entering tiny cottage number one. The girl had stared directly at the phantom and the specter could not help but chuckle, in spite of its anger at the danger she represented. Human eyes could not perceive the ghost, not unless it wanted them to. Glee bubbled over and laughter that could only be heard on another plane of existence rose into the night. Laughter that rustled the leaves of the mighty oak like a breeze only that single tree could feel. The branches swayed as if something large and invisible embodied them.

The ghost reflected over the decades. They had all been so easy to manipulate; paralyzed by confusion, fear, pride...guilt. All but that last one. Stubborn, yes...but her time had passed, just like the others. Now that the end was drawing near the spirit also longed for peace, though it had no idea what form that peace might take. Nothing must interfere. Not even this most unpleasant, unexpected fool.

Yes, she was a threat…this one. A threat which must be dealt with.

Chapter 6

The smell of cold, musty, re-circulated air assaulted me as I entered cottage number one. After I located the light switch next to the door, psychedelic wallpaper was next to attack.

"Yow!" I winced, slammed the door and locked it behind me. Though the cottage appeared to be clean, its interior was indeed very outdated. The open room contained a small Formica table graced by a huge ceramic owl lamp in front of a single front window. There were three vinyl kitchen chairs, two pumpkin orange and one a torn lime green. The wall behind the bed was metallically papered and along the other cheaply paneled wall, a worn gold couch rested beneath the air conditioner, next to a tiny, scarred dresser which boasted a cracked mirror and a thirteen inch black and white TV. I ran my hand over the ancient set.

There was a small walkway between the couch, the dresser and the foot of a queen sized bed. The bedspread could best be described as late 60s acid trip, and the carpeting was an early 70s shag; the color of which, upon close inspection, has most notably been seen coming out of someone's mouth in any number of Hollywood possession flicks. If this was any indication of the other four cottage interiors, I was sure to find finicky Cassie snoozing on the bench seat of our van in the morning.

Beyond a tiny closet, next to the bed, the carpet ended and gave way to shabby linoleum and a little kitchenette with a small window above the sink. I washed my face and brushed my teeth in the adjacent bathroom and considered a shower, but the tub reminded me too much of other well known horror films, so I slipped out of my bra without removing my barbeque sauce stained t-shirt, shimmied off my Capri pants...noting the splotch of chocolate ice cream on the rear (How did that get there? I'd been so careful!)...and kicked off my shoes at the edge of the bed. I did not want to risk my bare feet touching the rug.

With a few cursory glances and sniffs I found no evidence of cat poo, so I hoisted Petey up next to me and was suddenly glad of his company. He had been sneezing since we entered the room, and now his little nose was running. I wiped it with the edge of the sheet and tried to make him nestle his warm little body against mine, but when his sneezing subsided he began to vigilantly stare at something across the room.

"Stop it, Petey. You're giving me the creeps." I knew from my paranormal dabbling that animals were often sensitive to the supernatural. Petey continued to stare across the room and began to whimper, and it wasn't until I slipped on my shoes and turned the ugly owl lamp around to face the opposite wall that he settled down. Scratch, scratch, scratch. Turn, turn, turn. He sleepily plopped down on the offensive bedspread, sneezed, yawned, and was out like a light. My watch matched the wind up clock on the night stand. Eleven-fifteen. I had forgotten to flip the switch next to the door, but as I eyed the matted carpet and the light switch from across the room, I elected to sleep with the owl lamp on. Before long Petey's soft little Puggy snores and the incessant tick, tick of the alarm clock had lulled me off to dreamland.

* * *

I'm not sure what woke me up. Be it the smell of Petey, the freezing cold room, or the fact that the owl lamp was off, but around three a.m. I sat straight up in bed. For a moment I thought the bed had tremored, but I dismissed the movement when I heard Petey groan in the darkness. I sensed him roll to his side and heard him emit an unhealthy blast in my direction. Damn ice cream! I thought of Cassie sleeping soundly in the cottage next door and pinched my nose shut. I toyed with marching him over to cottage number two, knocking and running, leaving Petey on Cassie's doorstep to deal with. Instead I jumped from beneath the covers without thinking and my stomach rolled as my feet hit the nasty carpet.

I made my way to the lamp. The bulb must have burned out. I jiggled the base, attempted to tighten the bulb, and clicked the switch on the lamp itself. Nothing. Great! My bag was still by the door and Petey's leash was somewhere behind it. I felt for it in the moonlight illuminating around the edge of the drapes. "Good gravy!" I groused. "Come on Stinky. Let's go out." I felt for my shoes and tugged on the stained Capri pants before leashing Petey up. His belly felt bloated as I lifted him to the floor from the bed. When I picked him up another stream of warm gas grazed my arm.

"Gross!" I resisted the impulse to drop him on his head and clumsily set him down.

We trundled to the door and out into the night. Petey was wide awake now and scampering about looking for a good spot with a fair sense of urgency. I realized I had not taken my contacts out before drifting off to sleep and had apparently lost one. One eye focused while the other remained blurry. Crap! I was always paranoid about one going behind my eye and getting lost in my head, or some crazy thing like that. I firmly believed that had to be possible, no matter what anyone said. People got stuff stuck in their eyes all the time, right? Right…I reasoned with myself. Exactly why I never used tampons! But, shouldn't my eye hurt? I didn't think my eye hurt. Or did it?

I felt my brow bead with sweat and racked my brain trying to think if I had seen any news reports about this very situation while I closed first one eye and then the other, distractedly following Petey to the edge of the woods behind the cottage. I couldn't come up with anyone I knew who had lost a contact in their eye, thereby consequently losing an eye, but my bowels roiled with anxiety just the same. Was there a hospital in Spring Valley? My chest tightened and I unconsciously patted my hip. Where did I put my pack? This was ridiculous.

Petey and the end of the leash disappeared into the brush and trees. We were out of the moonlight and in the cover of shadow. I heard him rooting and rustling around. I was so sleepy and freaked out about my contact lens that I didn't even have the sense to be wary of my surroundings. Suddenly, about fifty yards away, behind Cassie's cottage, someone leapt from the trees. I shrieked, tripped over Petey and went down in the brush with a thud.

I scooted until my back was against a tree and I was sure we were out of sight. I hugged Petey to my chest, closing my blurry eye and trying to make out the identity of the person in the milky moonshine who hesitated in the shadow of cottage number two. It was the silhouette of a man, a tall man. He had burst from the brush with such speed that he appeared to be disoriented. He crouched for a moment and looked around, then ran swiftly in my direction.

I shrank against the trunk of the tree, willing Petey to be quiet. Had we been seen? I hoped not. The figure was almost by us when I realized it was Roger. He turned to look behind him, slack jawed with panic, eyes wide as if he had seen a ghost, then he bolted up the slope to the main house. I waited several moments to see if he were being followed then scurried into cottage one with Petey still in my arms.

I entered the cabin and unconsciously flipped the light switch on the wall, slamming the door behind me and locking it…jiggling the handle…and leaning against the door to catch my breath. I only began to relax after Petey and I had checked under the bed and the kitchen sink, in the shower and the closet, and I had located my missing contact lens in my tangled hair while removing cockleburs.

After removing burrs from the dog as well, I burrowed beneath the hideous blanket with the warmth of Petey beside me, the dim bulb of the owl lamp shining from across the room.

Exhausted, but curious about Roger, my mind wandered. I felt myself begin to relax and drift off after an hour or so. Then, in that murky place between reality and sleep I realized with a chill…the light switch that controlled the ugly lamp had been off, *pressed down*, when I re-entered the cabin, but I had definitely left it on at eleven fifteen when I fell asleep.

I spent the wee hours of Monday holding Petey and watching the slow tick, tick of the wind up alarm clock next to my bed until the sun peeked around the drapes. Then I finally nodded off.

Chapter 7

Monday

Still a little sick to his stomach, poor Petey woke me up at eight, needing another trip outside. I assumed my eyes were achy and burning since I had hardly slept, but for some reason my legs also itched.

I spent a few moments next to the door flipping the light switch up and down and watched, disturbed, as the lamp obeyed without a hitch. Then, I opened the door, peering left and right before allowing Petey out into the yard. He made a beeline for the tree in front of my cottage then scampered right back. Knowing Petey, now that he was empty, breakfast was foremost on his mind.

I found some plastic bowls in the kitchenette and left a bowl of water and a bowl of dry food for Petey in the corner on the linoleum, then shuffled into the shower. Still creeped out by the events of the night before, I left the bathroom door and shower curtain open while I quickly washed my hair and rinsed off. Angry red welts were forming on my legs, and I noticed more itchy blotches on my arms. Poison ivy! I hastily thought of my backless bridesmaid dress then shrieked in horror when I examined myself more closely in the mirror. I had taken out my remaining contact last night and my left eyelid was now slightly swollen and blistered.

Knowing Petey's coat would be contaminated as well; I haphazardly rinsed him in the shower and toweled him dry. Next I hastily dressed, and donned an old pair of glasses that I always kept in my purse for emergencies such as this.

Petey was on my heels as we dashed up the knoll. Whoa! Gretchen's house was even more impressive in the daylight. Bright white with its enormous porch columns and Victorian architecture, it roosted on the hill on a massive stone foundation like some great living creature, well aware of its own magnificence. I stopped for a moment to consider the elaborate carvings in the eaves and the complicated roof structure as the composition stared aloofly back at me with cool, glass eyes. The van was still parked beneath the behemoth oak tree, which, I could now see, was a blaze of shiny autumn orange.

I craned my neck and looked up into the array of twisted, thick branches. All the leaves clung with life to the branches, none of them succumbing to the season, ready to die and drift to the ground. I thought I detected movement, a rustle high up in the labyrinth. A squirrel no doubt, or maybe that cat. Petey sneezed. Tearing my eyes away I banged at the van window, which, predictably, was opened a crack. Sure enough, Cassie's tousled black bob presented itself. She reached for her own glasses on the console and threw open the sliding side door.

"Holy macaroni!" she exclaimed. "What happened to you?"

"Poison ivy…I think." I was still breathing heavily from my quick ascent up the hill and bent over to catch my breath, my hands on both knees. I should work out more.

Petey scampered into the van and Cassie shoved him back out. "Where did you…"

"Not now…I'll explain later. I have to see if Gretchen has some lotion…and I think I'm going to need a doctor to look at this eye. Can you drive me into town in a little bit?"

"Sure, why not?" Cassie yawned, pulled the door closed, and fell back onto the seat.

Next I ran upstairs, shouting as soon as I cleared the landing. "Mom! Mom!"

"In here, honey." The door at the top of the stairs was cracked and I raced Petey to it, finding Mom lounging safely in the beautiful French blue floral room I had left her in the night before. She was sipping coffee; a half eaten croissant rested on dainty china on the coverlet and a half read novel was open beside the plate. "What happened to you?" She cried, leaping from the bed and heading toward me. Then thinking better of it…she drew back a little. Just the compassion I had been looking for. Still, the concern on her face was a comfort. No matter how old you are there is something about a little "mom" sympathy that no one else in the world can replicate. I resisted the urge to fall into her arms.

"Poison ivy…I think. Don't come any closer!" I warned. "Can Petey stay with you? I need to get some drops for this eye." I pulled her medication from my pack and, taking care not to touch the pills themselves, opened the compartment for Monday and deposited them on the plate next to her breakfast.

Mom drew back as if I had the plague. She regarded Petey warily, who was already making himself at home on a plush chaise lounge in the corner.

"I showered him off. I think he's okay now. But I'll get some dog shampoo in town."

"Where's that little kennel?" Mom was just as allergic to poison ivy as I was. "Hey, if you're going into town could you develop my pictures? I saw one of those one-hour counters at the pharmacy." She returned to the bed and popped her pills in her mouth, indicating, with a wave of her hand, two plastic vials of film on the dresser by her camera bag.

I grabbed the film and shoved it into my pocket as I bolted back down the stairs to retrieve the kennel from the van. Cassie was gone but a bed pillow and blanket remained. She must have gone back to cottage number two to shower.

As soon as I had Petey settled in Mom's room I went looking for Gretchen. She wasn't at the hotel desk, in the sitting room, or the dining room. Maybe she and Roger were still in bed. I quietly crept toward the back of the house longing for a cup of coffee and a phone book so I could seek medical attention. I entered the butler's pantry and fell short. Angry, low voices could be heard coming from the kitchen.

"You know what I'm talking about," Roger hissed. The mild mannered fiancé didn't sound so friendly and loving this morning. I crept a little closer.

"Stop it, Roger. Stop it right now!" The sound of Gretchen's voice catching broke my heart. I immediately felt hostile toward Roger. I always thought they got along so well. I felt a knot form in my throat and quietly tried to clear it.

"I can't. We've got to figure this out."

"There's nothing to figure out. You're acting crazy."

"*I'm* acting crazy?" Roger started to raise his voice. The floor creaked beneath my feet. I felt like something was pressing around my neck.

"Shhh," Gretchen cautioned and sniffled.

"I'm not the one…"

"Shhh…." she urged again.

I coughed to catch air and couldn't hide myself any longer so I called out as if I had just entered the pantry and then pushed my way quickly into the kitchen.

"Roger? Gretchen? Oh, here you are."

They were seated at the kitchen's booth. Gretchen wiped her eyes and turned her head away. It took them both a moment to switch gears and force a smile, but there was no hiding her tear streaked cheeks.

"Good morning, Al!" Roger called heartily. "Want some coffee?"

"No, thanks."

"Breakfast?"

"No, thanks." I glared at him then tried to get a better look at Gretchen. Roger looked mildly perplexed and she wouldn't meet my gaze.

"Actually, I think I need a phone book. I walked Petey last night, around three a.m.," I looked meaningfully back at Roger. "Somehow I've contracted poison ivy. It's in my eye." I pointed dramatically at my face. Roger frowned as Gretchen jumped to her feet.

"Oh, Al! I'm so sorry. Let me get you some lotion. There's an eye doctor near town. Let me find the phone book." She pushed past me quickly, anxious to get out of the room. I was sure she made a beeline for the bathroom to splash cold water on her red, swollen face.

Roger shifted uncomfortably in his seat under my stare.

"That's too bad, Al. Coffee?" he offered again.

I shook my head slowly.

"Are you sure you don't want some breakfast?"

I shook my head again. "You need to be careful, Roger. I think I got this rash from the weeds around the woods behind the cottages. Maybe you should check yourself out."

His orange head tilted as if he didn't understand my cold tone, but his eyes were sharp. Gretchen nervously re-entered the room and thrust a pink bottle and a small red book toward me. "Fortunately, I've never been allergic to poison ivy, Al." Roger said evenly.

"Good thing." I stared him down, and turned to Gretchen who was puttering around putting their dirty dishes in the sink. "I'll be back." I said, a little too seriously. Gretchen glanced at me quizzically before I rushed out of the room, almost knocking Cassie down in the hall.

"Come on. Let's go." I hissed.

"Owww! You're hurting my arm. What is wrong with you?"

"Shut up! Let's go!" I spat under my breath.

In the safety of the van I told her about the events of the night before as we barreled toward Spring Valley.

"Do you think someone was in your room? Roger? Could he have turned the light switch off?"

"Maybe. When we came down to the cottages he was with Gretchen, but I'm sure they have extra keys to all of the rooms. What time did you go to the van?"

"Ugh." Cassie shuddered. "Almost immediately. My bedspread was giving me a headache, even with the lights out. The person who designed my room was either color blind or severely stoned."

I giggled and resisted the urge to scratch my eye. "Mine isn't any better. Trust me. I'm sure they'll be gorgeous when Gretchen is done with them...but until then..." I shuddered dramatically and Cassie laughed.

The phone book for Spring Valley had only one eye doctor listed. From the little map of the county inside the directory his office was on the outskirts of town. We recognized the name of his street as one we had passed while searching for Gallows Road the night before and finally found his exact address on his roadside mailbox. A sign at the bottom of the long gravel driveway confirmed we were in the right spot. Dr. David G. Gordman. His office was obviously in his home. Surely he could write a prescription.

Cassie let me out of the van near the house while she parked in the little gravel lot adjacent to the doctor's backyard hammock. I raced up the porch steps and stopped cold. A wooden hand painted plaque hung from a crooked rusty wire on the screen door frame. "Closed. Gone Fishing." I was desperately knocking anyway when Cassie huffed up the steps behind me.

"You're kidding me!?" she exclaimed.

"Now what am I gonna do?" Cassie sensed my panic and took my hand. We headed back toward the van.

"We're gonna go back to town to the pharmacy. You can drop off your mom's film and we'll see what the pharmacist suggests." Her matter of fact manner calmed me down a bit. My body and face were itching like crazy and my eyeball burned in its socket. All I could think about was ruining Gretchen's wedding photos with my ugly red welts.

The ride back to town was short now that we had learned our way around the countryside. We pulled up in front of the pharmacy with the soda fountain. Cassie filled out forms to turn in Mom's film while I waited patiently to talk to the pharmacist.

Finally it was my turn, and though he had several creams available for my skin, he thought it best that an actual doctor look at my eye. I bought a bottle of medicated dog shampoo and Cassie and I took off with directions to my only other option…the emergency room of a medical center thirty miles away.

So, it was over the river and through the woods…actually, through the creepy four hundred year old bridge…and back out to the highway where we headed for a slightly larger town called Mason.

After a two hour wait in the very tiny waiting room of a very tiny medical center I was finally called back. Apparently, being the only hospital in a thirty to forty mile radius, they were not hurting for business. Cassie joined me as the nurse led us to a curtained cubicle labeled with the number two.

The nurse took my vital signs and medical history. Forty-five minutes later a very young doctor appeared. Very young. He might have been in his late twenties, like Cassie and I, but his cherubic face and lack of whiskers made me wonder if he weren't some sort of child genius. I was mentally calculating college duration and how long medical school should take a normal person when Cassie attempted a joke.

"Does your mother know you're here?" He didn't look amused. In fact he looked like crap. "Sorry," she murmured when he rolled his eyes beneath a tousled head of dark hair.

"No, *I'm* sorry," he apologized and stifled a yawn as he perused my chart. "I've had four hours of sleep in two days. The flu is going around and we're short handed. And yes, my mother knows I'm here." He turned his bloodshot eyes to me. "Okay, what have we got?"

I indicated my eye and skin and he slipped on a pair of latex gloves. "Hmmm. Any idea what you might have gotten into?"

"Looks like poison ivy to me." Cassie chirped from a metal and plastic chair next to my bed.

He ignored her and checked out the inside of my arms. "I'll be right back." He strode from the cubicle.

Cassie shrugged and pulled herself up from the uncomfortable chair. "I gotta go to the bathroom."

I was left to study my surroundings, trying to ignore the screaming baby behind curtain number one and the painful moans behind curtain number three. We were all separated by about six feet with a thin green curtain between us. I picked at a hang nail and hoped nobody was contagious. A couple of minutes later Cassie hustled back into my area.

"You're not gonna believe this! He's out there looking you up in a book?"

"Huh?"

"I passed the nurses station and he's out there looking at pictures of rashes in a freak'n book." Brisk footsteps approached and Cassie quickly plopped back down into the chair. The plastic back groaned in protest.

"Looks like poison ivy to me." The young doctor drew back my curtain and commented. It was all I could do to keep from giggling so I bit my lip. Cassie let out a snort and ducked her head down. She pretended to dig in her purse for something.

"Ya' think?" I asked. He completely missed my sarcasm.

"I'm pretty sure," he said seriously. "Have you ever had poison ivy before?"

"Yes."

"Did it look like this?"

"Yes."

He suddenly looked very pleased with himself as he handed me two prescriptions, one for my rash and one for my eye. With a few other tidbits of advice we were ushered back out to the waiting room where we erupted into laughter as soon as we were alone.

"I should have gone to the library instead of the emergency room!"

"How much was your co-pay?"

"Fifty bucks!"

"Unbelievable." Cassie shook her head and we got back into the van. "Oh well, you still needed the prescription for your eye." I agreed and we began the return trip to Spring Valley where we waited an hour at the pharmacy for my medication before finally heading for Getchen's late in the afternoon.

On the way back I realized we'd forgotten to pick up Mom's pictures. Oh well. I was exhausted and I didn't dare ask Cassie to turn around. Our first day of vacation had not gone well. Poor Cassie. Unfortunately this wasn't the first time we had taken a trip together and spent the day in the ER. Even more unfortunately, it probably wouldn't be the last.

Chapter 8

I was hoping to catch Gretchen alone but when we arrived Roger informed us that she and Mom had taken a walk together. After a few awkward moments with Roger, I excused myself and took Petey from the kennel upstairs and back to my room to bathe him.

Cassie lounged on my ugly bedspread reading an old magazine and we hollered back and forth over the running water and splashing dog. Luckily, Petey loved to bathe. In fact, he practically bathed himself. He would run from one end of the tub to the other, skidding to a stop, prancing and snorting. Soon we were both sopping wet. I pulled the plug and wrapped him in a couple of towels. He wriggled from my arms and ran around the room shaking himself instead.

"Your room's gonna smell like wet dog." Cassie observed.

"Is there any room left in the van?"

"Not for Petey."

"Actually, for me. I was thinking of giving him the room."

Cassie chuckled. "Well, he should be fine…aren't dogs supposed to be color blind?' We both laughed and then she grew serious. "So what do you think is up? Any vibes?"

I poured myself into one of the ugly chairs and dried my legs so I could apply medicated cream to them. "No. This property sort of gives me the creeps, but I think it's because these stories of the past just kinda hang over it. I love the house though. I don't think Roger and Gretchen are happy with each other right now. Of course, I'm going to take Gretchen's side over his no matter what. Something's cooking and I don't like the smell of it. I intend to find out what it is before Gretchen takes a walk down the aisle."

"Agreed," Cassie sighed and hoisted herself from the bed. "I think I'll walk over there and see if the girls are back yet."

"Hang on, I'll come with you." I pulled on a dry t-shirt and loose jeans and put Petey on his leash to keep him out of the weeds.

Cassie and I meandered up from the cottages, our feet crunching in the few fallen leaves. We found Mom and Gretchen seated at the picnic table behind the house having a conversation and some warm apple cider. Mom's camera rested close to her. She waved excitedly when she saw us.

"I can't wait to see some of the shots I took today. Gretchen and I walked back to the old cemetery on the property. The tombstones are amazing."

"A cemetery?" Cassie plunked down on the bench next to Gretchen who was nodding the affirmative. "You have a cemetery on your property? Who's buried there?"

"Mainly settlers of the area, and a vast majority of the Powells from various centuries. Plus a few other people. Servants, we think. Some of the stones are unreadable because they're so old. We think that the ones from the late 1800's might include hospice patients. Also, some of the nuns that were caretakers here. Roger and I plan to do research on the stones once the house is done and we have more time."

I unleashed Petey and he stood on his hind legs next to Mom, his little corkscrew tail wagging. "He just had a bath." I informed her. Petey whined his interest in sitting next to her on the bench and she bent to lift him up.

"How far is the cemetery from the house?" I inquired. I suddenly wished I'd brought some of my recording equipment from home. A midnight vigil in a deserted country cemetery sounded a lot more appealing than another night in my psychedelic bedroom.

Mom gestured toward the blaze of trees behind the cottages. "That way. Skirt the edge of the woods, and over that knoll you'll find the late Ms. Powell's old garden area. Go across the small field beyond it. There'll be a fence post and you can hear the spring's pool gurgling in the woods. Continue to skirt around the woods and the cemetery is on the other side of the trees near the edge of the property line. Probably a ten minute walk or so."

"Hmm," I gazed toward the trees thoughtfully, thinking of Roger the night before. The walk to the cemetery was probably a lot shorter if you cut right through the woods behind the cottages.

"Count me out." Cassie blurted.

"Huh?"

"Count me out."

"I don't know what you're talking about."

"I know what you're thinking and you need to wait for Alex if you want to do any ghost hunting. I'm not hanging out in a cemetery with you when I'm supposed to be on vacation."

"Oh, you're just scared because of the EVPs we collected last time you came out with me."

"EVPs?" Gretchen asked.

"Electronic Voice Phenomenon. You place a recorder in an area you're investigating and when you play it back later you can sometimes catch some pretty interesting sounds."

"Sounds pretty harmless, Cassie. What's wrong with that?" Gretchen inquired.

Mom was stroking Petey's ears. His buggy eyes were closed and his tongue lolled out of one side of his mouth in pleasure. If he were a cat he would have been purring. "Something, or someone, said Cassie's name." Mom told Gretchen.

"It did not." Cassie was clearly still agitated by the event.

"Actually, Cass…it did." Mom said calmly.

"Did not!" Cassie's jaw was set at a stubborn angle.

"Well did it, or didn't it?" Gretchen asked with interest.

"It did." Mom and I replied simultaneously with Cassie's rather indignant "Did not!"

"Let's change the subject," Mom urged. "Deloris, what did the doctor have to say?" She must have been irritated by our bickering…there was that first name again.

Cassie began to chuckle and I gave her a playful kick under the table. "He said I have poison ivy."

"Well, we already knew that. What's so funny?" Mom murmured, lifting Petey to her face, kissing his furrowed brow and then setting him on the ground. He scampered to relieve himself on the tree shading the table then began to peruse the statuary in the flower beds. I watched him circle a cement baby deer, bypass a jaunty little gnome, then sit parallel to a concrete squirrel, its tail aloft as it hunched over, cradling a nut between its little paws. Petey began shooting the squirrel little sideways glances and looking innocently back at us at the picnic table. I had watched him consider each lawn ornament and thought of the fairy tale of the little girl who ventured into the bear's house. Too big…too small….etc.

Cassie was filling Mom and Gretchen in on my hospital visit when Roger stepped out onto the back porch. Gretchen had been laughing and joking but I did not fail to notice how quickly she sobered when Roger appeared.

"Hello Roger!" Mom called. She was obviously oblivious to the tension. Cassie and I shot each other a meaningful glance.

"Afternoon!" he called jovially. "What do you ladies think about a trip into town for dinner tonight? I hear the Elderberry Inn has some excellent Monday night specials. Gretchen and I can check out our competition and we can all have a night on the town."

Gretchen shrugged and looked around the table. "Sounds okay to me. Girls?"

"Oh!" Mom clapped her hands softly together. "A trip to town would be lovely. Then you won't have to cook for us."

Cassie and I agreed and Roger stepped back inside. Petey had inched himself closer to the squirrel and now leaned suggestively against it.

"By the way Al, have you seen my reading glasses?" Mom asked me, her brow knitted. Lately it was not unusual for her to misplace things. I was noticing it more and more, but never pointed out the frequency to her. She seemed disturbed enough as it was, always second guessing even common mistakes.

"I thought you had them on this morning when I came into your room."

Mom looked thoughtful for a moment. "Maybe I left them on the covers and they fell onto the floor when I made up the bed this morning."

"I'm sure that's what happened," I smiled reassuringly. "If you don't see them before we leave for the inn, I'll help you look." Mom looked worried but smiled half heartedly in return.

We all chatted a little longer and as the sun began to set decided to retire to get ready for dinner. I procrastinated for a few moments, detached Petey from his new found love, slowly snapping the leash on him and hung back as Cassie started down the knoll to cottage number two. Mom had just gone inside and I saw no sign of Roger.

"So, what did you need to talk to me about, Gretchen?"

Her eyes grew wide and she glanced nervously toward the house. "I need to talk to you alone, later. You didn't happen to bring any of that EVP stuff with you did you?"

"Well, no, but Alex is coming in a couple of days and…"

"That might be too late," she whispered with such desperation that I felt a chill run down my spine.

"Gretchen. Can I speak with you for a minute?" Without a sound, Roger had stepped back out onto the porch. I saw Gretchen's eyes fill with tears and she blinked rapidly to hold them at bay.

"Coming!" She called forcefully, cheerfully, before hastily reaching out to squeeze my hand. "Later…we'll talk later." She turned, and, pony tail bouncing, bounded toward the house. Roger silently watched her approach and with a pointed glance my way over his shoulder, placed his hand on the small of her back and ushered her through the screen door.

My blood began to boil beneath my itchy skin as a wave of protectiveness toward Gretchen washed over me. I didn't know what was happening. I didn't know what I was seeing…but I most definitely knew I didn't like it.

Chapter 9

We had agreed to meet back up at the main house in an hour, so I figured I had time for a quick shower when I returned to my cottage with Petey. The room was no less ugly, and since there was the hint of a chill outside tonight I had turned the air conditioner down but left it on to keep the stale air circulating.

Having left the kennel in Mom's room I decided to leave Petey to his own devices while we were gone at dinner. He had scampered into the room and made himself at home on the revolting bedspread. He was on his back, feet in the air, snoring before I'd even selected my clothing for the evening. Apparently, his tryst with the concrete squirrel had rendered him exhausted. I took my clothes in the bathroom with me and hurriedly showered and washed my hair; patted myself dry and began to apply my poison ivy cream to my skin.

At some point I noticed Petey had left the bed and sat outside the bathroom threshold watching me get ready. "Petey, you perv." His ears were perked and his head cocked to one side. After a few more moments he began to whine. "What's the matter? Do you need to go out? Hang on." I said with exasperation and cleared my throat. I had that weird, tight sensation in my neck again.

Next, I administered my eye medication and slipped on my old glasses, bra, underpants and jeans then bent over the sink to brush my teeth. That's when I noticed my mom's reading glasses folded up and resting next to the faucet. That's weird. Had I grabbed them by mistake? I was wracking my brain trying to figure out when I might have had the opportunity, when Petey began to growl and bark.

"What's the matter with you?" I plugged in my hair dryer and coughed. Maybe *I* was allergic to something. That cat had been in our room. Taking a dry washcloth I began to wipe the steam from the mirror absentmindedly, watching Petey go berserk outside the doorway snarling, and pawing with great agitation. "You need to chill out mister!" I admonished, glancing back at my own reflection. The mirror had quickly begun to steam over again.

"Ah, poo!" Petey sneezed and looked up at me with a confused expression.

Just then the bathroom door slammed shut on its own, right in his little face. "What the hell?" From the corner of my eye I glimpsed movement in the reflection of the mirror left bare by running rivulets of water. I took a quick swipe at the remainder of the steam and water on the glass. The face of death stared back at me from over my shoulder. Long stringy black hair, veins protruding from a purple complexion, bloated features distorted in a silent scream. Horror fluttered wildly in my chest like a bird trying to escape its cage. Bile rose in my throat. Initially I was paralyzed, then, adrenaline won out. I turned from the sink and glanced at the tub. Nothing!

I turned back to the glass and there it was; the image was closer behind me. In blind panic I took two steps in the tiny bathroom and yanked on the handle of the door with shaky hands. It wouldn't budge. I felt as if I were in a dream, one where you must fight or run to survive but your arms have no strength and your legs feel like rubber. Shrieking, I struggled, as Petey howled on the other side of the door. I had never heard him make that sound before and my blood curdled. The flesh crawled on my bare shoulders as the bathroom grew cold. My throat was tight and I forced myself to glance back. Nothing was physically behind me, but in the mirror that was icing over the words 'I shall have him' was carved in the glaze.

I was paralyzed for an instant until I glimpsed movement again in the glass…in the reflection left bare by the etchings! With a primal scream superhuman strength prevailed. I yanked and the door abruptly opened; unfortunately, I lost my footing on the damp tile floor and felt myself falling…slipping backward toward that thing, whatever, and whoever it was…my hands clawing futilely at the open air. Then, darkness.

Chapter 10

I awoke in a full blown anxiety attack, with Petey humping my thigh and Cassie's panicked cries ringing in my ears. My head was killing me. Pain. That was good. It meant I had lived.

Oh, dear Petey. Dear sweet, sweet, perverted Petey. His eyes were about to pop from his head with exertion as his warm breath and spittle misted my abdomen. He had tried to warn me and now he was venting his stress and showing his concern the only way he knew how.

Cassie's hot rollers had her short hair sticking out all over, she was also only in a bra and jeans and was on her knees tugging at the little dog, spewing an impressive and creative combination of curse words.

Struggling to come out of my fog, I tried to speak. I tried to tell her to leave Petey alone. He deserved a good hump after what we'd just been through. That's when I discovered my speech was thick and the metallic taste of blood coated my tongue.

I was sprawled on my back next to the tub and had somehow taken the shower curtain down with me, the rod rested across the top of my head and the plastic sheet had been pulled from the rings. They were scattered around on the floor. There was a hole in the wall above my head. My chest felt tight and my hands and limbs were quivering. My wrist was throbbing and my face hurt. I was sure I had bitten my tongue in the fall.

"What's going on? I heard the screaming all the way up the hill! " It was Roger, his red hair awry; skidding to a stop on the linoleum outside the bathroom door, bug eyed at the sight of two half clad women and a horny dog writhing on the damp floor before him.

"Help me get her out of here, Roger! Damn it Petey, move! Al! What the hell happened?!" Cassie placed demands with the succession of a machine gun. Bossy multi-tasker…especially in a crisis. God love her.

"P…p…p…pills." I stammered weakly, as the familiar tunnel vision of a stress induced migraine began to set in and everything but my aching head went numb. My glasses had been lost in the fray and I squinted up at Cassie in pain. "Pills."

Roger maneuvered his way into the close space and took my right arm as Cassie took my left. They pulled me to my feet. Initially, I had been happy to remain on the bathroom floor, thinking I would either get my bearings or pass out again, and either scenario would be just fine with me. But, as I began to recall the image in the mirror, I couldn't wait to get up and out of the room.

They ushered me to the bed. Roger hovering nervously while Cassie retrieved a wet washcloth. My chest was sticky with blood and I gingerly touched my face, trying to survey the damage.

"Don't touch it." Cassie said and I moaned as she pulled my hand away and dabbed at my aching lip with the rough cloth. "I think your teeth are okay, but it looks like you're gonna need some stitches. Here take this and put pressure on that lip." She stuffed the cloth into my trembling hand and headed back toward the bathroom. "I just hope you don't have another concussion so soon." She muttered and disappeared around the corner.

"Concussion?   So soon?"   Roger asked, staring helplessly down at me.

Cassie yelled over the sound of running water.   "She bought this blow up exercise thingy and Petey came in and…well, it's a long story.   I'd never heard such an explosion…but we are talking about Al and Petey here. Thank God her boyfriend, Alex, is a paramedic, that's all I have to say."

I seriously felt like I couldn't breathe.   "Pills."   I managed to whisper again.

Cassie was back and leaned over me.   "No pills, honey. You're gonna have to breathe through this one.   Your prescription is old and I don't know what they might want to give you at the hospital."   Of course, she was right.   Yikes! My panic heightened, knowing I had nothing to rely on to get me through the surge of anxiousness coursing through my veins.   I started to whimper, making little puffing sounds around the washcloth, trying to get myself under control. "No hospital," I moaned.

Cassie glanced over her shoulder at Roger.   "Panic attacks."

He stared at me like I had two heads and simply nodded dumbly.   What next, right?

I looked imploringly up at Roger. "I can't….I can't," I stammered thickly.

"Can't what, honey?"   Cassie crooned gently, mopping blood off my chest with a fresh rag, she was in a panic herself and seemed oblivious to the fact that Roger was in the room and neither of us had a shirt on.

"I can't sleep in this room." I groaned over my fat lip and swollen tongue.

Roger looked from me to the cottage door. "Well, obviously not. Cassie practically took the door off its hinges."

Cassie shot him a nasty glare. "Well, what did you expect me to do? You should have heard her screaming. And Petey, he was howling *so* loud. I heard him all the way over in my cottage. That's what first got my attention. I was curling my hair and all of a sudden I heard Petey going crazy. It sounded like something was trying to kill him."

"No!" I dropped my bloody washcloth and grabbed Cassie by her bra straps with both hands, pulling her closer. "Something was trying to kill *me*." Cassie frowned and her brow wrinkled. She gave me a disturbed look and pried my fingers loose.

Roger was over examining the door. "What'd you do to it?" He inquired. The bottom hinge had been ripped from the wood and the door hung crookedly, barely intact, from the top hinge. A hefty chunk of the door frame was missing from the opposite side where the lock had been.

"I kicked it in." Her tone of voice unmistakably said "Duh!" She turned to me and smiled. "Remember that self defense class we took at the community center? Master Jim would be so proud. Roger, the van keys are on the dresser in my cabin. Will you go get the van so she can lay down on the way to the hospital?"

"Uh, sure. I'll pull the van down here."

"Good idea." Cassie said as he disappeared.

"Where's Petey?" I tried to sit up on my elbows but a wave of dizziness swept over me. I had no choice but to lay back down. The back of my head was tender and I fingered the growing knot. Cassie placed the cloth back in my hand and directed pressure on my lip.

"He's down here on the floor. We'll run him up to your mom then get you to the hospital. What happened? Did you fall? Why were you screaming?"

"I'm a miserable ghost hunter, that's for sure." I mumbled. I closed my eyes, but all I could see was that purple, swollen face; its mouth slack and open in either death or horror, so I popped them open again.

"You probably are," she agreed. "But, what does that have to do with anything?"

"Someone, or something, was in the bathroom. It was awful. Petey started putting up a fuss. I realize now he saw it and was trying to warn me but he wouldn't come in the bathroom. Then, the door slammed shut by itself. He was on one side, I was on the other. All of a sudden this woman was behind me. At least I think it was a woman. But she wasn't really behind me. I mean, she was there…but in the mirror. I could feel her, and she was getting closer, but I couldn't directly see her. It got so cold. I slipped trying to get the door open. I guess I hit my head on the wall behind me or something."

"Looks like you took the curtain down with you and the rod got your face. Your eye is turning black. It already looks worse than the time you got arrested for assaulting that birthday clown."

I felt my blood pressure rise and painfully rolled my eyes. Cassie was referring to the day I turned twenty-five and came home from a long day of work to find a startled clown standing alone in the middle of our living room. Typically, I used the kitchen door and cannot recall what compelled me to come in through the front of the house instead, but long story short…I mistook my surprise birthday party for a bizarre home invasion. My family and friends got tired of waiting to jump out of the pantry, where they had run to hide when they saw my car coming up the street. Hearing a commotion in the living room they found Jingles and I rolling around the floor breaking furniture. I had him in a pretty nice headlock but, while trying to defend himself, he still managed to blacken both my eyes. "First of all...you and Alex know I'm afraid of clowns so that wasn't really funny, was it? And, second of all...it was not assault. I was released and the charges were dropped."

"Okay, you're right, it wasn't funny...it was freak'n hilarious. I just meant, Jingles had a mean left jab and this time your eye looks way worse." Cassie glanced around the room and shuddered. "So, do you think she's still here?"

"Do I think who's still here?" I couldn't believe she'd brought up the clown incident at a time like this.

"The lady in the mirror. Do you think she's still here?"

"I don't think so. Petey sensed her first, and he seems pretty calm now. I don't really feel that chill in the air either. My throat got tight too. I started having that sensation last night."

"Okay, I'm back." Roger skidded into the room again.

"Let's go." Cassie stood and gingerly took my elbow to assist me into a sitting position at the edge of the bed. After an initial wave of dizziness passed, I attempted to stand and shuffled toward the door.

"I need my glasses. I had them on in the bathroom."

Cassie's eyes rolled toward the bathroom door. "Uh, Roger...could you find them please?"

Wordlessly he loped into the bathroom and appeared seconds later.

"They didn't fare very well I'm afraid." The left ear piece was broke in two pieces and the right plastic lens was out. "I think I can snap the lens back in."

Cassie sighed. "Bring 'em. Roger, grab her purse would you? We'll need her insurance card...*again*. And, Petey?"

Roger slipped the pieces of my glasses into his shirt pocket and picked up a squirming Petey, tucking him under his arm. He cleared his throat. "Don't you think you both should....uhhhhh.....maybe..." he swirled his free hand in the general direction of his own chest.

"What? Take a coat?"

"No, uh. Your....uhh...." he swirled his hand again and Cassie stared hard at him, then glanced down at herself and flushed red.

"Oh, crap! Yeah, right. Could you step outside please?" Suddenly regaining her modesty and composure she haughtily dismissed Roger from the room as if her lack of attire was entirely his fault, then she reseated me on the bed. She rummaged through my unpacked luggage and found a large t-shirt for me and my roomiest sweatshirt for herself. It was tight, but it would do for now. She slipped my jacket over my shoulders and we headed outside.

"Cassie, wait." I recalled the message on the mirror. "Go to the bathroom, see if something's still on the mirror."

"The mirror?"

"She wrote a message on the mirror. Something like, I will have it...no wait it was *him*. The mirror said... 'I shall have him.'"

Cassie wasn't thrilled with the prospect of returning to the bathroom, but she sat me down again and crept to the door. She peeked in to check the mirror. "Him, who? Nope, nothing. It's just damp and streaked. Look's like you wiped it off or something after your shower."

My shoulders slumped. I knew Cassie believed my story, I just wished I had some physical proof of the terrifying encounter. "Nevermind," I sighed. "Wait! Grab Mom's reading glasses off the back of the sink."

Cassie was reluctant to step into the tiny bathroom. I saw the upper half of her body disappear as she stretched toward the sink to grab the glasses.

"How'd they get in your room?"

"Good question. Let's just get out of here."

Chapter 11

Roger agreed to stay with Mom and help her watch Petey while Gretchen rode to the hospital with us. Mom wanted to come but I wouldn't hear of it. "Nope, I'm sure it looks much worse than it is. You stay here with Roger and grab some dinner. We'll be right back." I garbled as I reclined on the bench seat of the van.

Roger closed the sliding door and Gretchen jumped into the passenger seat with a baggie full of ice for me. With Cassie at the wheel we were off to the hospital; our second trip of the day thanks to me.

My lip was throbbing pretty badly so Cassie filled Gretchen in on what had happened. She paled and listened with horror, then burst into tears. "I'm so sorry. I don't know what's going on." She sounded so dismal it nearly broke my heart.

Cassie reached over and patted her knee. "You didn't do anything, honey. It wasn't your fault. You know Al's a magnet for crap like this. Never quite this severe..." her voice trailed off and her eyes rolled to look at me in the rearview mirror. I gave her a dirty look and she turned her attention back to the road. "You *are* a magnet for crap like this."

"What have you wanted to tell me Gretchen? Obviously something is going on around your place. There's tension between you and Roger, you're not your normal happy, go-lucky self, and now I'm actually seeing apparitions. That's certainly never happened before."

Gretchen rummaged in the glove box and came up with a fast food napkin. She dabbed at her eyes and sniffled. "It just seemed so silly at first. Roger and I have never been angry with each other. I mean, you know, normal relationship stuff, but not like this. He's always been so sweet, and considerate. But working with him the last few weeks...spending so much time together," she began to sniffle again and then sob. "It's like...it's like...I don't know him at all." Gretchen wailed into the napkin.

"Honey, calm down and tell us what's wrong. You know we'll help you if we can." Cassie urged.

Gretchen slowly regained her composure. "There are so many gruesome stories surrounding this property, but we got it at a really great price. No one in town even wanted it. Roger's mom didn't want us to buy it either. She seemed to hate that we had become interested in it when Buck mentioned a Lillian Powell had died and she's acted upset ever since we made the offer. I mean, she seems supportive...you know...but not really happy. But Roger is not a superstitious man. He doesn't believe in silly stuff like ghosts. No offense, Al."

"None taken." I mumbled, eager to hear where her story was heading.

"Anyway, a lot of the tragedies involved husbands and wives. It seems the men have met some pretty horrible fates over the years, at young ages, often at the hands...or allegedly the hands...of their own spouses. I didn't really want to know a ton of details because I just got a great feeling about the place the second we looked at it. Roger had come out first and really felt drawn to the property, so we were excited when we actually got the house.

"Not long after we moved in and started renovating, weird things began happening. Tools would be moved or misplaced." I quickly thought of my mom's glasses and Cassie caught my eye in the mirror again as Gretchen continued. "We left a carpenter alone for an afternoon and when we returned there was a note telling us he was quitting and wouldn't be back. Now he doesn't return our calls.

"Maybe it's all the money we're spending, or how hard we're working to get the place open soon, but it seems like Roger and I have started getting more and more testy with one another. He insists it's me and not him. He's even complaining that I'm sleepwalking and he's had to come and find me outside. I don't want to call him a liar, but I've never sleep walked in my life, at least not before we moved here. It's ridiculous."

Gretchen took a deep breath and blew her nose into the soggy napkin. "Just the same, I *have* felt weird. When decorating the house I just knew where things should go, or what color to choose. I almost felt like something was telling me how things should look. A couple of times, when I actually found some of the pieces I used to decorate in the attic or the cellar, I could swear I heard voices in the house. Sometimes I thought I heard my name, or it seemed to be people having a low conversation, but I couldn't find anyone. Whenever I was looking for whoever it was, I usually stumbled upon an old mirror, or a table that I knew would look perfect in the remodeling."

Gretchen hesitated, as if she had to force herself to divulge what she had to say next. "I'm so stressed out I'm not even looking forward to the wedding. I'm not even sure if there should be a wedding. I don't know what to do."

Gretchen started to cry again. Cassie and I had been silent throughout Gretchen's story, now Cassie reached over to pat her shoulder.

"Wow." Cassie said quietly. We were pulling into the emergency room parking lot. The trip had gone quickly as we listened to Gretchen's tearful tale. I had been so engrossed in what she was saying the trip through the creepy bridge hardly even bothered me this time.

"Gretch…it's clearly not you. After tonight, I can tell you that something paranormal is happening. Maybe the energy is just stressing the two of you out. We'll get to the bottom of it. Okay?" Gretchen merely sniffed, nodded and climbed from the van to open my door. She gave me a big hug.

"I feel better already. Just because I told someone."

"We'll get it figured out," Cassie said. "Don't worry."

"I'll call Alex and see what he suggests." I promised.

The emergency room was packed, but since I was so battered and my hair was matted with blood, they ushered me to the same curtained cubicle pretty quickly. Probably bad for business to leave people like me hanging out in the waiting room.

The nurse performed the necessary vitals, informed me that my lip had stopped bleeding but I would need stitches, and starting cleaning my wound while Cassie perched on one of the lovely plastic chairs and Gretchen stood over her, picking hot rollers from her hair and sticking them in her own jacket pocket.

I could hear a child whimpering behind curtain number one while its mother murmured gentle reassurances. From behind curtain number three, an elderly gentleman kept calling out for someone named "Beatrice." The hallway sounded busy and the nurses running to and fro looked exhausted. Finally, after nearly an hour of waiting, the doctor pulled back my curtain just as the kid next door started throwing up. Before the resounding "splat" could even be heard on the floor next to us, Cassie had covered her mouth and shoved past the young physician from earlier in the afternoon. Cassie didn't do vomit.

"Hot damn!" the old man hollered from behind curtain number three. The doctor merely grimaced and wrinkled his nose. He looked down at the splatter on his worn loafers and then blearily back up at me, trying to place my face. I instantly felt sorry for him and wondered how long he had until he could pay off his school loans and change professions. Mental note: Win the lottery - rescue small town emergency room physician from his thankless plight.

"Hi! Remember me? Two o'clock? Poison Ivy?" I tried to be upbeat and pleasant but when I smiled my lip split and a rivulet of fresh blood coursed down my chin. For a moment I thought he was going to turn around and leave. Instead, he took a deep breath and abruptly hollered, "Clean-up!" toward the hallway. Startled, poor frazzled Gretchen jumped about three feet off the floor, then nervously grabbed a tissue from the small stand next to the bed and handed it to me.

"Clean up!" the gentleman next to us echoed from behind the curtain and Gretchen jumped again. Before the doctor could step toward me a weary looking nurse pushed behind him with a mop and rolling bucket, disappearing behind curtain number one.

The physician glanced at the x-ray of my wrist lit up on the wall then approached me cautiously and suspiciously. "What happened this time?" He inquired, his hands folded behind his back as he leaned forward to examine my face visually. After several moments the doctor gently touched my neck and chin, and then began to roll my head slightly, beginning his physical exam.

"I fell. In the bathroom."

"Did you slip?"

"I think so. I must have. One minute I was wiping off the mirror...the next I was on the floor."

"Lose consciousness?" He gently fingered the bump on the back of my head.

"Uh, yeah. For a second, I think." I hated to admit it, fearing a hospital stay.

"Before or after the fall?"

"Definitely after."

"Hmmm." He plucked a light from his coat pocket and trained it on my eyes to study my pupils. "Follow my finger." I looked left and right, up and down, the best that I could with my swollen eyelids and lack of eyewear. "Feel nauseated...hurting anywhere else?" I shook my head gingerly, no.

"Not really. Just my wrist."

He grabbed my chart and started scribbling furiously. "Well, I think you're okay. But I'd like to do a CT scan just to make sure. We'll check you out and observe you while you're here and if all goes well you can go back home. I'll stitch that lip up first. Your wrist is only sprained. We'll get a brace for that." He glanced over at Gretchen. "Can I speak with Ms. Marche alone for a moment, please?"

Gretchen looked a little shocked and alarmed. "You said she's alright. She's alright isn't she?"

"She's fine. Just some routine questions."

"Beatrice!" The gentleman behind curtain number three abruptly bellowed again. Due to the apparent lack of privacy, I felt it was little absurd to ask Gretchen to leave, so I wasn't sure where my exam was heading.

- 94 -

"I'll be right outside. I'll look for Cassie." Gretchen slipped out of the curtained cubicle.

"Miss Marche, I'm required to ask the following, especially in light of your injuries. Are you in any way afraid for your safety, or in a relationship that is abusive?" He acted so concerned that I snorted with nervous laughter and my lip started to dribble blood again. He handed me a fresh tissue. I thought of sweet Alex and how lucky I was to have even remotely landed a guy like him. For a moment I considered telling him what had actually occurred in the bathroom, but he could probably legally commit me. I could see it now. 'Well doctor, I thought a ghost was about to kick my ass...but it looks like I kicked my own ass trying to get away.' Nope, probably wouldn't fly.

"No, not at all. I'm fine. I just fell."

"I just want to double check. Do you feel you might need to speak to a counselor or..."

"Probably," I interrupted him, trying to lighten up the atmosphere. "But not about this."

I apologized when he looked annoyed. "I'm sorry. I know these are reasonable questions, and I'm not making light of legitimate cases of abuse. I do appreciate your concern, but, I'm really fine." He looked doubtful, and perhaps a tad disappointed in my dismissive attitude. "This isn't the first time I've been to an emergency room twice in one day. Trust me."

Just then the tired nurse arrived with a rolling tray of sterile tools and a couple of syringes. The doctor turned away and busied himself with fresh latex gloves looking so tired and forlorn that I suddenly felt the need to share something with him, offer him some sort of interesting tidbit to liven up his evening. Like when someone tells you a terrible secret and you are compelled to share something…anything… personal of your own, to make them feel less alone.

"I think I had an anxiety attack and passed out." I blurted quickly.

He peered back at me wearily but rolled the tray closer. "An anxiety attack?"

"Yes, I have an old prescription." True. "I get migraines when I'm under stress and I'm prone to anxiety." True. "I haven't had to take the pills in a while, but I think I might need a refill. I'm sure I had a panic attack. I've been under some pressure lately." Not a total lie, considering my ghastly visitor. "My mother is ill."

He pulled a prescription pad from the other pocket of his coat and approached me with new interest.

Chapter 12

Armed with samples of a new anxiety medication, and a clear CT scan, which Cassie deemed comforting evidence that I actually possessed a brain; we vacated the little medical center three hours later.

My wrist was sweating under the brace they'd put on me and my lip throbbed. I couldn't resist fingering the prickly black stitches on the ride home. It was nearing midnight and we were all exhausted for our own individual reasons. I was coming down from the adrenaline rush of my ordeal. Cassie was clearly worried about everyone and control freak that she was, having no solutions or clear course of action, she had lapsed into troubled, thoughtful silence as she drove. Gretchen, unsure of her future, frightened of the present, relieved that I hadn't suffered more serious, permanent damage, dozed with her head against the window.

I called Alex from the dark, bench seat of the van on my cell phone. He answered after two rings, sounding sleepy, sexy, but alert. His husky voice was a comfort and I suddenly missed him and being at home terribly. I imagined his tousled sandy hair, the soft, worn cotton of his favorite blue t-shirt stretched over his muscular back and chest. He slept in boxers and would throw back the covers and sit on the edge of the mattress to talk, switching on the superman table lamp that had graced his every bedside since he was eight years old.

Alex was a fireman and a warrior. He didn't snuggle rebelliously under the blankets in the face of a midnight phone call; he was ever vigilant and ready for action. Unexplainably, surprisingly, I began to cry, something that didn't happen very often in front of other people, and I felt a little embarrassed that Cassie could hear my sniffles. I like to think I've developed tough skin, due to my unparalleled magnetism for the odd and insane. Apparently not so much.

"Hello? Who is this?"

"It's me." I mumbled over my swollen lip.

"Al? Honey, what's wrong? Where are you?"

"I'm okay."

"Are you sure?"

I filled him in quickly, minimizing some of my physical details because there was nothing he could do for now. Naturally, perfect, protective boyfriend that he was, Alex wanted to come immediately anyway, but I wanted to get some sleep, and I didn't want to worry about him missing work or having to make the trip overnight. We finally agreed that he would finish his shift the next day and drive down Wednesday, as planned, but he would be bringing our ghost hunting equipment. Alex sounded excited by the paranormal turn of events but extremely worried none the less.

I explained my suspicions of Roger and promised we would stay on our toes, agreeing that providing I felt okay, I would do a little more historical research on the house before he arrived. We disconnected and I drifted off to sleep, wallowing in the afterglow of Alex's warm, protective voice, clutching my meds and wondering what the next few days might bring.

Chapter 13

Tuesday

Morning dawned bright and clear. A shard of sunlight stole between the curtains of less-than-lovely cottage number two and stabbed me mercilessly in what would later come to be called my "good eye".

Queen size Cassie snored next to me on the dilapidated mattress of our full size bed. Her bulk being greater than mine, the bed lay uneven and I had rolled to rest against her back in the night. I vaguely remembered clutching my edge of the mattress before I fell asleep, like a woman at the bow of a sinking ship, no doubt losing my fight to gravity as soon as I drifted off. Still, it beat sleeping alone. Especially, after yesterday.

I threw back the edge of the repulsive, outdated bedspread and started to flail my legs, pressing down with my elbows and rocking in an attempt to gain enough momentum to detach myself from Cassie's backside.

"What are you doing?" Cassie demanded and sat up suddenly. The bed lurched and the back of my head smacked the headboard.

"Ahhhh!" I cried out, curling into a fetal position and fingering the lump on my skull from the fall in the bathroom.

"Jeez, Al! Are you gonna make it home or are you gonna kill yourself?" I opened one eye and Cassie stood over me, hands on hips. Not a morning person. I repeat…not a morning person.

"I don't know," I groaned and blearily studied the textured ceiling above her head for a moment. "How's my poison ivy looking?"

Cass gave me the once over and shuffled off toward the bathroom. "You don't wanna know."

As usual, she was right.

It took two hours for us to make it up to the main house by the time we shared a bathroom and I applied my various ointments. I looked and felt less than human. My head was tender, my eyes and skin were swollen, blotchy and itchy and my enormous lip throbbed like there was no tomorrow. Anxious to check on Mom and Petey, I finally donned my less than attractive eyewear, now taped together courtesy of Roger, and we ascended the slight hill in the van, Cassie manning the wheel again.

Everyone was finishing breakfast in the kitchen when we arrived. I gave Mom her pills and bent to scoop Petey up from the floor, planting a kiss in the furrow of his brow the best I could without causing myself further pain. He tolerated me for a moment, taking great interest in my wrist brace, then tried to wriggle free when he saw Cassie had a piece of bacon. I suddenly had a new appreciation for Petey and felt a sense of comfort in holding his warm little body. He had seen the apparition before she was apparent to me. I sensed I might be relying on him to be my little spirit barometer again.

Mom fussed over my wounds while Cassie made awkward small talk with Roger and Gretchen. Roger was doing his best to be a congenial host, but I'm sure he couldn't help noticing our coolness, though we made every attempt at being polite on the surface.

They finished up the eggs and bacon and Cassie announced that she was ready to work on the desserts for the engagement dinner that we were throwing for the couple the next night. It was going to be a small affair but she always liked to work a little ahead, leaving no room for surprise before an event.

Gretchen had already purchased the list of ingredients we had e-mailed her and Cassie was chomping at the bit to get started on the cake and some of the fruit desserts. None of these being my particular responsibility, Cassie and I had agreed last night that I would forgo assisting and run into town to gather some information on the property before Alex arrived. Mom could stay and help Cassie and Gretchen. Petey could hang out in the kitchen or his kennel. We had not told Mom or Roger about what Gretchen had confided in us, or about the grisly spirit in cottage number one. My excuse to leave was to fill another prescription, pick up the developed film I left at the pharmacy the day before, and shop for some forgotten toiletries.

"Are you sure you should be driving in your condition?" Mom worriedly inquired. "Those glasses are really old, and now they're broken." Actually, Cassie was also less than excited at the prospect of me taking the van alone, but that had more to do with a prior incidence of theft than faulty vision and a recent head injury. A story for another time.

"I'll take you." Roger chimed in, as he filled a travel mug with coffee. "I have to run into the office to pick up some papers."

Alarmed I glanced quickly at Cassie. "Uh, I'm really not sure how long I'll be. You go ahead."

"It's no problem," he said cheerfully and leaned back against the counter to take a slurpy sip from his mug. I don't know why my nerves were so on edge but his slurping suddenly made me want to slap him.

"Really, you go on ahead." I insisted. Gretchen's eyes darted nervously from Roger to me.

"It's right on my way." This guy was either really good at playing dumb or he seriously didn't get it.

"I said I got it. Go on." My words were clipped, terse and to the point. His company was not desired.

Mom gasped a staccato "Deloris!" in astonishment at my tone. Even Petey had stilled, ceasing his usual panting and snorting, recognizing the moment for what it was…flat out rude.

Gretchen looked pained, for Roger and me, and I was immediately sorry. Cassie turned and started rummaging through the cupboards. Roger straightened and cocked his head, staring at a distant spot on the floor by the back door. He looked like a hunted bird, frozen for a moment, trying to will himself invisible. Then, fight for composure resolved, he cleared his throat without making eye contact with anyone, picked up his briefcase and gave Gretchen a brisk kiss on the cheek before striding from the house. "Have a good day," he said crisply, before the screen door closed with a 'thwack' behind him.

"Crap," I sighed. Gretchen started to cry and ran out of the kitchen.

"Deloris," Mom breathed again, her disappointment palpable. I suddenly noticed her t-shirt was wrong side out and backward. My itchy eyes welled with tears.

"I gotta go." I whispered and slipped outside.

Chapter 14

I hung out in the van at the bottom of the driveway for ten or fifteen minutes, giving Roger a good lead start, then I headed into Spring Valley myself. It actually felt good to get away and be alone, though I kept furtively checking the rearview mirror for signs of my purple friend in the seat behind me. There was way too much space in the back of that paneled van for my complete comfort and I felt my shoulders prickle at the thought of her. I was scaring myself, and absently patted the pack around my waist. In the light of day I hadn't taken any of the new anxiety meds, but they were there just the same…just in case. I was all about trying to control things myself…but a little backup never hurt anybody.

The first order of business was Mom's film. I thought I'd better get it before I got hung up with research and forgot. I grabbed a chocolate shake at the pharmacy fountain for breakfast, paid for Mom's pictures and headed down the sidewalk looking for the little county museum I had spotted when we first rolled through town. I nodded confidently at other pedestrians, but couldn't help feeling self conscious. Everyone smiled politely, but I was pretty sure mothers were pulling their children a little closer to them as I passed by.

The museum was hardly more than a storefront on the outside, but once I ducked into the cool dim interior, I knew

I had hit pay dirt. There wasn't a square inch of wall space left, artifacts and photographs were practically floor to ceiling. A maze of glass display cases snaked the room. It looked like a flea market and it smelled like a museum, musty with nostalgia. I could hear an elderly female voice resonate from somewhere. "I put ketchup in mine, but she insists on using fresh tomatoes. I think the ketchup adds a little extra something, but you can't get her to try anything new. No sir. Anyway, she's always complaining, that one." I drifted around the corner into the museum as my eyes adjusted to the dim lighting.

"Hello, dear, can we help you?" The female voice rose and startled me. I spied an elderly man and woman lounging in canvas folding lawn chairs behind an information counter just to my right. The woman held a cell phone close to her ear. "Gladys, I'll call you back. We've got a live one." I hadn't noticed where they were sitting at first as my sticky eyes adjusted to the dimmer lighting.

"Hi! How are you today?" I asked pleasantly, smiling as broad as possible as I approached them, the stitches straining painfully in my lip. The woman flinched when I got nearer, but her smile never wavered. She seemed happy to have some business. The man, who appeared to have been napping next to his motorized scooter which was emblazoned with veteran bumper stickers and an American flag, only frowned and narrowed his eyes. One index finger slowly rose to push his wire framed glasses up the bridge of his nose.

"What happened to you, missy? Car wreck?"

"Herbert!" the woman exclaimed.

"It's okay." I laughed softy and stepped closer to their counter. What a character! I struggled to maintain my painful smile.

- 104 -

"Well, what was it?"

"Herbert!"

"Oh, she doesn't care, Flossie. Do ya' girl? What the hell happened? Mean boyfriend?"

"Good Lord!" Flossie looked appalled. Her painted on lips were pulled down into a frown, and her painted on eye brows had knitted into one. She reached for a nearby brochure and started to fan herself. "I'm so sorry," she murmured to me. Then she gave up fanning herself and swatted him on the back of the head with the paperwork. "Herbert!"

I couldn't help laughing, though it made my face and head throb slightly. Flossie was mortified, but Herbert seemed encouraged.

"Damn it, Flossie! I told you she didn't mind. You can't walk around look'n like that and not expect people to be curious." They exchanged a cross glare then he turned his attention back to me. "Now then, what happened?" Flossie swatted him in the back of the head again and his bifocals flew off onto the counter. I felt the need to intercede before they were tousling on the floor. I was pretty sure Flossie could probably take him out.

I reached for Herbert's glasses and handed them over to him. "Hey, it really is okay. Just a case of poison ivy and a slip and fall in the bathroom. Nothing too exciting really. Par for the course for me. I tend to be accident prone, to say the least." Herbert looked doubtful and was still looking me over as Flossie rose from her chair.

"Oh, dear. You poor thing. You have stitches too. I do hope you've seen a doctor about that eye."

"Yes, ma'am. I took care of that yesterday." Flossie looked pleased. Herbert was losing interest in me fast. He adjusted his slouched position in the rickety chair and looked like he was already starting to doze back off.

"Well, good. Then what can we help you with today? Have you ever visited Spring Valley before?"

"No, I haven't. I'm just doing a little sight seeing on my own today. It's a fascinating town. I'm here for the wedding of a good friend."

"That's lovely. Let me show you where to begin. This area is very old, established in the 1600s, you know?" Flossie was bustling over to the far right corner at the front of the building, expecting me to follow. "See here? These are the first drawings and records from the settlement of the valley, and you just wind your way around to present day information. The exhibits end over there, with Herbert and I." I noted that their counter not only held informational brochures but also racks of souvenirs for purchase.

"Great, thanks."

"Where are you staying dear? The Elderberry Inn? They have a wonderful restaurant."

"No," This was my chance to get a local's reaction. "Actually, I'm out at the old hospice. My friend, the one who is getting married, is renovating it."

Flossie's eyes widened and she emitted a little gasp, but she maintained her professionalism and her smile. It looked a little too forced, but remained frozen on her face. I noticed a smudge of lipstick on her dentures. "Lilly Powell's place…on Gallows Road," she murmured thoughtfully.

"Yes, it's going to be an excellent bed and breakfast. Have you ever been there?"

"Just once, as a child, for a birthday party." I could tell Flossie was itching to get back across the room to tell Herbert where I was staying, but she graciously and professionally pulled me along and pointed up the wall at a series of photos. I recognized Gretchen's home immediately. "There I am." She pointed herself out of a group of about ten youngsters, dressed in pinafores and short pants, posing around a cake. "That's Lilly." A pretty blonde little girl in the middle smiled shyly at the camera.

"We have an entire section on the hospice, the spring waters, and the Powell's of course. They were one of the first families to settle this area you know?"

"Wow."

"Just follow along dear." She pointed about the room with a crooked, arthritic finger. "Herbert and I will be right over there if you have any questions."

"Thank you."

The museum did indeed boast a variety of photos, with little cards indicating dates and names of former townsfolk. First were a series of drawings depicting the early 1600s, no doubt the people who originally settled the area. There were cases with dishes and old farm tools and displays of toys and clothing, jewelry and documents. I saw drawings and photos of the old bridge throughout various phases in time.

I lingered over a display regarding the importance of the agriculture in the area, and eventually came across the promised expansive photography section on the Powell family, the hospice, and the healing spring waters. I saw images of the nuns and patients, and black and white photos of the spring itself, then, in chronological order, photos of the Powells, mostly women and children. Most pictures were in front of the house, beneath the huge gnarled oak tree. Family reunions perhaps, the women looking stern, the children lined up, or in one photo chasing an indiscernible pet up the porch steps.

The section ended with a large color portrait of an elderly Lillian Powell, the last of her line. She was a handsome woman, even in old age. Hard to believe a woman with her looks had never been married. A fluffy tan cat rested on her lap and Lillian smiled wanly for the artist, who had captured the hint of a mischievous sparkle in her eyes. I studied the portrait, the cat in particular, uneasily, and then released a heavy sigh.

Though the photos were interesting, the museum was not as useful as I had hoped. I approached Herbert and Flossie again. Herbert momentarily opened one eye then went right back to snoring. Opossum.

"Well, that was very interesting. Thank you." I slipped a couple of dollars in the dusty, nearly empty donation jar. "Do you have any other information on the house itself, or the property?"

"Oh, not here, honey. Not anymore. That's over at the library. But can we interest you in any souvenirs?" I glanced thoughtfully and politely at the array of pens, key chains, bumper stickers and recipe books with no intention to buy.

"Oh, no thank you. I appreciate your time though."

Flossie looked disappointed. "Alright, honey. Come back again."

"Thanks!" As I turned to make my way toward the door, an author's name caught my eye on a thin purple paperback on display. *Reflections of a Generation, Prose and Poetry by Lillian Powell*. "Wait a second." I turned quickly. "This book. It's by *the* Lillian Powell?"

"Oh yes, she fancied herself a bit of a poet."

Herbert stirred in his chair. "Fancied herself as more than that." He grumbled.

Flossie pursed her lips. "He's just jealous because he had a crush on Lilly when we were kids and she wouldn't give him the time of day. She always said she wouldn't get married...never, ever. Said that since we were all very young."

"Did she say why? That's a weird decision to make as a child."

"Oh, she never really said. Just made it clear that she wasn't interested any further than dating. As a young woman she moved to New York for a while. She returned when her mother was older and ill. Turned a lot of heads, but never gave anybody the time of day. Including Herbert. She just seemed eccentric. Maybe she was afraid the boys were just after the family money. Published this book about a year before she passed away. It's only been marketed locally of course. The poetry's good, but what you might call 'deep'. Over the heads of a lot of folks in these parts. I'm afraid we don't sell too many copies."

Herbert was alert again. "I think it was the curse. She didn't want to love nobody because of the curse."

"Oh, that's ridiculous." Flossie twittered nervously and her cheeks seemed to color with embarrassment.

"Is not. Didn't want to be born male in that family. No siree." Herbert let out a long whistle and rolled his eyes. "Didn't want to marry one of them Powell girls either."

"The curse? I know there was some misfortune...but what's this about a curse?" I kept my voice light, but felt excitement bubble up inside me.

Flossie laughed and slapped her knee. "He's so silly. A curse in Spring Valley. Imagine. Some people just like to make up stories. Gives the area a little more color." She smiled demurely at me and out of the corner of her mouth growled, "Shut-up" at Herbert.

"It's no story." Herbert pouted and laced his fingers across his ample belly. I noticed the buttons of his overalls were straining on the sides. "That family has had more than just a run of bad luck. It's that witch curse."

"A witch curse?" I pressed.

"That's all I know," Herbert asserted. "My family helped settle this area too and that's what my grand pappy told me. That's what his grand pappy told him. Someone in that family crossed a witch at one time or another and the property has been cursed ever since." I thought of the apparition in the bathroom and involuntarily broke out with goose bumps.

Flossie looked annoyed. "Just a story, dear." She said to me. "Besides, it doesn't matter now. The family is gone. All the sadness is in the past."

"Some people say there's a stain on that land." Herbert was caught up in it now and he enjoyed my full attention. "With all the tragedy in the family and the sickness of the folks who stayed out there, you better believe there's a stain on that land. You tell your friend to be careful. She must be the one marrying that Richardson boy."

"Herbert!" Flossie's eyes darted around in disbelief. I suspected she might be looking for something heavier than a brochure to swat him with.

"I'll take the book." I blurted. "As part of my wedding gift to the new property owners. How much is it?"

I purchased the book and left Flossie and Herbert bickering behind me. Hmm...nobody had said anything about a curse. That put a new angle on things.

Chapter 15

I'd spent more time in the museum than I had thought and by now it was approaching one o'clock. My stomach was growling so I stopped by the Elderberry Inn. I'd heard enough about their wonderful food and had decided to try it for myself.

After the most awesome cream of potato soup I had ever eaten, seated at a corner table for two close to the kitchen (which I'm sure was not an accident due to my unappetizing appearance), I headed to the library. I found it took me forever to eat with my giant bottom lip and by the time I left the inn it was nearly two o'clock.

I'd never met a library I didn't like. In fact, I loved libraries. This one was a testament to its time and could not have fit more perfectly into the ambience of the little town. At first blush I guessed the building to be at least 100 years old. The cornerstone confirmed my suspicions; the library was 125 years old. Gray stone and granite, the structure boasted two fierce looking lions to either side of the short set of outer steps. The building appeared to be two stories tall, with two turrets in the front of the structure and enormous mahogany doors bedecked with stained glass. Above the doors the words 'Spring Valley New Library' was chiseled. I wondered where the "old" library had been housed and mounted the stairs with the same sense of anticipation I had felt as a little girl.

Basically an only child, with professors for parents; books were a comfort zone for me, my first and favorite form of entertainment. It was like entering a church. Quiet and cool; row after row of knowledge and imagination between the covers of every volume, worlds upon worlds just waiting to be discovered. I stood for a moment in the tiny foyer and took a deep breath, allowing the familiar musty scent wash over me, and then I pushed through the second set of swinging doors.

Marvelous high ceilings and a stone fireplace with open doors on either side dominated the main room. Comfortable chairs were pulled together on a worn Persian rug, creating a sitting area where end tables held magazines and discarded books waiting to be returned to their shelves. This room held the circulation desk and reference volumes, and I could see the beginning of the non-fiction section which a sign indicated would continue into the next room, to the right and beyond the fireplace, along with the fiction section.

Through the doors to the left of the fireplace I glimpsed an alcove and the top of a set of winding stairs leading down. These apparently led to the children's library below, housed in what would technically be the first floor were it accessible from outside.

I noted that the computer terminals were discreetly tucked along a back wall in the main room, accessible, but out of clear view so as not to mar the library's old fashioned charm. An enormous old wooden card catalog graced one wall. I wondered if little yellowing cards still occupied the alphabetical drawers, or if the index was just there for effect.

Colonial landscapes and portraits of presidents such as Washington and Lincoln hung about the room. A huge portrait of a dour looking man sat upon the mantle of the fireplace.

Just as I suspected, a darling little old woman graced a high stool behind the check out counter. Beyond her one of the turret rooms appeared to be the office of the head librarian, as indicated by a bronze plaque. The birdlike creature smiled demurely at me, her black dress with white collar buttoned to her chin, and her blue hair rinse offering up a wonderful haloed glow with the light shining through it from the window behind her. She was so hospitable that she didn't even blink or mention my blotchy skin and bruises.

"Hello, I'm visiting your town and would like some information on the spring waters. Is there a particular section I can look at?"

"Of course, honey. We have an entire room dedicated to the county, and genealogy too." She never left her perch, merely indicated a closed door behind me that I had not noticed with a graceful wave of her hand. Ah, the second turret. "If you need any help Prudence will be in and out, dear."

"Thank you." I crossed the space to the closed door. Another bronze plaque indicated that I was about to enter the Powell Room. I quietly pushed open the door to find another fireplace, with more comfortable looking chairs and a chintz sofa pulled close to it. This time a dour looking Puritan woman surveyed the book stacks of the Powell room from above the mantle. A balding man who appeared to be around sixty years old glanced up from his book from one of the Queen Anne chairs near the hearth then quickly immersed himself in his reading again.

The center of the room held an enormous table with at least twenty sturdy chairs and some reading lamps. The florescent lighting above was scarcely brighter than the sunlight seeping through the only window of the turret. Tree branches crowded close and shaded the window from the outside, but a male child was curled up on the window seat nodding off over a magazine in the little warmth of fall sunshine that struggled through.

I approached the first set of shelves, tiptoeing on the hard wood floors. The artwork on the wall behind me appeared to be very old, some with surprisingly violent scenes of Indian attacks, revolutionary and civil war battles and sour faced pilgrims. There were also men working in the fields or women and children attending to various domestic duties. One painting, completely out of character, was a black night scene of women in long white sleeping gowns, their hair undone as they danced feverishly around a blazing bonfire. Their gestures were wild, and their eyes wide as if in a trance. On the outer circle, in the glow of the flames, a dark gray devilish figure leered, no more than a shadow, barely visible, except for the whites of his eyes. I shuddered and scurried between the shelves to the lone computer terminal, against the back wall.

My search turned up a little bit on the springs and the Powells, and soon, armed with a list of Dewey decimal numbers I began to actually peruse the books. To my disappointment, though there were many volumes, I wasn't finding out much more than I had at the museum. I had determined that I was going to have to ask for help when I sensed a presence behind me in the close space of the shelves. Maybe it was Prudence. I wondered if she would be a twin to the little darling behind the counter, perhaps with a pink tinge to her carefully curled hair. With a small smile on my battered mouth, I turned to greet her.

"Ahhhhh!" I didn't mean to scream out loud, nor did the person looking back at me I'm sure.

- 114 -

"Sssshhhhh!" The man in the front of the room shushed loudly and I pressed my hand as tightly against my tender lips as I dared.

"P…P…Prudence?" I stammered in a whisper.

She gulped and nodded, returning my whisper. "I'm sorry. I didn't mean to scare you."

"Oh, no. That's okay. I'm sure I look just as scary, not that I mean you look scary, just that I look scary, and…well, never mind."

Prudence just regarded me warily for a moment, looking me up and down then sniffed. "Is that potato soup in your hair?" she finally asked with a crinkled nose. I realized she was trying to make me feel uncomfortable.

"Maybe." I didn't flinch and resisted the urge to pick at my hair.

Suddenly she gave me a friendly grin, displaying a beautiful set of straight, white teeth. Over the black lips pierced with an array of fine metal hooks, I glimpsed a silver spike through her pink tongue. For a moment I was mesmerized and studied the human pin cushion before me. I counted twelve earrings running up each ear and one of those huge spacers in her left ear lobe, which created a hole about the size of dime. Yowza! Both eyebrows were pierced above dramatic black makeup, which made her porcelain skin only whiter, in contrast to the big diamond stud glittering in her right nostril. Beneath all the cutlery and baggy black boys' clothes, painfully thin Prudence was really a very pretty girl, who I guessed was in her last year or two of high school.

"Can I help you find something?" The spike clicked again her teeth with the second syllable of 'something.'

"Uh, yeah. Actually, I need some information on the old hospice, and the resort by the spring. The Powell property."

- 115 -

"Really?" Prudence started to walk through the stacks, glancing sideways at the shelves and running her finger over the numbers labeled on the book spines. "You're in the right section."

"Well, I really want some good background information. Like who owned the property before the Powells. What was on the grounds before the present house. Stuff like that. My friend owns the place now and I'm just curious about its history. Do you think I need to try the court house?"

Prudence turned and silently studied me a moment more. She looked intrigued.

"What happened to your mouth?"

"Bathroom accident." I didn't want to elaborate. It wasn't really any of her business. I respected Goth kids, and might have been one myself if it had been in vogue at the time, but closer to thirty than naught, I found myself adopting somewhat of a stereotypical bias that they were all a little macabre. Possessing this opinion sickened me and made me feel old, but I felt it just the same. I resisted the urge to pull a few hooks from her lip and utter "You crazy kids!"

"Hmm. I could show you some things that aren't out in circulation. Is there a particular reason you're asking?" Shrewd kid.

"No, just curious." Prudence smiled again and just stood there staring at me, sizing me up. What? Did I have to bribe her for information?

Suddenly, she looked around, grabbed my un-braced wrist and pulled me along the back side of the room and around the shelving. She cracked open the door, and seeing that the woman at the circulation desk was busy checking out books, pulled me toward the alcove with the spiral stairs.

"Where are we going?"

"Shhh." Prudence cautioned and tiptoed down the metal steps so carefully that her chunky black boots didn't make a sound. "I'm the upstairs page," she whispered, "but there's nobody working downstairs this afternoon, so I can get you in." In where?

The hall downstairs was dark, the only light coming from the doors leading to a brightly decorated children's library. Prudence tugged me past those and retrieved a set of keys from a janitor's closet. A few more paces and she opened a creaky door and flipped on the dim light to what appeared to be a storage area for periodicals. Shelves and shelves of yearly magazine volumes labeled in cardboard holders stood sentinel in the room. Prudence and I zigged and zagged until we reached another door near the back corner of the dark room which smelled of aging paper. She studied the ring of keys, going through them one by one with deft, pale hands, bedecked with silver rings and black fingernails. She thoughtfully selected one in the gloom and eyed me coolly. "Something's going on out there isn't it?"

I gave her the sternest, most adult glare I could muster with my googly eyes and fat, blotchy face. "Do you have something to show me or not? I could ask the lady at the desk what's down here you know?"

She didn't budge and we stared each other down for a moment or two. "Hey," she leveled, "I'm just curious. I've been fascinated with that place and all the rumors since I was a kid." Awww…hardware aside, she was starting to remind me a lot of….well…me.

"What do you know about the hospice, or the people who built the house?" I asked, starting to warm to the girl.

"Only what I've heard. Information that you can just

about find in any book upstairs. But, another library page and I...she doesn't work here anymore...found this room one day."

Prudence went ahead and slipped the key into a rusty door handle and it turned with a scrape. A dank scent assaulted my nostrils and she disappeared momentarily into the darkness beyond and pulled a cord, illuminating a single weak light bulb hanging from the ceiling. The stone room was barely a closet containing a wooden stool and several cardboard boxes. "This stuff was stored in here when the museum moved to the smaller building on Main Street." That made sense and seemed to coincide with what Flossie had said.

"Why isn't this stuff displayed at the museum, or in the collection upstairs?" I entered cautiously and reached into a box containing stacks of old pictures, haphazardly thrown in piles.

Prudence shrugged. "It's all kind of personal. I don't even know if it's supposed to be here. I think it got lost, or left, or something. Somebody thought that Lillian Powell requested it not be displayed and then when she got sick nobody ever got it back to her. Of course it doesn't matter now, since they've all died out and all. Now, what's going on that a stranger to town is so interested in the Powells?"

"Can you keep a secret?" I whispered conspiratorially. Prudence licked at one of the little rings on her black bottom lip in anticipation. Her eyes widened.

"Yeah."

I decided to give her a grain of information, but nothing personal about Gretchen...just in case Prudence was a gossip monger. "I think I saw a ghost last night. That's what happened to my face, besides the poison ivy. I panicked and fell in the bathroom in one of the cottages on the property."

"Wow." Prudence barely breathed the word. "What did it look like?"

"A woman…with long dark hair. I know, that's not very specific, but that's all I've got. I'm sort of an amateur ghost hunter and I'm just looking for some background information."

"Wow." Prudence said again. She crinkled her brow as if she were debating something within herself. Then, decision made, she hefted the top box of pictures near me and pulled a battered, black leather volume from the nearly crumpled bottom box. "Obviously I can't let you take this with you, but you can look at it and tell me what you think. I've got to get upstairs, but I'll be back to let you out in a little bit." She put her finger to her lips and quickly pulled the door nearly closed behind her. In several seconds I heard the main door to the periodical room close and lock.

'Let me out? Crap!' I thought wildly and touched my waist pack for support. Why'd she have to lock the door? What time did the library close? What if I was stuck here? Okay, okay. Calm down. Trust the girl and read the book. Trust the girl and read the book. I had a cell phone if I needed it. I took a series of deep breaths and settled myself on the little stool. Before long I was so absorbed in what I held that I wouldn't have cared if Prudence left me there all night.

Chapter 16

I paused in the kitchen doorway and observed Cassie at the counter skillfully wielding a pastry bag of icing, putting the last artful touches of bright green leaves on the red roses atop the engagement party cake. I heard Mom giggle from the kitchen booth as she added sugar to her coffee. Petey snored softly from under the table.

"There is no such thing, Gretchen. I don't believe it. Uhhh…uhhh. It doesn't exist."

"There is so. I have one."

"It's a myth." Cassie replied. "Like a Sasquatch, a UFO, or dead movie stars who are supposedly alive and well, hiding in plain sight. I have to see it to believe it." I saw Mom snort gleefully, and then cough, as her coffee almost came out of her nose.

"That's ridiculous! What does that have to do with what I'm talking about?" Gretchen countered.

"Girls, you've been talking about this for half an hour." Mom said gently, tilting her wrist and indicating her watch.

"What *are* you talking about?" I strolled into the room, took a finger full of icing from the edge of the bowl near the sink, and plunked it into my mouth.

"A comfortable bra." Cassie said matter of factly.

"Seriwously?" I garbled around the icing.

"Seriwously." Cassie mimicked me, grunted and pulled the icing bowl out of my reach as she surveyed her cake.

I swallowed hard. Cassie made great icing. "It's true. I have one too."

"Oh, for heavens sake!" Cassie exclaimed. "Let's just change the subject!"

"Well, I do." I plopped down next to Mom who started picking dried soup out my hair until I handed her the photo packets I had retrieved from the pharmacy in town. She immediately opened the top envelope and started sifting through them.

"It's awfully late in the afternoon, Al. Did you have a productive day?" Gretchen asked me pointedly.

"Very." I said with meaning. We both nodded slowly. I could tell she couldn't wait until we were alone so we could talk.

"We were going to try and eat at the inn again tonight, but I haven't heard from Roger yet. Apparently he decided to stay at work this afternoon." Gretchen said quietly.

"Gretch, I'm so sorry about this morning."

"Yes, Al. What exactly had gotten into y…y…you..." Mom suddenly stuttered and turned pale. She was staring at the picture in her shaky hand.

"Oh my God!" Cassie dropped her decorating utensils and rushed to the booth.

"Mom! Mom!" I shook her shoulder gently. "Are you okay?"

She sat stone still for a moment, then finally her rounded eyes met mine and she thrust the snapshot toward me.

Gretchen leaned forward and Cassie stood close. The photo was of me and Mom, with Petey in her arms, on the bridge. Cassie had snapped it when we stopped on the way into town. But, we were not alone. White, fuzzy wisps were all around us, and leering over my shoulder was the blurry, purple image of the face I had seen in the mirror the night before. It was unmistakably a woman's face.

"It's her!" I exclaimed. "It's her! The ghost in the bathroom last night!" Cassie took the photo from my hand to study it closer and I grabbed the rest of the pictures from the pack in front of my mother. They were all clear as a bell.

Mom's hand slapped the tabletop forcefully and Cassie, Gretchen and I all jumped, so intent and horrified by the picture that we were startled.

"I knew something was up! Why didn't you tell me?" Gentle creature that she was, Mom really looked angry and hurt.

"Mom, I didn't want to worry you. We weren't sure what was going on yet."

"I knew you weren't shopping all day. You don't shop."

"And when she does, she doesn't do it well." Cassie quipped and attempted a smile to break the tension. Mom and I cast a quick frown and a glare her way.

"What, just because I have a problem you have to handle me with kid gloves? Is that what everyone thinks?" Cassie and Gretchen were studying the grout between the floor tiles. "I'm not an invalid you know…at least not yet." Mom's eyes were welling with tears.

"Good gravy, Mom, I know that. I'm sorry. We should have told you. I didn't mean to leave you out." I wrapped my arms around her frail frame and gave her a gentle hug.

With that Cassie, Gretchen and I filled Mom in on everything that had happened so far…then I took over, extolling the day's events, and enjoying the fact that everyone hung on my every word, especially when I retrieved the contents of my oversized purse and placed the old, black volume from the library on the table.

The book Prudence had shown me was a treasure trove of information, but it raised more questions than it answered. It seemed to have had many contributors over the last century or two, and though many of the documents were faded and worn beyond recognition, many remained intact. I had not had time to get through the entire book, but what I read implied that there was more than just coincidence and bad luck involved in the many tragedies surrounding the Powell family; whether it was insanity or pure evil I could not be sure. Someone had collected these snippets and who it was and how the collection had ended up in the basement of the local library would probably remain a mystery.

I had started to make notes about the book in the near darkness of the library closet, jotting down names and facts on the back of an envelope I found in my bag…hoping for a clue, something that might ring a bell later. Then, I realized my bag was just big enough to hold the book. Feeling a little guilty I had stuffed it inside the large purse I was carrying and perused piles of old photos while I waited for Prudence to return. If Gretchen didn't want the book I vowed I would somehow smuggle it back into the library before we left town. In the meantime, deep down I felt that it might provide some clues as to what was happening on the property.

Eagerly we spread the volume open in front of us finding that the first page appeared to be a family tree of the Powell's, but something had been spilt on the top half and all of the names couldn't be read. Shoved between the subsequent pages was a verse of Psalms torn from the Bible, a pressed rose, whose petals had crumbled into dust, leaving only a blackened dry stem, and a scrap of embroidered cloth that we assumed had once been part of a handkerchief. There was a large 'P' sewn onto the corner.

Each fragile page revealed fascinating pieces of the past, saved and added to the book by a variety of Powell women. It was a chronological history of the family's ancestors, from military records to birth announcements, and sadly scads of obituaries, many for young men.

It was amazing to find a brittle, faded letter in delicate script that pre-dated the American Revolution. It was to Mary, from Albert. He spoke of his trip to Europe and his fear of the political climate. He inquired about their children and expressed his undying love. Apparently, his trip home had been delayed and he was worried about how she and the farm would fare through the winter without him. He discussed their servants briefly and charged her with traveling to pay their taxes in his absence in the springtime.

Next a few pages of a journal of expenses. I assumed them to be Mary and Albert's since the date was only two years after his letter. In an even hand the cost of lamp oil, fabric, seed, and all of the expenses for running a plantation were meticulously recorded. The listings were fascinating; shoes for the children, physician fees, a mule and gunpowder were all carefully accounted for. The final entry was for a casket with a shaky notion: 'for Albert.'

Following were political flyers, calling cards, and a scrap of paper with a recipe for fruit punch. Documents recording children's progress in school, a funeral announcement for someone named Jonah and a Civil War dated letter of sympathy from none other than Abraham Lincoln himself. A lock of blonde hair, tied with yellowed ribbon.

There were crude pen and ink drawings of a cat, then of Gretchen's house and the tree in front of it. A page or two from a school sampler and a bill for a grave marker carved in 1857, followed by the wedding announcement of David

Powell and Etta DuBois. Faded photos of serious looking men, women and children began to appear from the mid-late 1800s and forward. More obituaries as printing became readily available and the women appeared to keep better records. Mom and Gretchen confirmed that they had probably seen all of these names in the cemetery on the grounds.

Next, a receipt from bills paid to the Hamilton Insane Asylum in Ohio from the late 1930s and 40s...the patient's name was Blanche. Clipped copies of newspaper articles about the fire of the guest house that had been a sanatorium and the death of Blanche's husband, Jack, followed. There was even a small article about Blanche's trial and sentencing to the mental institution in Ohio. Near the back of the book we found flyers about the spring waters and the resort, even some old menus.

From a worn satin pouch Gretchen pulled a small tarnished locket. She opened it to reveal a tiny scrap of cloth that was yellow and gray in some spots from age, but it was still clear to see that the fabric had once been lavender or violet. I suddenly felt extremely ill.

"Put it up!" I blurted, holding my stomach and swallowing bile.

"Why?" Gretchen questioned.

"I don't know. Just put it up. I feel sick."

Perplexed, Gretchen slipped the item back into the pouch and hastily tucked it between two pages.

"You're really pale, Al." Cassie commented as Mom reached over to check my forehead for a fever. Finding me cool to her touch her attention returned to the book.

Cassie withdrew a black and white photo from a stained envelope. She slipped it to Gretchen. "Does this place look familiar?"

Gretchen studied the photo and flipped it over to check the date. In faded pencil someone had written 1912.

"It's the sitting room. It's literally *my* sitting room," she breathed with disbelief. She passed the picture to Mom who looked it over intently then handed it to me. The furnishings were nearly identical and placed in the same spots Gretchen had chosen for the pieces she had doggedly hunted flea markets and antique stores for. Even the arrangement of books, hurricane lamps and flowers on the fireplace mantel matched Gretchen's style of decorating. And to top it off, the exact same mirror appeared to rest above the fireplace. In the photo a fluffy cat sat regally on the hearth rug.

"I found that mirror in the attic…one day when I heard the voices," Gretchen said unsteadily. "That cat looks like Caramel."

"It looks like the cat I saw in a portrait with Lillian Powell at the museum too." My nausea was slowly subsiding.

"Where is that cat anyway?" Cassie inquired. "I haven't seen a cat since we got here."

"She was in my cottage the night we arrived. She ran out when I opened the door." I recalled. "Petey sneezed up a storm."

"Roger's allergic to her too. But, I haven't seen her since before you came. Maybe she got locked in when I took clean towels to your cottage, and she's been hiding out since. Probably angry. Poor kitty." Gretchen peered at the picture again. "She could be this cat's kitten, but it was too long ago."

"Gretchen, didn't you say you just had a feeling as to how to decorate? That the pieces just seemed to fall into place?"

"Well, yes. But I'd looked through so many books and magazines. And I've always dreamed of owning my own place like this. I just assumed all my dreams and hard work were paying off. At least at first. You think something led me to make the decisions I did, don't you?"

"Looking at the picture it certainly seems like a possibility. Maybe you're just picking up vibrations lingering from the past or something. Like a residual haunting. Maybe that's why you and Roger are so tense."

As if on cue, the phone rang. Gretchen ran to answer it and came back to the table crestfallen. "Roger says he still has some work to do and he won't be home for dinner."

"I'm *so* sorry." I groaned. "You know I just didn't want him to be upset that you talked to us. I didn't want him to know where I was going today, or what I was really doing."

"It's okay." Gretchen flopped back into the booth. "Roger's just such a private person. He didn't even want anyone to know we were interested in this place until the deal was almost clinched. He's pretty sensitive too. Normally I think it's kind of cute. Lately it's been irritating as hell."

"Well," Cassie clapped her hands together and headed toward the refrigerator, trying to lighten the mood. "As our mystery thickens, let's see what surprises lurk in here that we can wrangle up for dinner."

"Cass…no," Gretchen protested. "You've been cooking all day. I'm up for pizza. Who's with me?"

Mom and I raised our hands simultaneously.

"Great. I don't know about the rest of you but I need to chill out tonight. Do you want to go out…or eat in? Surprisingly enough, a pretty good place actually delivers out here. It's a little restaurant that's on up the highway as you head to the lake and the state park. Roger and I really like it."

We agreed to stay in and Gretchen phoned in our order as Cassie opened a small bottle of wine. Mom and I trekked into the sitting room, comparing the old sitting room photo with the present day décor. Before long, we were all lounging and relaxing, deep into some serious girl talk, with two half empty boxes of pizza on the coffee table and a second bottle of wine uncorked.

The windows were cracked open to let in some of the fresh fall air and the night was just barely cool enough for the pleasant fire which Gretchen had built. Petey snored on the hearth rug and a little tipsy, Cassie, Gretchen and I had resumed our former argument over the comfort of certain undergarments. I was totally relaxed and had not been this itch free in two days, having thrown caution to the wind (knowing I would certainly not be taking any pain pills now) I had downed three small glasses of wine by myself. Mom, who stuck to hot tea, was curled up on a settee in the corner by the bookshelves beneath a beaded standing lamp, to peruse the book of Lillian Powell's poetry I had purchased at the museum. Soon I noticed the book tip in her hands as she nodded off to sleep.

It was getting late and there was still no sign of Roger. Though Gretchen appeared to be enjoying herself anyway, and Cassie and I were still doing our level best to distract her from her problems, I knew she could not help but be upset. After all, her wedding was only days away, her relationship with her fiancé was strained and her guests were seeing ghosts. Ghosts which had no problem appearing on film no less. Pretty brazen.

Finally, the phone rang and Gretchen left, re-entering the room several minutes later with a little more bounce in her step. She had changed into her pajamas and washed her face while she was gone. With her hair pulled back and the freckles on her pert nose she looked like a vulnerable, tired little girl.

"It was Roger. He apologized for being so mopey. He's going to head for home soon." She sat down in a chair near the fireplace and breathed a long sigh, like someone was deflating the air from her.

"Good. I'll let him know I'm sorry when I see him." I rubbed the back of my neck. It was feeling stiff again.

Gretchen wrinkled her nose. "I'm sorry things are so awkward. Like I said, he really is sensitive…probably too much so."

"No, I totally offended him. I'm just feeling protective toward you right now. Alex will be here tomorrow and we'll try to get to the bottom of this so you can have some peace on your wedding day…and beyond."

Cassie yawned and stretched. "We'd better get your mother upstairs and head down the hill ourselves or I'm liable to fall asleep right here. It's such a cozy room, even if it was eerily recreated from the past."

Gretchen's brow knitted as she surveyed the room. I noticed Petey stirring on the rug behind her but I thought nothing of it until his buggy little eyes popped wide open.

"Ahhh…poooo," he suddenly sneezed.

"God bless you!" Gretchen turned in her chair to look at him and Mom opened one eye to peek across the room.

"Ahhh…poooo!" He sneezed again, looked around with annoyance, wrinkled his nose, and tried to tuck his face between his paws and go back to sleep.

"Ahhh…poooo!"

"Good gravy, Petey!" I exclaimed. "Do you need to go outside?" Cassie was right, maybe it was time we all headed for bed.

Petey stood up and rocked on his little feet. "Ahhh…pooo! Ahhh…pooo! Ahhh…pooo!" He groaned and swiped at his nose with a forepaw. He had everyone's attention now. Mom had sat up blearily on the edge of the settee.

"Poor, Petey!" Gretchen cried and bent to pick him up. She stopped in mid-stoop. "Look," she whispered and smiled, gesturing slightly to the archway leading to the foyer. "It's Caramel. That's why he's sneezing. Isn't she precious? I wonder how she got in."

We all craned our heads and Cassie stood to get a better look. Mom was the closest to the door and she grimaced and pulled her feet back onto the furniture, hugging her knees to her chest.

Caramel was enormous, fluffy and none to precious in my opinion. I saw Cassie's head volley quizzically from the cat to Gretchen who had a silly enamored look on her face. The animal sat imperially in the doorway with an expression of disdain for all other life forms before her, Petey in particular, who was convulsing with sneezes and rolling in misery on the floor.

"Here, kitty, kitty." Gretchen inched across the floor, hand outstretched, toward Caramel who simply regarded her coolly with narrowed eyes. I had never seen an animal look so incredibly evil and contemptuous. Something niggled at the corners of my brain. It was unsettling and alarming. If I had been Gretchen I would have been chasing the creature from my house with a broom.

Just when Gretchen got close enough to touch the cat, Caramel hissed and swiped, raking her claws down

Gretchen's wrist and hand. Disturbingly, Gretchen didn't move, she continued to coo to the beast. Caramel immediately began mewing sweetly and licking her arm.

"Yikes! I'm gonna puke." Cassie yelped as Mom gasped loudly.

We could see the blood beading up on Gretchen's skin from across the room, but Gretchen hadn't flinched, and just as quickly as the welts oozed crimson the cats pink tongue lapped up the blood. Gross.

"Now, Caramel. Tsk…tsk…is the puppy dog upsetting you?" Caramel cast a glance of pure loathing toward Petey on the fireplace hearth then appeared to smile as she returned her attention to Gretchen.

Poor Petey was limp from sneezing. His tongue hung from the corner of his mouth and tears dribbled into his wrinkles as he huffed and puffed between fits. "Ahhh…pooo!" If he had been human I was sure he would have been reduced to sobs by now.

I crossed over and picked him up with concern. "He needs to go outside before he has a heart attack." Gretchen was still intent on cajoling the freaky cat who now hatefully eyed me. Petey was wheezing in my arms and as I walked toward the archway to get out of the room every instinct within me said to retreat back to the couch. Every muscle in my body willed me to find another exit from the room. But, short of walking through a wall, or jumping out a window, there was no exiting without passing the malicious feline. I swallowed the ever growing lump in my throat and stayed as close as possible to the wall.

With a low snarl Caramel squared off on me, everyone but Gretchen appeared to be holding their breath as I hugged a wilted Petey to my chest and tried to inch out into the foyer. No wonder Roger hated this cat. The she-devil's tail sliced the air and the hair stood up on her arched back. Her lips parted and pulled taunt, revealing her fangs, slightly tinged with Gretchen's blood. I could almost imagine how those teeth would feel sinking into the flesh of my throat…in fact, based on her expression, I was actually anticipating it…when Petey apparently had enough bullying.

His limp body abruptly wriggled from my arms. In mid sneeze he hurtled toward the floor. "Ahhh…" The cat's eyes widened as Petey fell toward it. Then Petey landed on Caramel "…Poo!" Mom screamed and kitty-cat pieces could not be discerned from doggy-dog pieces as they rolled around in a blur.

Suddenly Caramel sprang from the fray and shot down the hall. Petey remained, panting, too pooped to pursue. Cassie and Mom were silent, horrified, while Gretchen appeared a bit dazed.

I knelt down to hug Petey. "My unlikely hero! Again!" With bulging eyes, he bestowed me one sloppy kiss before he sneezed and fainted on the hard wood floor.

Chapter 17

Wednesday

I was somewhere between dreamland and reality. Me and Aunt Rose were riding top down, in a convertible that is, through Arizona at sunset, the wind whipping in my hair and Rose's bouffant swaying as an entire entity in the balmy heat. I don't know how I knew it was Arizona…I just did.

Rose let out a shrill "Yippee!" as she put the pedal to the metal and I glanced at the side mirror, glimpsing the town we'd just left as it erupted into a massive fireball. Amazingly, all I could think about was how pleasant the warm desert air caressing my skin…wait a minute! I cracked one goopy, bleary eye and couldn't believe the shadowy sight before me. Alex loomed over the bed, running his forefinger tentatively over my bicep, with a grimace on his handsome face. I broke out in goose bumps.

"Hey, baby." I croaked with a surprised, sleepy voice and turned partway over onto my back.

He sat on the edge of the bed, gave me a good once over with those sexy blue eyes of his, and leaned in to kiss my shoulder. It was probably the only place he felt safe putting his lips. "I thought you said you were okay. You look like hell."

"Thanks, a lot."

"I didn't mean it that way." He reached out to tousle my hair and grazed a sore spot on my head.

"Owww! Owww! Owww!"

"Sorry."

I realized the sagging bed was half empty. "I'm alone. Where's Cass?"

"She's up at the house. I brought Petey down so you wouldn't be by yourself." As if on cue, Petey jumped up on the end of the bed from the floor, turned around three times and flopped down next to me with a sigh.

"How long have you been here?"

"Just an hour or so. It's still early. I left around 2 a.m. and drove straight through. Bob finished my shift. I'm going to help Roger spray for weeds behind the cottages, so go back to sleep. Petey can be your paranormal barometer, and I'll be right outside if you need me."

"I'm so glad you're here. Something really creepy is going on. There's this cat, and…"

"Shhh, I know. I brought all our stuff." Alex said, referring to our ghost hunting equipment. He gently touched my swollen lips with an index finger and I broke out in goose bumps again. "Cass filled me in on what happened last night with the cat. Pretty gross. Go back to sleep. I'll be right outside."

I was a little irritated that Cassie had stolen my thunder. I had been dying to call Alex the night before but I didn't want to disturb him at work. At any rate, I felt so relieved just having him close that I didn't even argue. Let my knight in shining armor go out and slay the dreaded poison ivy as I slumbered. I curled up next to Petey's warm little body and Alex pulled the blankets up to my chin. Soon I was lulled back to sleep by Petey's soft gentle snores and didn't wake for at least another couple of hours.

The steady whir of a weed whacking machine sounded behind the cottage and I could hear the deep timber of Alex's voice and then, his muffled laugh.

Petey seemed pretty comfortable on the bed, still snoring away. Apprehensively, I padded barefoot to the bathroom to brush my teeth, unafraid that my toes would become ensnarled in mystery shag. The carpet in this cottage was actually a newer, sculpted style and not so matted or sticky. Teeth clean, I checked the time. Mom wouldn't need her meds for about another hour, so I bravely decided to take a shower. I started the water and peeled off the big faded blue t-shirt I had been sleeping in. It was one of Alex's discards, with giant white peeling letters of EMT emblazoned on the back. As I waited for the shower to warm up I considered the bathroom door with my blurry eyes and shivered at the thought of how I had been trapped before.

Slipping naked through the darkened cottage to retrieve my clothes from my bag, I grabbed my glasses from the nightstand and put them on top of the pile. Petey was still sawing logs. Suddenly a great idea occurred to me...not brilliant, but great. If the ghost could slam the door, she would have a little more trouble if a one of those ugly chairs were wedged in the way. Yes, Cassie's room sported a set almost identical to the lovely grouping in cottage number one. In fact, the table was exactly the same...but, instead of the leering owl, this lamp was an enormous 1950s baby doll, and the frilly, faded shade was her pink hat. Vintage to be sure, but the big, grinning plastic baby was extremely creepy none the less.

I dropped my pile of belongings on the floor, turned the freaky cherub toward the wall, and hoisted one of the ugly chairs. These were heavier than I thought. I tried to hold the cold plastic upholstery away from the naked skin of my belly and my arms were aching before I made it halfway past the foot of the bed. Once I had one chair in place, I realized the need for a second. They would fit tightly with the backs against the opposite door frames and their seats jammed together. I would just have to climb over them, no biggie. Of course, I knew the spirit could move the chairs as easily as she could hold the door closed, but if I showered with my glasses on and the curtain open I could watch for the chairs to move and it might buy me some time to get out of the bathroom. Huffing and puffing, I retrieved the other chair and shoved it into place. Ha!

I dusted my hands against one another, impressed with my own ingenuity, and before I had climbed halfway into the bathroom, another great idea struck me in mid straddle. I could faintly hear Alex whistling a disjointed tune outside while he worked. I should open the little kitchenette window over the sink so he could hear me if I screamed.

Clumsily, I maneuvered my way back over my obstacle course and parted the dusty kitchen drapes that covered the little three by three window. I had to pull the blinds up to get to the sash. The sunlight temporarily seared my sticky eyes and I could see even less. I realized I couldn't reach the lock and struggled on tip toes for a few seconds before hoisting myself with my arms up on the rim of the counter in front of the sink. I leaned and balanced on my abdomen, feet off the ground for several seconds. Though I could now reach the lock I couldn't twist it. Alex shouted something outside but I couldn't hear Roger at all. Uuuggghh! The damned window was stuck tight. I ignored my throbbing wrist.

Determined to get the job done, I pushed hard with my straighten arms and was able to get one knee up on the counter, then two. Soon I had a knee on either side of the sink and was struggling with the lock. Once it was freed, I balanced precariously, the steel rim of the double sided sink cutting into my knees as I straddled the basin, breaking a sweat as I tugged and pushed on the stubborn sash. Climbing onto the counter was definitely easier when I was a kid and there was the promise of cookies hidden somewhere.

Lawn equipment sounded outside again, some distance away. I began to hammer with my fist on the wooden corners of the window to loosen it. With a creak and a groan the window parted about two inches. Ahhh…progress. A cool breeze chilled my bare thighs. I cupped my hands in the new space, planted my knees, gritted my teeth, closed my eyes and straightened my arms, arching my back with a tug. Straining, straining. Still no use. I heard Alex's faint laughter again and opened my blurry eyes, noticing and appreciating the male backside just outside my window, clad in tight blue jeans, made tighter by the fact that he was bending over grappling with some sort of tool.

"What are you doing?" Alex's voice demanded from somewhere behind me. Startled, I twisted my head to the left and squinted at the sunlight trying to squeeze around his big, buff form in the open cottage doorway. Crunch! went my glasses beneath his dirty hiking boot. Petey was about three feet behind me on the floor, panting, his tongue lolling about as he gazed up at my bare behind.

"Huh?" My mind was slow to work it out. So, if that was Alex in my cottage, then outside was…? I suddenly lost my balance and my right knee slipped into the sink. My body splayed across the glass and my right eye, pressed painfully against the window, met the incredulous, slack jawed stare of Roger…two feet away…receiving a full frontal Deloris, and not appearing all that impressed.

I felt the entire window casing start to give way as old rotten wood and glass creaked beneath my weight. With a shriek I mustered all the strength I had, lurched backwards and fell off the counter. Unfortunately, Alex had rushed forward to catch me and the back of my skull smacked him in the forehead. Thwack! We fell to the cold linoleum groaning, a tangle of arms and legs. As I struggled to sit up, I caught sight of Petey circling us in delight, a smorgasbord of body parts available to him.

Chapter 18

Needless to say, I couldn't get near Roger with a hundred foot pole for the rest of the day. It was like he evaporated until it was time for the guests to arrive at the engagement party, then he appeared in his suit in the foyer attending graciously to Gretchen and everyone else, but avoiding eye contact with me at all costs. Who could blame him? I still hadn't apologized for my rudeness the day before and now I had taken the concept of 'awkward' to an entirely new level.

At least the evening was beautiful for the party. Golden setting sunlight washed across the porch of the house and the fall breeze caressed the leaves of the enormous oak tree out front making a continuous, soft rustling sound. The day had not been too hot…or too cold, but comfortable and pleasant.

Gretchen was stunning in a cream colored lace evening dress that clung to her lithe form perfectly. Her eyes sparkled with excitement, and her usually pony tailed hair was now an elegant cascade of curls across her shoulders. She was going to be a beautiful bride and Roger was lucky to have her. His arm rested protectively, proudly, around her waist as we all waited just inside the front screen door, watching as the engagement reception guests arrived in ones, twos and finally a group of three.

First the ones. There was Mona Hampton, fresh from the nearest airport in a black limousine, having flown in from Chicago that day. The car rental must have cost a fortune…but it appeared that Mona was the type that would spare no expense for making a grand entrance. Swanky and single, Mona was a magazine editor and had been a friend of Gretchen's in college. Cassie and I heard plenty about her over the years, but we'd never actually met. Mona looked to be about a size two. Her highlighted brunette hair was pulled back into a sleek up-do, and she sported bright red lipstick and a low cut filmy black dress with a very short skirt.

Mona was svelte and sexy. She slinked into the house like a stealthy jungle cat…and she appeared to have arrived hungry. Unfortunately, by the time she had greeted Gretchen and Roger, it seemed she had looked down the line and acquired an appetite for Alex. She sailed past Mom's extended hand, as well as the rest of us, and cruised toward my boyfriend like a guided missile. I hated her on impact. She grabbed his elbow and steered him right out of the receiving line toward the sitting room, inquiring as to where the cocktails could be found.

I could have caught flies in my gaping mouth but hardly had time to trade a bitchy glance with Cassie before George Tomlin scuttled up the walk. He had grown up with Roger in Connecticut and they had apparently been best friends for years. George was short and stout with an intelligent, yet nervous air about him. Small of stature, but rumored to be a mathematical giant, George greeted everyone pleasantly and inquired where the restroom could be found. I didn't see him again until the appetizers were being served.

Roger's mother arrived third. Slightly heavy-set, Helen was the stuff comfortable grandmas are made of. Her short, salt and pepper hair was slightly curled and her blue eyes were framed by deep smile lines. She looked careworn and a little frazzled, but was a darling woman, warm and friendly. She and Mom took up with each other immediately.

Buck Thistle, Roger's law partner at Douglas Docking's firm in Spring Valley, sped up the drive in a little red convertible. He leapt from the car without opening the door. Buck was broad shouldered with a slim waist. Obviously, a jock; probably football. Cassie licked her lips in anticipation as he strode confidently up the walk in his neatly pressed suit, the material of his jacket straining over his expansive chest and biceps. He nearly jerked the door off its hinges before Gretchen could push it open for him. He kissed Gretchen briskly on the cheek and began pumping Roger's arm as if he might strike oil. "Congratulations old buddy! Good to be here…good to be here."

Buck's large teeth were perfectly straight and glaringly white. He smiled and pumped all of our arms as introductions were made, his eyes darting around the room, never directly meeting any of ours. "Buck Thistle, good to meet ya'. Buck Thistle, happy to make your acquaintance. Buck Thistle…has the Colonel made it yet?" He inquired, interrupting my mother as she murmured her name in reply. What a butt kisser. I took another look at Cassie and she looked a little disgusted.

"Not yet, pal. Help yourself to a drink." Roger responded heartily to Buck's verve. I imagined laid back Roger had quite a time trying to match Buck's enthusiasm around the office. So, with that, Buck Thistle, mover and shaker, moved and shook himself right into the sitting room; where I heard him loudly introduce himself to someone else. Alex still had not reappeared; maybe Buck was pumping his arm out of its socket. Then Mona would have to find something else to hang on, I thought cattily.

Within moments the Colonel in question had arrived. Colonel Douglas Dockings, Esquire, and his wife Edith bustled up the walk. The bearded Colonel was tall, rotund and reeked of pipe smoke. He was jovial enough, though I almost couldn't understand a word he said, as every sentence ended in a hearty chortle. Edith was just as petite and demure as he was animated. A small, woman, with bird-like features, her grey hair was pulled back severely, and little curls were plastered to her forehead. She was so soft spoken you had to lean in to hear her mumble her hello's.

Harold and Dot Stephens, Roger's aunt and uncle, were next. A handsome couple in their sixties, they seemed nice enough, perhaps a little stuffy. Apparently, Harold was Helen's younger half brother from her mother's second marriage. A successful banker from a town not terribly far away from Spring Valley, he had managed to retire early and spent most of his days at the nearby lake on his large boat, or traveling with Dot overseas.

And, last, but not least, Roger's cousin Harry Stephens Jr. arrived with his family...wife Kathryn, and daughter Rebecca. Harry was Harold and Dot's only child and he apparently made his living in banking, just like dear old dad. Harry's demeanor was a bit like Buck's, while Kathryn was mousy, and seemed like a cold fish in comparison to her outgoing husband. I estimated their little girl, Rebecca, to be around twelve or thirteen years old. She quietly brought up the rear, offering her hand maturely to each of us.

Dot began fussing over her son Harry the second the family arrived. I noticed Harry's wife Kathryn stiffen as Dot straighten Harry's tie and clucked over the uneven bows in Rebecca's hair.

Soon the lower level of the house was full of chatter. Though the food was pretty much ready and Mom and Cassie had already slipped into party mode, mingling with the other guests during the cocktail hour before dinner; I however, felt the need to skirt the room, busying myself with tasks like making sure the appetizers were coming out of the kitchen in a timely manner, or checking to see if the bartender needed anything. We had made the meal, but Gretchen had hired a handful of servers from the local country club to run the show after our cooking was done so that we could enjoy ourselves too.

I was surprised to find Prudence, from the library, in the kitchen, looking halfway normal in her uniform, hair pulled back conservatively and her make-up toned down. Some of the hardware was missing too.

"What are you doing here?" Pru was filling a tray with chocolate covered strawberries and I had just caught her popping one into her mouth.

"Sorry," she covered her mouth and mumbled over the fruit. After a big swallow she said, "My cousin works at the club, but she had a family emergency. I used to waitress at the Elderberry Inn…so I offered to fill in. Besides, after meeting you, I couldn't pass up a chance to get into this house. It's amazing." She didn't mention the big, black book being missing so neither did I.

I left her to her work as I went to help polish some spots off the wineglasses coming out of the dishwasher. Maybe it was the insecure control freak in me (making sure everything was running smoothly), maybe it was the investigator in me (catching snatches of conversation, making assumptions about the other guests, keeping an eye on Gretchen and avoiding Roger), or maybe it was the fact that I was self conscious about my monstrous appearance. It was probably a little bit of the three…but mostly the third. If it walks like a loser and talks like a loser…it's a loser. I was definitely a loser tonight. I had a brace on my dominate hand, my left eye was still nearly swollen shut, and my right eye was black and bloodshot, as my jaw jutted out unnaturally because my mouth was still about three times its normal size. The stitches looked like little black spider legs growing out of my lip…and they were starting to itch.

To make matters worse, I was bumping around the house like a drunk since Alex had stepped on my glasses. They now sported a cracked lens in addition to the swathes of electrical tape that Roger had used to reattach the ear piece after my fall on Monday. In an attempt to conceal my battered face and optical issues, I had elected to wear my unruly hair down and struggled most of the afternoon to arrange it into some sort of style. Unfortunately, sight impaired, I had incurred a nasty self inflicted curling iron burn which resembled…of course…an enormous hickey. Ultimately, I soon realized all my efforts had been in vain because the heat from the kitchen had kinked the ends of my hair beyond mortal repair. My bangs, on the other hand, had fallen flat and were oily. By the way my shirt was sticking to me, I was pretty sure I had sprayed deodorant on my head and hair spray under my arms. Blind as bat, the aerosol cans had looked pretty much the same.

No small wonder I felt like hiding under the dining room table. Folks weren't exactly racing across the room to get to know me either. I had traded the smart little dress I had planned to wear for a long sleeved white blouse and black slacks, attempting to cover up the poison ivy. My makeup was smudged on the collar, and not only was I itching and sweating profusely, but I looked like one of the staff. Gretchen's friend Mona had actually drifted by and handed me her empty plate a few minutes before, while she was making another bee line for Alex with a fresh drink.

I tried to tell myself that I would probably never see these people again, that I was only here to support Gretchen, and that the avocado dip I had labored over was divine, but that still didn't make up for the way I really felt. Ugly and dorky.

Alex was supposed to be casing the house so we could set up equipment after everyone had gone. Instead, he was seated in a big comfy chair in the sitting room and Mona was standing over him like a little nursemaid commiserating about the lump on his forehead. She even had one of the waiters bringing him fresh ice in a baggy.

Luckily for me, Alex was decent to the core and I could trust him completely. In addition to being friendly, smart and gorgeous, he was absolutely clueless and truly had no concept of the effect he had on women. Unfortunately tonight, his naïveté only seemed to encourage Mona, who was putting on one hell of a show in an effort to monopolize his full attention. I hovered on the perimeter of the room, fixing a meaningful glare on him, but he was yet to look my way. That's when Cassie sidled up from nowhere.

"What ya' do'n?"

"Nothing." I grunted through clenched teeth. Cassie followed my line of vision and took a long drink of her cocktail. Mona was laughing loudly at something Alex had just said. Her laugh resembled a honking bicycle horn, a trait which Alex would never be able to stand, no matter how drop dead beautiful she was. With this I consoled myself. At one point she even had the nerve to glance over at me before directing her concentration back on Alex. She laughed uproariously again. Honk. Honk.

"If you could have one super power, what would it be?" Cassie inquired quietly.

"Setting people's heads on fire with my eyes." I blurted without hesitation.

Cassie smiled smugly and shook the ice in her empty glass. "It's the very best one." I was so intent on sparking a flame in Mona's perfect up-do with my one good eye that I didn't even notice Cassie gliding away until she had completely disappeared.

Well, I wasn't going to just stand here alone like an imbecile. Let's see, Edith Dockings dozed in the chair opposite Alex, a half empty glass of wine tilting dangerously toward the floor in a dangling bejeweled hand.

Her husband, Colonel Douglas Dockings Esquire, had George Tomlin cornered like a wild animal. George was switching his weight from foot to foot like he had to urinate again and his wire spectacles kept slipping down his little nose, slick from the perspiration running out of his thinning, sandy hair. That guy was a sweater. Tonight I shared his pain. George appeared pretty uncomfortable but the Colonel was oblivious and relentless.

I observed that the Colonel was one of those people who always had a story to tell, no matter the subject, and he never really made eye contact with his polite prey, giving them less of an opportunity to escape once they had fallen into his clutches. Colonel Dockings ended every sentence in an indecipherable bluster. It looked like George was trying to follow along and appear interested, but he was mostly bewildered. I suspected Edith Dockings had the falling asleep thing down cold…if only to keep her sanity.

Harry and his parents had monopolized a waiter with a tray of shrimp puffs. The poor man stood patiently as they scarped down the food, having a conversation as if he were part of the woodwork. Prim Kathryn was being completely ignored by her husband and in-laws, but seemed to be enjoying her time with Buck Thistle…maybe a little too much from the way she was guzzling her martini and playfully slapping his lapel. Though he was smiling and laughing, Buck's eyes were scanning the room for someone better to talk to. What an ass.

Glancing through the foyer into the dining room I saw my mother chatting with Roger's mother, Helen. They were already seated at the dinner table, and from the look of things it was a serious subject. I spied Gretchen and Roger at the foot of the stairs having a conversation that had 'do not disturb' written all over it. So, that left little Rebecca Stephens, all by herself in the far corner of the sitting room perusing the book titles on the mammoth shelving by the windows. Poor kid, she looked pretty bored, and since I looked like a leper, I decided to rescue both of us from loneliness. I slid across the room and made my move.

"Hey, what's up?" I managed to make my voice as normal as possible in spite of my gigantic lip.

Rebecca turned and her face lit up like a Christmas tree. "Hi!" she lisped through the most enormous set of orthodontia I had ever seen. "What happened to you?"

"Poison ivy and a fall in the bathroom." I said robustly, like a nine year old showing off my scars.

"Cool. I'm going to be a doctor. I have allergies *and* asthma. What do they have you on? A steroid I bet. Steroids can make you gain weight. They can also make people go crazy. My uncle's a psychologist and my aunt is crazy. She's a ny…a ny….a nymphomanic." Rebecca exclaimed triumphantly, and loudly.

Too much information. I squinted down at her with my best eye. "Really? How old are you?" I had mistaken

- 149 -

Rebecca's aloofness for sweet self consciousness. Apparently I was wrong. Upon closer inspection this kid had precocious brainiac written all over her. I had just unwittingly opened a can of worms and they were spilling all over the floor around me. I started to inch a little bit away from her toward the foyer.

"Almost thirteen. I used to want to be a vet or a psychologist, but Mom says if I'm going to spend that much time in school I might as well be a doctor. Besides I could specialize. Urology pays well. So does obstetrics. I might even be a pediatrician. My neighbors let me baby sit their kids all the time and I'm really good. Do you have any kids?"

"No." I took another step back.

"Too bad, because I'm really good." Awkward silence. "Hey, is that your boyfriend?" Rebecca pointed toward Alex. Edith had vacated her chair and Mona had it pulled close to Alex. I squinted and found that their knees were practically touching!

"Yeah." I said thoughtfully.

"Hmm?" Rebecca mused, and considered them with a tilted head. That's what I was thinking. This kid was reading my mind. "Anyway, I won the sixth grade science fair last year. I dissected a baby pig." Rebecca smiled smugly. The ugly head of the overly gifted further reared. Did this kid ever watch cartoons or play with dolls or anything remotely normal for her age? The base of my skull started to throb. I'm not great at math unless I'm measuring ingredients, but right now I was calculating how many feet there were from Rebecca to the front door. "Did you know pigs are actually very smart?"

"I think I heard that."

"A sow can have two to three litters a year. That's a lot of pork. And, when they orgasm it lasts for half an hour."

"What did you say?"

"I said, when they orgasm it…"

"Don't believe everything you hear, kid. I gotta go." The last time I moved that fast I was chasing our stolen catering van. Right now I wasn't sure what was disturbing me most, Mona, practically in Alex's lap…or the word orgasm rolling effortlessly off a twelve year's lips.

"I read it on the Internet," Rebecca called to my retreating back. When I was twelve I'm sure I hadn't even known that particular word existed…much less what it meant. Anyway, go pigs! Who knew…rock solid romance and when they died they got to be bacon. You couldn't do much better than that in life. Mmmm…bacon. My stomach growled and I made my way toward the kitchen.

I observed that George had made his escape from Colonel Dockings. He, Roger and Gretchen were now visiting with Buck Thistle. Kathryn Stephens was across the room eyeing Buck, but smiling politely while her mother-in-law, Dot, jabbered about her looming knee replacement.

I bumped headlong into Cassie and the Colonel in the hall near the butler's pantry. Cassie had a fresh drink in one hand and a cigarette in the other. I nearly ran into the hot end of it. "Why are you smoking?" I exclaimed, interrupting their conversation. She had quit right after college.

"I always smoke when I drink." Cassie replied, slurring the word "smoke". I tried to open my poison ivy eye a little wider so I could glare at her.

"Why are you still drinking?" I inquired incredulously. She hardly ever did and we'd had quite a bit of wine the night before.

She shrugged. "I feel stressed out for some reason. I'm just trying to take the edge off." She had a good point. For a couple of seconds I considered taking a sip of her cocktail.

Seizing the moment of silence, the Colonel puffed on his pipe and extended his hand. I stepped closer to grasp it and observed a chunk of my dip in his mustache and a stain of chardonnay on his white beard. My stomach rolled.

"Al Marche, as I recall?" A puff of cherry tobacco smoke drifted my way and my nose began to itch. Why was everyone smoking in the house? Did Gretchen know about this?

"Yes, sir. Are you enjoying the evening?"

"Well...well..." He stared off to a distant corner for a long moment. He was still as a statue and Cassie and I involuntarily leaned toward him. Maybe he had a seizure disorder. After half a minute he abruptly took a deep breath and, startled, we jumped back a pace. "Liquor and tobacco. Two vices that often go hand in hand... haw...ho...haw...ho...hmmm...ha.ha." Cassie and I strained our ears, leaning forward again, trying to recognize any decipherable syllables in the last of his sentence. It was sort of like watching an old crank-up car sputter to a stop. At last, another blustery breath and then, "Which reminds me of the time my unit was surrounded in this little village near the border of..."

Cassie rolled her eyes at me and swayed as she took another drag off her cigarette. "Fascinating," she drawled. The Colonel was already deep into his tale and ignoring us completely.

"I gotta go." I sacrificed Cassie and slipped away to the familiarity of the kitchen, where I was assured that everything was under control and dinner would begin within ten minutes. The staff supervisor from the country club practically threw me out, no doubt tired of having me underfoot. I checked my watch. For a repulsive woman without a country, ten minutes seemed like a long time to wait. Should I take a walk outside, wilting flowers in my wake and frightening small forest creatures? Or, should I suck it up and rejoin the group? I thought of Alex, at the mercy of Mona, and quickly decided to rejoin.

The Colonel and Cassie were gone from the hall. My mother was still in deep conversation with Roger's mother at the table in the dining room, but Edith Docking had taken a seat and was sitting idly nearby. The four elder Stephens, Buck and George were now chatting with Gretchen, Roger, Alex and Mona. Phew! At least Mona was batting her eyes at Buck instead of Alex now. Dowdy Kathryn was currently sizing Alex up. Good luck, lady. That left tipsy Cassie alone with Rebecca by the bookcases. Awww…crap!

Rebecca was chattering like a magpie while Cassie leaned against the wall and stared down at her in disdain, one arm loosely crossed, sipping at least her third fresh drink. I'd lost count of the cocktails but I had seen enough nature biographies to realize this didn't look good. Cassie's eyes were half slits. She was raising and lowering her glass slowly, like a crocodile that didn't want to startle its dinner. Cassie was my best friend and a wonderful woman, but she rarely drank hard liquor, and when she did, she was not usually a very friendly drunk. This kid didn't know what was about to hit her. I edged closer, knowing instinctively that Cassie had already sensed my approach from the corner of her eye.

"We all have yards and yards of intestines anyway. So if you stretched them out…"

"Get this kid away from me before I kill her." Cassie growled at me. Rebecca merely smiled superiorly. I think she might have thought that was a compliment.

"Anyway, If you stretched them out…" Relentless.

"Seriously. You're mak'n me sick." Cass moaned.

"If you stretched them out…"

"Beat it, freak!" Cassie bent and snarled in Rebecca's face. The chatter in the room ceased as all eyes turned to Cassie. Rebecca looked like she'd been slapped. I doubted she'd ever been spoken to as anything other than a thirty year old. Thankfully, a waiter stepped into the room at that moment to announce dinner. Rebecca scuttled over to her mother's side as the entire Stephens family glared reproachfully in our direction. Cassie put her cigarette out in her drink and sauntered carelessly from the room into the entry hall. I attempted a pleasant smile for the crowd, which, of course, was more of a hideous sneer, then lowered my eyes and shuffled after her, smacking my head into the side of the archway on my way out. I was actually a bit relieved. Now Cassie and I were *both* outcasts.

Everyone awkwardly took their seats in the dining room. The plates were marked with little labeled table tents, no doubt Gretchen had labored over the seating assignments, boy…girl, for the most part, so that everyone could get to know someone new. Roger took one end of the table while Gretchen graced the other. The Colonel was to the left of Gretchen, then Mona, next Alex (go figure…Mona had probably run in and switched table tents with someone), Roger's mother Helen, my mother Flora, Harry Stephens and Cassie sat to the right of Roger. To Roger's left was Edith Dockings, Harold Stephens Sr., myself, Buck Thistle, Kathryn Stephens, George Tomlin, and Dot Stephens. A chair had been pulled up for Rebecca to the right of Gretchen at the corner.

Dinner conversation was slow to start, but by the time the salad plates had been cleared people were starting to warm up to each other. The Colonel had monopolized Gretchen, while Mona monopolized Alex. Helen and Mom were still getting along famously, while Cassie, Roger and Harry Stephens bantered back and forth about a variety of topics. Edith Dockings was practically nodding off in her soup, while Harold politely searched for things to say to me. I was having trouble eating and conversing simultaneously so soon we had fallen into an uneven silence. Eventually, Harold and Buck began talking over my head about politics. I was pretty sure Kathryn had one hand on Buck's thigh while she ate awkwardly with the other, and I think George had seen it too. He was sweating again and making little sideways glances to the right under the table while Dot deafened his left ear with stories of Harry as a child. Rebecca still seemed in shock over Cassie's outburst and, being ignored by the adults again, she was picking quietly at her food.

I was preoccupied, concentrating on spooning soup over my ginormous lip without getting any in my hair and vice versa. That's when I overhead Mona asking Gretchen questions about the history of the house and the property.

"You said it has a violent past, Gretch," Mona pretended to shiver and clasped Alex's bicep with both hands. He continued to eat his soup and winked at me from across the table. He was trying to be polite and no doubt thought Mona was a simpering moron…but I still wasn't happy. "Tell us a ghost story, Gretch. You know how I like to be scared."

I noted that Helen stiffened and started concentrating on stirring sugar into her tea, vigorously. I saw my mother give

Helen's wrist a comforting pat. What was that all about? Everyone else seemed eager to hear a tale…except maybe Gretchen and Roger, who just looked down the length of the table willing one or the other to start.

"Well," Roger finally began, "I'm not really sure we have any ghost stories to tell. Let's just say the family that owned this land had a very unlucky past, especially the men. Many died young, and their wives were either accused of murder, or lived on as widows never to remarry again. There is one story of a poor woman who was committed to an insane asylum after her husband's death. She claimed she had been possessed by evil spirits who told her to murder him and she couldn't control herself. It's said that she killed him and attempted to burn the house out back down around herself and his body, but she was rescued and sent to an institution. The woman we actually bought the house from was the last of the line, never married, and never had any children."

"Ooooohhhhhh," Mona shivered dramatically again. "Did any of the deaths happen in *this* house?" Just then a crack of thunder and lightening sounded outside. Everyone jumped in their chairs and a round of nervous twittering began. Mona grasped for Alex so abruptly that the hot roll he had been gingerly buttering flipped from his fingers and landed across the table in Buck's soup. The hot liquid splattered, missing everything on the table but the sleeve of my blouse where I rested my arm, of course. I felt the stitches in my lip pull as I smiled at the blatant look of irritation on Alex's face.

"Uh, sorry, Buck." Alex muttered.

"No problem," Buck replied tersely, fishing the bread out of his bowl with his spoon.

In the clearest sentence I was yet to hear him speak the Colonel twisted to look curiously out the now darkened window. "It wasn't supposed to rain tonight." The chandelier overhead flickered in response.

Gretchen was staring down at her silverware as if in a daze. Roger glanced at her and seeing no help coming his way attempted to change the subject. "I hadn't seen that it was going to rain either. Maybe it's just a quick storm moving through. You know, we need it though. The weatherman said we were down in precipitation by about six or seven inches this year," he babbled nervously.

Mona was relentless. "Well, were there any deaths in *this* house?"

Roger looked increasingly uncomfortable. His mother shot him a pained look. "We don't actually know….."

"You don't know?" Mona laughed at Roger. Honk, honk. "That would have been the first thing *I* would have checked on!" She continued to honk and glanced around the table for support over Roger's obvious stupidity. Although I wasn't super wild about Roger, I really hated Mona right now. Cassie rolled her eyes at me and I was irritated to see that she had another fresh cocktail in front of her. In fact, now that I though about it, I found just about everyone in the room completely infuriating. I thought of Petey in his little travel kennel upstairs and suddenly his company seemed the most preferable, second only to Mom's, of course. She gave me a reassuring smile as thunder cracked outside again.

"Hey," Harry Stephens suddenly exclaimed. "What's wrong with Gretchen?" Everyone had been watching Mona and Roger's exchange, but now all heads swiveled in Gretchen's direction. I had heard the expression of blood running cold, but I never understood until that moment. My heart had stopped in my chest and my blood indeed felt like ice water in my veins.

Gretchen's eyes were rolled back exposing only the whites of them. Her head lolled on her shoulders from side to side. The rest of her body was stiff, leaning back in the chair until I was sure she would fall over were her fists not clutching the tablecloth anchored by so many dishes.

Roger jumped to his feet but froze when her head started to droop, "What the…?" The chandelier began to shake and flicker madly while names spewed from Gretchen's lips in a voice that was not her own. I felt that odd choking sensation begin again and grasped my neck. It was as if someone was tightening a noose around my throat. Gretchen's expression could only be described with one word…demonic.

"Rachel and Richard, Robert, Suzanne, Constance and William, Mary and Albert, Rebecca and Jonah, Etta, David, Blanche and Jack, Martha, Walter, Kenneth, June, Bradley, Elizabeth, Roger…Roger…Roger…" Gretchen's head rolled grotesquely and saliva ran from the corner of her mouth as she croaked out Roger's name repeatedly.

Everyone had been silent…horrified, petrified, and then suddenly complete mayhem set in. I sat glued to my chair as the chaos ensued around me. Prudence and been entering with the entrees and dropped a full tray of plates and food in the doorway. Our eyes met briefly with meaning. Rebecca started crying and Dot pulled her away from Gretchen's side as if she had been exposed to the plague. Mona was practically in Alex's lap and he had to push her off to catch Helen when she fainted. Roger's complexion had gone from his normal pasty to beyond pale. He could not have had a drop of blood left in his face as he stood, mouth gaping, in front of his overturned chair.

People were screaming and bumping into each other; furniture was clattering as they scrambled toward the entry hall. My Mom was pushing in the opposite direction past the Colonel to make her way toward Gretchen who was now limp and perspiring.

"Holy macaroni!" Cassie hiccupped and I watched her slide off her seat onto the floor as the lights went out and the entire house was consumed in darkness.

Chapter 19

Weak and dazed, like someone coming out of a seizure, Gretchen didn't remember a thing. She spent a solid ten minutes on the hall restroom floor retching God only knows what into the toilet. Then, while the house settled down, she lay pale and quiet under an afghan on the settee in the sitting room. Helen and my mother finally coaxed her to bed. I felt so sorry for her.

Roger was clearly shaken, and not a very attentive fiancé in my opinion. He left Gretchen in the care of others and busied himself elsewhere, avoiding the sitting room except to occasionally peek in from the doorway. Perhaps he was afraid to approach Gretchen, and who could blame him, after the eerie way she spewed out random names, ending with his own repeatedly.

Alex helped out in the dining room, clearing broken dishes and food from the floor. A couple of chairs were actually damaged as the stampede of guests attempted to exit the house.

The electricity had not returned and we had every available candle lit. The house had cleared out quickly and the only person staying over now was Helen, Roger's mom. With hasty excuses, Roger's other relatives chose to spend their night at the inn in town. The wait staff cleaned and picked up the kitchen with a frantic sense of urgency. No doubt, embellished stories would be flying around town by morning. Exactly the kind of publicity Roger and Gretchen didn't need for their new business.

I mostly stayed with Gretchen, hovering with concern, but Pru found me and pulled me aside before she left. For a tough little Goth girl enthralled with the supernatural, she seemed as shocked and freaked out as everyone else.

"We need to talk…tomorrow. I need to check on something first. Can I call you?" I hastily gave her my cell phone number and she was on her way.

At midnight, when we were sure Gretchen was sound asleep in the master bedroom, we had a little powwow in the sitting room by candle light. Cassie seemed completely alert now. She was nursing a headache and acting mad as hell at no one in particular. She put Roger on the spot immediately.

"Okay, spill it."

He was tense, guarded, casting a quick glance toward his mom before giving Cassie his full attention. "Spill what?"

"Whatever is going on here? Gretchen told us you two are having trouble."

"My relationship with Gretchen is nothing I intend to discuss with you." Roger snapped back. "Any of you!" He shot a nasty glare my way and curled his lip. Cass looked like she was going to fly across the room and strangle him.

"Roger," Helen said tentatively, "We're all upset."

He sighed and practically poured himself into a chair near the fireplace.

"Look Roger," I felt I had finally found my opportunity to make some peace with him. "I know this is very uncomfortable for you. And, I know I've treated you badly. I've been suspicious and rude. Two of your cottages have been damaged…not to mention what happened this morning…"

"What happened this morning?" Helen asked.

"Roger saw Al naked." Cassie blurted.

"But not on purpose." Alex interjected quickly.

Cassie looked quizzical. "I've been thinking about it, Al. I don't know that you should apologize for this morning. I mean, it wasn't on purpose, and a lot of people *have* seen you naked."

"But never on purpose." Alex interjected again.

"I was just saying…"

"Okay, people, this really isn't the direction I was trying to steer the conversation, but thanks anyway." I stared Cassie and Alex down for a moment, and then focused my attention back on Roger. He and Helen sat quietly next to one another, sickened expressions on their faces. Mom looked tired and was barely listening. So used to our banter, she just smiled and shrugged at Helen.

"I was just saying…" Cassie murmured, crossing her arms over her chest and slouching in her chair.

"It wasn't on purpose…" Alex reiterated under his breath.

I ignored them both.

"Anyway, the point is, I'm sorry, Roger. I know you're a private person and I know this investment is a huge risk for you, but Gretchen is my friend." Cassie cleared her throat loudly. "Our friend," I continued. "And this is really scary stuff. We know you love Gretchen, but you have to put your pride aside and lay all the cards out on the table. We have to get to the bottom of this, at least for Gretchen's sake. We just want to help."

Apparently speaking from the heart had been the best tact to reach Roger. He dropped his head into his hands and his shoulders sank a little. Some of the tension seemed to drain out of him.

"You can trust us." I said softly.

Helen drew a chair close and stroked Roger's back softly. "Go on, son. It's alright."

"I don't know what's going on?" He choked back a sob. Now it was truly obvious just how very distraught he was. "She always wanted something, just like this." He gestured around the room and looked at each of us in turn. His face was drawn and hopeless. "I would do anything for Gretchen. Anything. Now we have the chance to have it all and it's going straight to hell. We've never really fought before. I just love her so much and I want to take care of her. I want to give her the family she's never really had." I glanced at Cassie and saw that her anger had subsided; a tear glinted on her cheek. Roger continued.

"The first week or two that we lived here it was great. We were so excited. But, as we started to work on the house that damn cat showed up. That was our first fight. Apparently I'm allergic…but Gretchen kept letting it in…or it kept getting in, I don't know which. Anyway, then she was so damn stubborn about how the furniture should be placed, what colors the walls should be. My input didn't mean a thing, so finally I just let her have at it. No compromise. I mean, it's all turning out beautifully, don't get me wrong. I've just never seen her that way and I felt less and less like the project was mine too. She spent hours looking for just the right pieces, or refinishing stuff she found in the attic or the cellar. I finally did whatever she told me to do. There was no use arguing over anything. Besides, whenever I tried to help I'd take a break and come back to find my tools put away, or things I had arranged would be moved. Apparently, she just didn't want me around."

Despite my growing uneasiness over the last few days, my heart strings were unraveling. Roger looked miserable, and it was clear he was not having an easy time divulging his private matters to a group of people he hardly knew. He looked to his mother for reassurance and she nodded her encouragement.

"Then, Gretchen started acting super weird. Emotional. Grouchy. She was sleep walking, and she's never done that before, that I know of. I'd wake up and she wouldn't be in bed. I'd find her outside, under that big old tree, like she was in a trance. At first the episodes seemed harmless and few and far between. Gretchen doesn't believe me, because she never remembers doing it. I'd just lead her back to bed. But, it started happening more and more, so one night I took her picture outside and the flash of the camera woke her up. She looked so scared and confused, just standing outside in the cold in her nightgown. I felt like a jerk, but I had to prove it to her. She started to cry and said 'What am I doing out here? What's wrong with me?' I tried to calm her down and led her back to bed. Then, the next morning, as usual, she didn't remember a thing and my digital camera was missing. I still can't find it. I wanted to attribute the sleepwalking to stress, or excitement over the wedding; anything, so as not to upset the apple cart. It's no use. I've been staying awake a lot at night. Watching her. For her safety. Rousing her when I think an episode is starting. Now she accuses *me* of acting weird and overbearing. Neither one of us has been getting a lot of sleep so we've been more and more tense with each other."

Roger looked squarely at me. "The first night you were here I got up to get a drink of water. I was in the kitchen and she drifted into the room, turned off the house alarm, and headed outside without even speaking to me. It was happening again so I followed her. This time she didn't go to the tree in front, she walked to the graveyard beyond the woods. Right past the spring waters, all the way to the graveyard, in the dark, in her sleep, like she was on auto-pilot. I didn't think she saw me behind her, but suddenly she turned and started chasing me into the woods. I don't know why I ran from her exactly…the look on her face was just…not Gretchen," Roger shuddered visibly and wrung his hands. Helen reached to hold them still. "You saw me, didn't you Al? That's how you got into the poison ivy."

"I'd let Petey out." I admitted. "Then you came running by and I hid in the brush."

He nodded solemnly. "I don't know when she quit chasing me. By the time I got back to the house she was sound asleep in bed. I don't understand how she got back so fast. I almost felt like it wasn't her I'd followed. Maybe someone that looked like her lured me into the woods." Roger hesitated and studied the floor. "What they say must be true. This land is cursed or something. I've never believed in things like that…but something's come over Gretchen. Something I can't explain."

"We'll get to the bottom of this, Roger." Alex piped up confidently. "Gretchen is worried too. She asked Al to have me bring some of our paranormal equipment. She understands something is wrong. We'll start gathering data and try to have this figured out before the wedding on Sunday."

Instead of looking buoyed by Alex's words Roger gave a half hearted smile and hung his head further. "Sunday. There may not be a wedding on Sunday folks."

"You can't just give up on her, Roger." My mother murmured from the perimeter of the candelabra light.

Roger glanced back at her in the gloom. "I'm afraid she's given up on me, Flora. Last night, after I got home so late, we had an argument about the cat. I saw the scratches on her arm and told her I was going to catch the damn thing and take it to a shelter and have it put down. She got hysterical. She told me if I touched a hair on that cat's head she would leave me. She said that she wasn't even sure she wanted to be with me anymore anyway. I slept out here and got up early to clean up the brush behind the cottages. Even though we made up this afternoon before the reception, somewhat, she seemed completely serious last night. I don't know how much longer I can go on like this."

"Maybe we should all move into town and stay at the inn." Helen suggested.

"No!" Roger shouted abruptly. "This is my house. Nothing is going to make me leave it. We've invested too much already."

"Hang in there, buddy." Alex slapped him gently on the back. "We'll get it figured out. How about we all get some sleep and we'll regroup in the morning. Al and I planned on setting up some equipment tonight, but it's late. I think we'll wait and start tomorrow." Alex looked to me for confirmation. "We'll get at it first thing in the morning." I nodded and stifled a yawn. It felt good to have Alex here, taking some control over a situation that seemed completely impossible right now.

"There might be a perfectly natural explanation, Roger." Alex continued. "Maybe the spring water creates some type of vibration that sensitive people are susceptible to. I've heard of mineral deposits in the ground that can cause events that seem to be paranormal at first. Maybe there's faulty wiring in the house. Strong electrical energy can cause events and sensations that seem paranormal too."

Roger rose, looking exhausted, unconvinced and perhaps a little annoyed by Alex's confidence that there might be a simple, physical explanation for Gretchen's behavior. I could only imagine how his mind was working right now. Either the land he had put his last cent into was foul, or his fiancé had lost her mind…or both. Suddenly he glanced at me.

"You didn't just slip in the bathroom did you?" My eyes must have said it all. "I didn't think so."

"Why? Have you seen something? Has something else happened?"

He just shook his head and shuffled dejectedly from the room.

Chapter 20

One thing was certain; I couldn't leave Mom alone in that house now that Gretchen's behavior was so questionable and we were obviously dealing with something pretty powerful. Helen had taken the second upstairs bedroom while Cassie and I decided to share the third, since Roger's relatives would no longer be staying.

Alex helped us move our things up from Cassie's cottage, and though he had taken the keys to cottage number three for himself, the two of us were holding vigil on the large divan in the sitting room after everyone else had gone to bed. I felt safe having him close and was relieved when he suggested we stay up a little later to strategize our investigation.

"Well, what do you think?" I inquired. Alex was leaning upright in the corner of the couch, his feet on an ottoman, and one arm encircling me as I curled against him, my head resting on his chest. I had removed my wrist brace and had my injured arm draped across his stomach.

Alex closed his eyes and pinched the bridge of his nose. "I don't know," he sighed. I felt him crook his neck to look down at me. "I don't know," he repeated thoughtfully. We were silent for several minutes and Alex absentmindedly began to run his fingers tenderly over my swollen, bruised skin. "It seems like this thing has made a target out of you. That makes me angry."

"I'm okay," I murmured sullenly.

"Yeah, you look like you're doing *great*." Alex said sarcastically, then chuckled and gave me a gentle hug. He was attempting to lighten my mood. It wasn't working.

"I want to go home," I found myself saying.

Alex grew quiet, and then sounded surprised when he finally spoke. I was actually a little surprised by what I had just said myself. "What? Com'on, Al. We love this stuff, right?"

"This is different. This isn't spooky, or intriguing. It's not thrilling, or even sort of fun. This is actually pretty horrifying. I mean, Cassie was acting completely out of character tonight, I feel weird, Gretchen…well, I don't know what to think about what just happened to Gretchen. I was suspicious of Roger, but now I feel sorry for him. I'd be lying if I didn't tell you that I'd really like to throw Mom and the dog in the van and head home. But…" I felt my eyes growing heavy. Alex was warm and his breathing had grown more even and steady.

"But, we can't leave Gretchen alone with this," he finished my sentence sleepily.

"We can't leave Gretchen alone," I agreed, then drifted off myself.

Chapter 21

Thursday

After only a few hours of sleep, Alex and I awoke in the sitting room. The sun was just breaking over the horizon and the rest of the house remained quiet. The power appeared to be back on.

While Alex ran down to his cottage to change, I peeked in on Mom, finding her fast asleep with Petey coiled on the pillow next to her head. He opened one eye, assessing what my intentions might be. When I didn't enter the room he closed his eye after several moments. Apparently he didn't need out.

Next, I crept into the pretty pink paisley bedroom Cass and I now shared at the end of the hall. She was snoring loudly and remained oblivious as I donned jeans and a sweatshirt, grabbed my digital camera, and slipped back downstairs to start some coffee and meet Alex.

As I approached the butler's pantry I noticed the door to the master suite was open about a foot. I couldn't resist peeking in. A few feet into the darkened room I spied poor Roger, uncomfortably bent on the love seat in their television area, his lanky frame folded in every direction so he didn't spill over onto the floor. He must not have had the courage to share a bed with Gretchen. He looked cold, so I retrieved the blanket that had slipped off of him and draped it over his body.

Later, Alex and I took our coffee out back, hand in hand. It was a cool, peaceful morning, with just a hint of winter in the air and that sense of expectancy, of change to come. I loved that about autumn…when the seasons were slowly relenting to one another. Frost gleamed on every blade of grass, yet the leaves held vigilantly and colorfully to the trees. It was like walking a fine line between two worlds. Jeans and a sweatshirt felt just right in the crisp air, and though the rising sun promised warmth with every gathering ray, they would be just right later on. Leaving our empty mugs on the picnic table, we decided to check out the cemetery for ourselves.

Alex and I often had long stretches of time when we did not speak, just roamed quietly in the same direction. That was actually the beauty of our relationship. We were generally in sync. With Alex, I am sometimes able to experience rare moments in which my constant feelings of angst disappear and a fleeting notion of complete peace settles over me. These moments are usually disturbing to me when they have passed. I feel I have let my guard against the universe down, even though I realize it's okay, in fact more than acceptable, to relinquish control occasionally and let Alex steer the course for awhile.

Some people think you should find someone who completes you; your other half. I have no idea what that really means. I think you should find someone who enhances who you are. I was pretty sure that I'd found that person in Alex.

We meandered until we'd crested a knoll, coming across an old tool shed with peeling green paint and several slats of board missing. The grass was overgrown around the little lean-to and a rusted out wheelbarrow was tipped up against one wall on its flattened tire. Broken clay pots were stacked by the door. Next to the shed was a fenced in area that was obviously Lillian's old garden plot, it was perhaps an acre or so of land.

A weathered old scarecrow hung limply from an upright bamboo rod. From the look of its worn, faded rags, the scarecrow had endured many seasons. Few fronds remained of its cornstalk arms and legs which swung loosely in the slight morning breeze. I could not tell what the head had been comprised of. It fell forward and a black felt hat, nearly rotten, was snagged atop the rod, covering any face that might have existed. Alex took a couple of pictures with his camera and we moved on toward the trees.

Off in the distance I could see the remains of the large guest house foundation. Grey pieces of stone erupted randomly from the dirt like unearthed bones. Those quarters, burnt to the ground decades before by the insane Powell ancestor, had housed the nursing nuns and guests seeking health and comfort from the supposedly healing waters in the forest. Vowing to explore the layout later, Alex and I reached the woods, skirting their edge until we found a well worn pathway. It was darker beneath the trees…and chilly. I had been keeping an eye out for the crazy cat so I could show Alex, but I hadn't seen her yet.

We heard the bubbling spring before we could see it. Old wooden arrows, that had once been painted red, were nailed to trees at various intervals, confirming that we were headed in the right direction. Before we knew it, we had reached a small clearing where the water accumulated into a clear pool. For some reason, in my imagination the bathing area had been much larger, but the spring gurgled over a formation of stones and trickled into the pool which was not much bigger than a hot tub. I could see where large rocks had been brought in to landscape the area naturally. They were placed in the water as steps and for seating when bathing. In spite of the cool air, the crystal clear water was inviting and I would have had no problem jumping in had it been a little warmer outside.

Spying another path beyond the edge of the bath, we headed into denser trees. This trail was barely visible and had not been maintained at all. I clung to Alex's hand tripping occasionally over roots on the ground and dodging low hanging limbs in the air when he indicated them. I knew that Mom and Gretchen had said you could walk around the woods to get to the cemetery, but it was too late…we were in it now. Burrs clung to my sleeves and it suddenly occurred to me that I might be re-infecting my poison ivy. I wondered if this had been the path Roger took when Gretchen chased him from the graveyard, and where it picked up on the other side of the spring to lead behind the cottages.

We walked for five or ten minutes and though the trees seemed to thin, we were still under cover. Alex stopped to take a picture of a squirrel and I forged forward. Within a few steps my toe caught on something solid and I found myself tripping head first, spread eagle onto the ground.

"Mmmm…" I grunted with surprise as I landed hard. As often as I fell down you'd think I would have perfected some sort of technique by now. I lay stunned, trying to assess the damage.

"Are you okay?" Alex had closed the space between us quickly. I rolled over, sat on my butt, surveying the sizeable rip in the muddy knee of my new jeans. I looked up at him like a forlorn child.

"I just bought these."

Alex smiled down at me and for a moment I forgot where I was. Dimples in all the right places. Yum. He was well aware that the turn around rate for my clothing was pretty tight. Whether I fell down a flight of stairs, spilled food, or spilled food falling down a flight of stairs, I had learned long ago not to invest a huge amount of money in anything I put on my body. He extended his big warm hand and I accepted it with my cold, grimy one. "You're not bleeding are you?" He pulled me to my feet.

"No, I don't think so." My brow knitted as I wiped my dirty hands on the rear of my pants and studied the ground behind him. "I'd swear I tripped over something." There weren't any roots, but something jutted up in the middle of the path. It had been camouflaged by some vines and undercover. "That's what I fell over." We knelt and pulled away the greenery.

"It's a grave marker," Alex breathed reverently. "At least what's left of it." You could tell by the shape of what was left broken off in the ground that he was right. We searched briefly around the path but couldn't turn up the rest of it.

"That's weird. Why would you bury someone in the middle of the woods?" I said, on my knees, pulling sparse plants on the forest floor away from the base of the stone. "It's away from everyone else."

Alex shrugged and knelt with me, then practically lay on the ground. "I don't know, but I can feel some of the lettering. Maybe…i..n..h..e..l..l. In hell? That can't be right. We should come back later, with some shaving cream."

Using shaving cream to read old stones was a trick we had learned one evening when setting up for a ghost vigil in a local Crescentville cemetery. An amateur genealogist was employing the method to read and photograph old family gravesites. He showed us how he sprayed some foam across the upper portion of a stone and spread it down across the words with a shower squeegee. It was amazing, the foam filled the crevices that had been too worn or full of moss to read and they became completely legible.

I froze in place, shivering and rubbing my arms, looking all around me at the ground. It seemed like the temperature had dropped about ten or fifteen degrees in the last few minutes and I had that weird choking sensation. I cleared my throat and habitually reached for my absent waist pack.

Alex glanced up and saw me hugging myself and rose. "Come on. Let's go." He placed a gentle arm around me and I calmed, welcoming the heat of his body as we pressed carefully on side by side.

I was relieved when we finally erupted from the woods into the sun and came across the little graveyard. Large cedar trees dotted the area. The stones, well over a hundred, were lined up randomly in rows or clusters on about two acres or so of flat land between the trees and an old barbed wire fence thick with weeds. The fence ran before us and to our right, back into the forest from which we'd come. It was obviously the property boundary between the Powell property and the farmland surrounding it. In the distance I could see cattle dotting the hillside.

In the corner, on our side of the rusty wire barrier, a huge elm shadowed several of the graves. A large white marble angel, her wings folded down and her weathered hands in prayer, stood atop a pedestal not far from the back fence just a few yards from the elm. The stones were aged to varying degrees. A few were broken in two like the one I had fallen over in the woods, but the tops of these were accounted for as they leaned against their sunken bottom halves. Many markers were in good shape and easily readable. Lillian Powell's grave was obviously the newest with slightly mounded dirt and sparse dry grass. Her marker was rose colored, flat and set into the ground. We approached it reverently.

Lillian Elise Powell was buried next to a Martha Stella Powell who had died approximately thirty years before and around thirty five years after her apparent husband, Walter. Having never married, I assumed Lillian had been buried next to her parents. If only the family tree from the book I swiped at the library had been clearer.

A few feet away were markers for a Kenneth and June Powell. Kenneth had been born two years before Lillian and I wondered if he might not be her brother.

The Powell graves covered the north side of the lot. There were several stones that simply said infant, and true to local lore, all of the men seemed to have died young, in their twenties or early thirties. On most of the stones, though the women had lived long past their mates, they either kept their last name of Powell, or hyphenated their names. A custom I did not believe was common in those times.

Over toward the elm tree and fence, on the south edge of the property, there were several names that did not appear to be family related. I wondered if they were patients from the hospice era of the property; sick people with no family. A handful of stones clustered near the angel indicated the graves of sisters in Christ who had cared for the ill.

We found Blanche, the Powell who burnt down the guest housing around her husband Jack's body, his cause of death unknown due to the fire. She had been institutionalized in Ohio until a few years before she came back to Spring Valley to be cared for by her family. She was buried next to her husband.

The oldest stones we could make out without a rubbing or the shaving cream method; were those of a David and Etta. He passed away in 1782, she in 1841, at the ripe old age of ninety-one.

The fact that Gretchen had spat out many of these names last night was not lost on us. Alex and I kicked around a couple of theories. Perhaps the names were fresh on Gretchen's mind from her walk with my mother only a day or so before. Or perhaps, during her renovations of the house, she had come across Powell family documents and just did not recall seeing them. Either she was really stressed out and couldn't remember, or she was truly under the influence of a spirit.

Alex and I left the graves behind, determined to come back later. We decided to skirt the woods as Mom had described and head back to the house for breakfast. We were so intent on our conversation about the Powell's that my cell phone startled me when it rang in my jeans pocket. I didn't recognize the caller, and then I remembered giving Prudence my number the night before.

"Hello," the connection was less than ideal.

"Al?" Prudence's voice crackled from the other end of the line. I stopped walking and plugged my opposite ear with my index finger. A big black bird had landed on the tree above me and was squawking like there was no tomorrow.

"Yeah, it's me. What's up?"

"I told you I needed to check on something last night."

"Yeah?" I was practically yelling over the ruckus the bird was making. Alex was trying to take a picture of it but it kept jumping from branch to branch.

"Well, how open would your friend be to a séance at the house?"

I sighed. "A séance? I don't know. I really think this is getting beyond a lay person's realm, Prudence."

"Oh, I'm not talking just some average people getting together and holding hands while trying to talk to the dead. I'm talking a real life psychic medium."

Now she had my full attention, though getting Roger and Gretchen to agree to any such thing might be a much different matter. "What did you have in mind?"

"Edna Shine. She's a legend around these parts. She was a school teacher for sixty years, until she lost her eyesight. She retired when she was eighty-two. She's almost ninety now, but her third eye is still going strong."

"Peaceful little Spring Valley is certainly an unusual place; untimely deaths, apparitions, psychics. Half the town doesn't want to talk about it…the other half thinks the land is cursed. You're sure this lady is the real deal?"

Prudence laughed. "Oh, she's the real deal alright. I had her as a teacher in the third grade, before she retired. She can tell you what the weather's going to do before the weatherman. I saw her send Ira Perkins to the nurse's office for an appendicitis attack an hour before his stomach even started hurting. He was just sitting there working on a worksheet and she called him up to her desk and sent him to the office with a note. The next day he didn't come to school and it turns out a little later his stomach actually started hurting, his mom came and picked him up and he went home, started throwing up and they had to remove his appendix that evening. Emergency surgery they called it. He almost died. It wouldn't have been an emergency if his parents had taken him straight to the hospital like Edna suggested."

"Hmmm, interesting. Well, let me talk it over with my friends. I haven't even seen them yet today. They may or may not be happy about dragging more people into this after last night. Too many witnesses."

"Just let me know. I've already talked to Ms. Shine and she said she'd be happy to come. She lives close by. She actually knew several of the Powells, and a couple of their children were in her classes many, many years ago."

"I've got your number now. I'll talk to everyone today and call you if they're interested. Thanks, Prudence."

After we hung up I explained our conversation to Alex and we walked on. We passed the overgrown garden area as the annoying bird flew overhead, and then perched on a fence post, squawking belligerently. We agreed to talk to Gretchen and Roger, and though the prospect of a séance was sort of exciting, we really wanted to see what we could turn up through our own investigation first. Of course, it was entirely up to Gretchen and Roger anyway.

"What's with that bird?" Alex wondered. We stopped to consider it and cautiously took a few steps toward the post. The black thing spread its wings, held them open and quieted down, though it continued to make soft noises in its throat, eyeing us the entire time.

"Is it a crow?" I asked. "It's huge."

"Looks like it, but...what the hell? Run!" Unexpectedly, talons extended, and the creature's wings outstretched further than imaginable. It flew right at us. I was screaming my brains out and Alex was shouting hysterically as we sprinted toward the house, our arms waving wildly in the air. Alex was a couple of paces ahead of me when I felt the thing pass me over and I saw it swoop at the back of his head. He let out a startled yelp and picked up speed. Then the crazy bird circled swiftly, left Alex and flew low, straight toward me, I squealed in terror and zigzagged toward the little tool shed.

"Al!" Alex hollered. Turning, he realized I was not behind him anymore. I was running in circles, and lurching like a lunatic, cussing and waving my arms, trying to stay low and keep up my speed as the bird buzzed my head emitting a maniacal screech. Seeing the rake lying in the deep grass too late, I anticipated the inevitable. Thwack! My right foot felt like a hot knife had been driven through it, but that pain was nothing compared to the smack of the old wooden handle striking my nose. I hit the ground and quickly curled into a fetal position, howling and holding my face. I could taste and smell the coppery trickle of blood in the back of my throat and on my swollen lips. My eyes stung and at first were so watery I couldn't see, so when Alex reached me and touched my arm, I was startled and came up swinging.

"Al! Ohhhhffff!" Apparently my elbow connected with his jaw.

Suddenly, the bird returned. It roosted atop the shed and cackled softly down at us, almost as if it were laughing. Angry, Alex picked up the rake and hurled it at the crow. The bird gracefully sidestepped the tool, which landed with a clatter on the rusty metal roof of the shed, before sliding down and nearly whacking me in the head.

Taunting us with one last cackle, it spread its wings and soared away. We could hear its cries as it disappeared over the tree tops back toward the cemetery.

Alex helped me limp across the remainder of the field and down the knoll while I held my head back and pinched my bloody nose shut. At the back of the house we found Cassie sitting at one of the picnic tables eating a piece of toast. Petey, eyes protruding and tongue lolling, was entranced with the cement squirrel in the landscaping. He barely looked up as we approached.

"What's up?" I asked Cassie and plopped down next to her.

She eyeballed my muddy, ripped pants, my bloody nose and sweatshirt, and red, watery eyes, and decided to ignore my question. "What's up with you?"

"You couldn't hear all of that?" Alex exclaimed in disbelief. He knelt and started to untie my shoelaces. The metal rake had gone right through the bottom of my sneaker. Now I had another problem. I resisted as Alex tried to take off my shoe.

I hated feet, mine in particular, and had taken great care to ensure Alex had never been this close to them in broad daylight. Having lived in a pleasant state of ignorance until around the age of twelve, I first became aware of the situations at the ends of my legs at Mary Beth Henley's birthday slumber party. Seated in a circle, playing a board game, I suddenly noticed everyone else's pretty, straight, painted toes and it immediately occurred to me that my feet were heinous. I remember quietly looking around then down at myself and thinking, "What happened?" I spent the rest of the evening with a blanket over my lap and hadn't worn open toed shoes since. Now Alex was kneeling before me, dangerously close to slipping my sneaker from my heel.

"I'm good!" I kicked at him with my other leg.

"You are not good. You're leaving a trail of blood."

"Back off!" I really didn't want him examining my hooves. He held my ankle firmly and stripped off my bloody sock. Okay. There it was. Wait for it…hmmm…oddly he appeared unscathed, at least for the moment. I reminded myself that the guy charged into burning buildings for a living so this might not be the worse thing he'd ever witnessed, but on another level I was pretty sure he would find some excuse to end our relationship by the week's end.

Cassie was watching us with a wry smile on her face. She was reading my mind.

"What are you looking at?" I snapped.

"If you weren't stressed out all the time you wouldn't be so accident prone," she retorted and tossed Petey her toast crust, which he ignored in favor of my bloody sock.

Cassie and I watched as Petey snuck up behind Alex, swiped the sock from the ground next to him and, looking quite pleased, pranced happily toward the hollow beneath the back porch steps. Unfortunately, he ran head long into a spider web, spit out the sock in a panic and raced out into the yard, frantically rolling around on the ground. Within moments he laid catatonic, legs outstretched, his sides heaved from exertion.

"He's messed up," Cassie commented and turned to me. "So are you. Are you gonna tell me what happened or not?"

"I shouldn't….but I will."

I quickly filled her in about the graveyard, and the bird, and Pru's suggestion of a séance. Cassie only yawned loudly.

"What's wrong with you?" I asked, thinking she should at least be excited at the prospect of a séance.

"That dog kept me up half the night." Cassie scowled and gestured grumpily at Petey who was now humping the concrete squirrel in earnest. "At first I thought he missed you or Flora and was just being annoying, and then I thought of your purple lady friend and I started to wonder if he sensed something in the room. About four a.m. I finally put him in with your mother." Cassie yawned again. "I haven't heard a peep out of Gretchen and your mom was in the shower when I let Petey out. I guess Roger's mom is still asleep. If you're okay, I think I'm going to go in and take a nap."

"She's okay," Alex stood and gently palmed my head with one hand, tilting it back so he could check out my nose, "But, we're still going to take a trip to the ER." I groaned. "When's the last time you had a tetanus shot?"

Cassie rolled her eyes.

"I know I got one last May, remember? After the catering van was stolen." Cassie grimaced at the thought of the incident and I stuck my tongue out at her as far as I could over my big lip. "It wasn't my fault."

"It was totally your fault," she asserted.

"Was not."

"Was too."

"Was not."

"Who leaves keys in a running vehicle?" She challenged.

"It wasn't running!"

"Who leaves keys in *any* vehicle?"

"I just ran into the convenience store to get a soda."

"Yeah, well, you're lucky the cops found the van or our insurance could have been cancelled and we would have been out our only work vehicle."

"We got it back."

"All our equipment was gone, and the bumper was missing."

"So, what?"

Cassie shuddered dramatically. "So, what? So, all that was left inside was a halter top…a sandal…an empty vodka bottle…and a container of mustard."

"Big deal, they had drunken sex and made a sandwich…or vice versa. Who cares?"

"We carry people's food in that van!"

"And I hosed it out!"

"Stop yelling at me!"

"Stop yelling at *me*!"

"Girls! That happened two summers ago. Get over it." Mom admonished, stepping around Alex with her hands on her hips. We were arguing so loudly that we hadn't even heard her come outside. She turned pale when she saw my swollen nose and bloody sweatshirt. "Deloris, what now?" Roger's mom peeked around from behind the other side of Alex and gasped.

"What do you mean, 'What now?'!" I whined. Why was everyone picking on me?

"She was attacked by a bird," Cassie said calmly, like it happened everyday. I stuck my tongue out at her again for no apparent reason, other than it felt good to do so. We never fought over truly stupid stuff like this. Why was Cassie so testy? For that matter, since when was I so sensitive?

"And, now she's going to the emergency room." Alex added. Mom looked confused as she sized up my bloody foot.

"I'll fill you in." Cassie told her.

"What's wrong with that dog?" Helen suddenly exclaimed and pointed toward Petey, unconscious in the landscaping.

"Is he breathing?" I asked.

Helen craned her neck. "Yes."

"Mmm, he passes out when he gets overly excited. We've been to three specialists, but no one can figure it out."

Helen initially looked concerned but since the rest of us didn't appear worried she smiled and joked, "Ever give him mouth to mouth?" Nobody laughed. I looked sideways at Alex whose complexion reddened as he studied the ground around him intently.

"Only the first time." I replied.

"I see," Helen said uncomfortably under her breath. She watched as Mom knelt to softly stroke Petey's head. Soon his little eyelids began to flutter.

"See, he's okay. Come on, Al." Alex changed the subject and touched my shoulder. "I'll help you to my car."

"But, I've been to the hospital twice already. In fact, actually, I think they gave me a tetanus shot when they stitched up my lip. I don't wanna go!"

"I don't care. Stop whining and MOVE!" He reached to take my elbow and I jerked away.

"Ha…ha," Cassie taunted. "At least I don't have to go this time."

"This vacation sucks!" I groused, picking up my bloody shoe and hopping toward the porch.

Chapter 22

Alex drove me to the emergency room for the third time in almost as many days and I was starting to sniffle by the time we got there. The pain was subsiding, but Cassie had hurt my feelings. As I checked out my face in the passenger visor mirror I saw that both my eyes were now turning black and I had a swollen purple knot in the middle of my nose that had erupted into a big bloody sore where the skin had split.

"I'm going to be the ugliest bridesmaid ever!" I wailed.

"No you're not." Alex tried to console me as he pulled carefully into the hospital parking lot.

"Yes, I am."

"Trust me, you're not."

"Oh, yeah? Well who could top this?" I gestured hysterically toward my reflection in the tiny mirror.

"My cousin, Pat."

"Your cousin Pat was the ugliest bridesmaid ever? Your cousin Pat could top stitches, poison ivy, two black eyes, and possibly a broken nose? Not to mention the fact that there is no way my foot is ever going to fit into the freak'n designer heels Gretchen picked out for us. Your cousin Pat...the bridesmaid...could top all of that?" I ranted.

"Yep." Alex said calmly and rolled up his window.
He started to get out of the car and I huffed, "Well? How? How could Pat top the disaster that is *me*?"

Alex slammed his door, walked around the car and opened mine. I glared up at him. "Pat's not a bad lookin' dude…but he makes one hell of an ugly bridesmaid."

I had to smile in spite of myself as Alex bowed, took my hand, and helped me from the car as if I were his queen disembarking from a gilded carriage. He made sure I had my balance, closed the door and gently pinned me against his car for a moment.

"All kidding aside," his handsome face had grown grave as his easy grin collapsed into a strong chin and pursed mouth. Alex tenderly held my face, leaned close and tilted my head so he could look deep into my eyes. I noted that the usual cheerful twinkle in his had evaporated in the intensity of his gaze and I braced myself for one of our rare serious moments, absentmindedly grateful that his body weight held me firmly in place. My knees were turning to jelly. "I love you, Al. I love you and I worry about you. I can't always be around to protect you…or to provide emergency medical services." The corner of his mouth twitched and the twinkle surfaced for a moment then he grew somber again. "So what I'm saying is…don't argue with me now…just let me take care of you."

Uh, okay. I nodded dumbly as his lips touched mine lightly, softer that the whisper of a butterfly's wings. Then he scooped me up and carried me toward the hospital doors.

The emergency room was not busy and we got right in. In fact the receptionist was the same lady I had seen twice before. She didn't even call a nurse, just grimaced, had me a sign paper and told me to go back to curtain number one. Apparently, since I was a regular, I no longer required an escort.

This time I was surprised to find that the doctor was a quiet, elderly gentleman, with a neatly combed shock of thick, white hair and wire spectacles. He looked almost as exhausted as the zealous young physician I had seen before. This doctor read my chart quickly and began his exam. My nose was not broken…only badly bruised. My foot wound was flushed, medicated and bandaged. I got a shot of antibiotic in my hip, just in case, and the doctor confirmed my tetanus booster was administered during the last visit.

"Be careful now," he murmured with a smile and disappeared behind curtain number two with no further questions. I hadn't heard them bring anyone else in. Maybe he wanted to chortle over my chart in private, or maybe he was just going to take a nap.

"Happy?" I shot Alex a frosty glare.

"Ecstatic. Let's go. Now I'm hungry."

Alex wanted to use the restroom on the way out so I waited in the hall. I leaned against the wall, tilted my head back and closed my eyes. I was stressed out and completely surprised I had not come down with a migraine yet. Yet, was the key word. I reflexively felt for my waist pack and of course, I did not have it. Ah, breathe in, breathe out, breathe in, breathe out, I willed myself. 'You're at a hospital if you need something,' I rationalized with myself. I was breathing through my mouth, of course, because my nostrils were solid blood clots.

I heard a slight noise and opened my eyes. The young doctor that had treated me before had rounded the corner and stood in the hall, his mouth agape. Before he could utter a sound, Alex stepped from the restroom and took my arm.

"Ready?"

Some kind of realization seemed to overtake the young man's tired face and he nodded slowly. We all just stood there for a couple of awkward seconds, then the intern shot daggers at Alex with his eyes, and he looked sadly at me. He shook his finger menacingly at Alex then turned away and disappeared down the hall without a word.

"What was that about?" Alex looked puzzled.

"Forget it. Let's go." I sighed. "Good gravy!"

Chapter 23

We returned in the afternoon to find Cassie back in the kitchen. Not knowing what else to do, she was burying herself in wedding reception preparations. We hugged apologetically. "I'm sorry Al; I don't know what's up. I just feel so…so…emotional."

"Me too. Bad vibes."

"Bad vibes." She agreed and started to cry. We hugged for a long time.

This was getting to be too much. Stoic Cassie generally kept her emotions in check. In fact, I tried to remember the last time I actually saw Cassie seriously upset about anything and thought it might have been our junior year of high school when Darren Winder stood her up for the homecoming dance. He didn't pick her up and he didn't call. He didn't come to school on Monday either. I was enraged and waited in the dark parking lot of the Burrito Barn that night for him to leave work. I gave him a bloody nose and whacked off the driver side mirror of his muscle car with a baseball bat as a souvenir for Cassie. Not a moment I was necessarily proud of, but to this day she kept it on her living room bookshelf.

We sniffled and made up for a little while longer then I left Alex to make himself a ham sandwich and stay in the kitchen with Cassie while I checked on Mom. Helen was sitting with Gretchen in the master bedroom and Roger was no where to be found. They assumed he had left for town and gone to the office. I located Mom upstairs crawling around on her bedroom floor muttering. Petey followed her, assisting with whatever she was doing with an intense, concerned look on his little face. I watched her backside round the end of the bed and Petey slipped out of sight beneath the dust ruffle.

"Mom? What's wrong?"

Her head popped up over the mattress...hair mussed, cheeks flushed, eyes watery. "My walking shoes. I left them right here yesterday. I know I did." A tear slipped down her cheek. "I know I did," she whispered desolately and disappeared beneath the bed again.

I dropped to my hands and knees and started crawling with her. Having no respect for me whatsoever, Petey quickly mounted my thigh.

"Get off!" I said tersely and gave him a shove.

The shoes were nowhere to be found. I checked the adjoining bathroom. "They're not here, Mom. Are you sure you didn't leave them downstairs?"

"Of course not!" She looked confused and angry. "I took them off to get ready for the party last night. I didn't come back up here until we all went to bed. I remember. I think." She looked around the room helplessly, biting on a thumb nail. "I remember."

"Hey. Don't get upset. We both know you hadn't been in the cottages and somehow your reading glasses ended up on my sink. Remember? I think this might have something to do with Roger and Gretchen's problems. Don't worry, they'll turn up. Let's go bug Cassie and see if she needs any help." She looked doubtful as I ushered her toward the stairs, so, to distract her, I told her about my earlier phone call with Prudence and asked her opinion of a séance.

The afternoon passed slowly as everyone busied themselves with little tasks, trying to be productive. By the time Roger arrived home around six o'clock I had taken to chewing antacids like they were candy. My stomach was churning with anxiety and a headache threatened behind my left eye.

"Hey, Flora," Roger held up Mom's walking shoes as he entered the kitchen. "Aren't these yours? I almost fell over them on the porch steps." He smiled good-naturedly.

Mom gasped and we exchanged a glance. "I was sure I left those in my bedroom yesterday. I'm sorry. I hope you didn't hurt yourself."

"Oh no, I'm fine. I just didn't think you'd want to leave them out all night."

We were all having a brief conversation about the various items of Roger and Gretchen's that had come up missing, only to be found some place else later, when Gretchen appeared in the doorway in a nightgown and housecoat. Helen was behind her. "You're home. I heard your voice." She said tentatively to Roger. He didn't meet her gaze and mumbled something about trying to get ahead at work and needing a shower. Edging around Gretchen and Helen in the doorway he retreated to the master bathroom. Gretchen's eyes reddened and she hung her head. Helen put a comforting hand on her shoulder.

"He's afraid of me." Gretchen sniffled.

"Oh, honey, he's just tired." Helen reassured Gretchen and led her toward the booth seating. "This is hard on everyone. Come on. You need to eat something."

Cassie and I busied ourselves with heating up soup and toasting cheese bread in the oven, while Mom, Helen and Alex watched us, keeping Gretchen company at the table. Though everyone was tense, the tone of conversation was purposely light, for Gretchen's benefit, mainly consisting of tales of Petey's exploits. The subject of our discussion was curled up on the rug in front of the refrigerator keeping his eyes trained on Cassie and I, should we drop something. No one mentioned the events of the morning. Gretchen tried to be polite as everyone attempted to engage her in conversation, but she seemed so preoccupied that she didn't even ask about my swollen nose, or limp.

Roger ducked back into the kitchen with damp hair and in more comfortable clothing and was a lot more attentive toward Gretchen. She had opened up somewhat to us but became almost silent as Roger hovered over her. Her hair snarled and freckles standing starkly out against her sickly pale skin, Gretchen took about three bites of soup, tolerated our banal conversation for another few minutes, and then wanted to go back to her room.

Helen had been busying herself mothering over both Roger and Gretchen. She was a frenzy of nervous energy throughout the meal as she ladled soup, cut bread, and jumped up and down to get more tea for everyone. I felt sorry for her. It was obvious she really liked Gretchen, and she was upset that things weren't working out smoothly for her son.

Cassie barely seemed able to contain her simmering emotions and was alternating between subdued grumpiness and forced enthusiasm. Mom seemed a little quieter than usual and as we ate I realized with a pang of guilt that I hadn't remembered her morning pills before Alex whisked me off to the hospital. Though she'd had her dinner dose, she seemed a bit withdrawn, and I wondered if the stress of everything wasn't wearing her down. I caught her casting worried, furtive glances toward her shoes which now rested near the back door.

Everyone was so tense; the pressure seemed to build throughout the meal, so the time never seemed quite right to bring up Edna Shine. Eventually, tired of pretending nothing of consequence was going on, Roger retired early, as did Helen. Mom chatted with Cassie while she cleaned the kitchen, and me and Alex started setting up our paranormal equipment.

The house was pretty big, so we did the best we could to make the most use of the few cameras and recorders we had. One video camera was placed in the entry hall pointing up the stairs, one motion camera was in the sitting room, pointing out into the entry way so that part of the dining room and the front door would be caught on film, and, finally, one motion camera pointed down the hall toward Gretchen and Roger's bedroom and the back of the house. We placed a recorder on the dining room table, and one in the kitchen on the counter. The other two recorders and digital cameras would go with us. We decided to check out the graveyard in the moonlight and see if we could get some electronic voice phenomena. After that, we were going to stake out the cottages for a little while.

Once Petey and Cassie were upstairs in the pink room playing quietly with some of his toys, and Mom was relaxing in bed, with a cup of tea and Lillian Powell's poetry book, Alex and I turned on the equipment and headed outside together.

I was happy I had thought to grab a jacket. The night air was becoming brittle and little wisps of fog were curling around our ankles. There were no stars to be seen but the moon was full and bright, lighting up the landscape. The main house stood like a sentinel in a spotlight, casting a large shadow behind it. I leaned on Alex for support as I hobbled next to him up the slight hill. Our cameras and recorders dangled heavily from their neck straps and rattled against one another.

"You can go to bed you know. You probably ought to rest that foot."

"Not on your life. I don't want to miss out on anything. Besides, as long as I'm with you I'm A-OK." I said buoyantly.

"Thanks, babe." We trudged slowly on, but even with Alex next to me I had to admit I was anxious. We hadn't seen the cat since the other night, and there was that crazy bird to consider so I kept casting furtive glances around us. Whether I was looking for kamikaze crows or devil cats, I wasn't sure. Maybe it was just the brilliant moon at our backs, but I kept feeling like something or someone was watching us. I had that prickling sensation around my shoulders and the back of my neck.

We had crested the top of the knoll behind the house and had just passed the garden area when Alex blurted, "Oh, crap!" He was patting his pockets down frantically.

"What?"

"That's weird. I think I left the batteries for my recorder in the bag in the house. He started rummaging through the little camera bag on his hip. "But I remember picking them up. I counted them."

"Oh, honey," I huffed with false exasperation. This was actually a welcome respite. It was hard plodding along trying to breathe through your mouth because your nose was swollen shut. I was out of breath and trying not to show it.

"Come on." He turned toward the house.

"I can't. I'm worn out. We'll just use my recorder."

"I haven't put the batteries in that one either." He said apologetically.

Hmmm…stay or go, stay or go? It wasn't like Alex to forget the batteries. He was always so organized. I cast a glance toward the moonlit hillside and noted the throb in my foot. The main house was no longer visible.

"You go. I'll wait here." I said bravely.

Alex sized me up for a moment. "Are you sure? I'll run and be right back. Or, do you want a piggy back ride?"

"No…just get. But, hurry. I'll either be standing right here or headed toward the graveyard. I won't get far like this." I gestured toward my injured foot. "You'll catch up quick enough."

Alex didn't look too sure, and I really didn't feel too sure, but we had no choice. "Okay. Holler if you need me."

"Okay."

With that, he took off across the weeds, sprinting past the garden shed, and down the hillside. I watched him go and felt that eerie 'being watched' feeling increase. My shoulders were involuntarily rising up to meet my ear lobes with tension. 'Don't be stupid,' I coached myself under my breath. 'The moon is huge. It's almost bright as day out here.' I placed my hand on my waist pack and turned slowly in little quarter circles, warily scanning the pasture around me. Off in the distance a train's whistle wailed and I heard a cow's muffled moo. The fog slithered through the grass. I wouldn't have minded a cow's company right now. A cow that would calmly stand and chew cud while I hid behind it. Anything so that I wasn't the only warm blooded mammal out here in the middle of this damned field.

I looked intently toward the tree line but saw nothing lurking amongst the trunks. Humming beneath my breathe I took a few cautious steps toward the cemetery. 'No sense waiting, I can't go very fast. Alex will be right back,' I reasoned.

I always hummed Christmas carols when I was very tense or nervous, most often when I was driving in the snow. Tonight, I suddenly felt like belting out a tune or two so I began to hum. Hmm…Hmm…Hmmmm. Hmm…Hmm…Hmmmm. After a few halting steps anxiety continued to roil in the pit of my stomach and I felt the need to switch to something a littler more religious.

I had managed to limp near the edge of the trees when behind me a noise no louder than a whisper halted my progress. Afraid to turn around, I simply froze for a moment. The lonely howl of a coyote came to my ears and I felt like someone had run an icicle down my spine. I waited a few beats of my heart more, chided myself nervously at my jitters and overactive imagination, and plugged forward, tentatively. There it was again. I had that squirmy, tickly feeling across the back of my shoulders. The feeling you get when something or someone is standing a little to close. As my throat began to tighten I turned quickly. Nothing…thank you, God!

"Alex?" Every muscle in my body was tight. "This is stupid." I felt incredibly small and vulnerable in the middle of the field, yet extremely exposed, like I had a target taped to my back. My chest was a block of cement and that creepy, crawly shiver ran through my torso repeatedly. A group of clouds slid across the moon, blocking out its milky light. I felt my limbs going numb with anxiety. It was really dark now. "Alex?" There it was again, a dry, rasping sound. Barely audible, but definitely out of place, and in my heightened state of awareness, it resembled fingernails on a chalkboard.

"Alex?" My voice wavered and my eyes strained. Mist had risen further from the ground and without the moonlight the landscape was rapidly becoming murky. Gulp. The fog began to lick above my ankles and up my legs.

Oh, there he was. Whew. My muscles loosened with relief as I detected movement a few yards away in the gloom from the direction of the house, but my relief was short lived. Alex wouldn't answer me and that crisp raspy noise was getting louder. The figure edging closer to me was lilting with a peculiar jerky sway. Bile rose in my throat and I felt faint as my body seemed to recognize what was happening before my mind could comprehend the nightmare bearing down on me. I was flooded with adrenaline. "Alex!" I screamed one last time and then it was time to make a decision. Fight or flight baby! I chose flight.

The crown of the hat. The loose swinging limbs. Too afraid to turn my back on the scarecrow that had left his garden post, I kept my head twisted and my eyes on him as I started hobbling madly in the opposite direction, toward the cemetery.

Little whimpers escaped my lips as the scarecrow picked up speed. He rustled and lurched as I struggled under the cover of the edge of the trees. I had just made it to the shelter of the woods when I yelped, having run headlong into a spider web that seemed to stretch over my head like plastic wrap. I thought quickly of Petey earlier that day and sputtered, turning in circles, swatting at my head, then every instinct told me to forget the damn spider. I had to get back to the main house…back to other people. So I started to double back, making an arc in the darkness toward the rubble of the burnt out guest quarters.

The words 'heart in my throat' couldn't even begin to cover it. Every time I glanced back the scarecrow seemed closer, his head bent intently, lolling with momentum. The hat tipped down as if he had to watch his legs to keep them going. It reminded me of a zombie movie, so unnatural, so unnerving and disturbing. My vivid imagination could only guess what his face might look like. Jagged teeth? A dark void? Somehow I knew he would throw me to the ground and tear me to pieces if he caught up with me; if I didn't have a heart attack first.

I managed to skirt the foundation of the burnt out guest quarters and huffed and puffed toward the direction of the main house. It was not yet visible, when I could swear a brittle frond of stalk swiped my face from behind. With a scream I jolted forward, threw myself down the slope, rolling painfully, then climbing clumsily to my feet took off at a fast paced limp, the pain in my foot searing, but nothing like the tightness of pain in my chest from fear. The moon finally broke free of the clouds and with a quick glance back, I could see the scarecrow's grey silhouette standing still at the top of the knoll. I could feel him watching me, eyeless, yet watching me…and then, the form retreated and vanished back into the moist, night air.

Finally, the house loomed close ahead. I could glimpse flashing lights and detected the distant sound of sirens coming from Gallows Road. Where in the hell was Alex? Howling for Mom, Cassie, anybody, to hear me, I bypassed the dark rear porch and steamed around the side of the old Victorian, just as an ambulance pulled up beneath the enormous tree out front. My mind flew in a million directions. Alex? Mom? My chest felt like it might burst and I couldn't speak. I turned and surveyed the area around the house. No sign of the scarecrow. I bent, hands on knees for a moment trying to catch my breath and allow my tremors of panic to subside. The paramedics rushed past me as if I were invisible.

Limping up the porch and opening the screen door I spied Alex bent over someone at the bottom of the staircase. The EMT's were breaking out equipment and Helen and my mother sat watching, huddled a few steps up on the darkened stairwell in their nightgowns. Helen was sobbing softly and Mom was looking concerned, hugging her close.

Cassie, black hair tousled, stumbled down the stairs with Petey on her heels. "Did I hear sirens?"

Roger was sprawled on the hard wood floor.

Chapter 24

"**W**hat happened? Where's Gretchen?" Alex and the other professionals were tending to Roger and barely paid me any attention. It appeared that Roger had fallen down the stairs.

"Go check on her." Alex ordered me and began to fill the other paramedics in, spewing medical jargon. He had kicked into hot, professional auto pilot. I really wanted his attention right now but resisted the urge to blubber uncontrollably all over him about my experience outside. I hobbled down the darkened hallway toward Gretchen's room to find her sleeping soundly. For the first time in days her brow was not furrowed and she looked at peace.

"Gretch."

"Mmmm."

"Gretch, wake up. Something's happened to Roger." She didn't stir so I nudged her arm gently. "Wake up."

"What? Al? Roger?" She stretched and rubbed her bleary eyes then looked sharply to the empty spot in the bed next to her.

"He's fallen, down the stairs or something. An ambulance is here."

"Oh my God!" Gretchen leapt from the bed, grabbed her robe from a nearby chair and pushed past me. She stopped in the doorway looking frantically both ways, then seeing the lights in the foyer, she dashed down the hall.

Roger was on a gurney about to be rolled out the door when Gretchen reached him. I wasn't far behind so I could clearly see his face contort with horror and his agitation. "Ahhh....ahhhh." He held up a hand to ward her away.

"Roger, what happened?" she gasped. "What's wrong?" Alex caught her and held her up short with one meaty bicep. "Let me go." She struggled briefly as Roger was rolled from the house. Alex had lifted her completely off the ground and she kicked uselessly at his shins with her bare heels.

"Roger!"

"He's okay. Let them get to the hospital and we'll meet up with them there.'

"Let go of me!" A siren wailed outside and the sound grew fainter as the ambulance sped away.

"Okay, okay."

"Has anybody been outside? You didn't see a scarecrow out there did you?" I had crossed to the window next to the door and peeked out between the lacy drapes.

Everyone glanced at me like I was crazy, and then Helen rose, fatigue and worry etched on her face, and started upstairs to change clothes. Mom began to follow.

Gretchen began to wail and wring her hands. "What's happening?"

I pulled her close to me. "Get dressed and we'll go after him."

She turned to Alex. "How badly was he hurt?"

"We can't be completely sure until he has some x-rays. He was unconscious when I found him so checking his head out will be a must. My exam was brief, but at first blush, I know his ankle is either broken or severely sprained."

Alex agreed to drive Helen and Gretchen to the hospital while I stayed home with Mom and Cassie. They changed clothes quickly and went off into the night. As soon as Mom was settled back in bed I headed for the foyer and grabbed the camera.

"You're not going to leave it running tonight?" Cassie inquired.

"I'm hoping I've already got what I need."

I took the camera into the sitting room and dimmed the lights. Cassie and I shared the couch and focused our attention on the little electronic screen while I rewound the tape and told her about my foray with the scarecrow.

Within twenty minutes or so the cause of Roger's fall had been revealed. I couldn't wait for Alex to get back. Even at that late hour I had no problem calling Prudence up to start the séance ball rolling.

Chapter 25

Friday

After watching the taped footage Cassie and I made the executive decision that no one would be staying alone any longer. This thing, whatever it was, was determined to do any of us harm, both physically and emotionally. There was at least some false sense of safety in numbers. We even took Petey out together.

Mom was sleeping soundly upstairs, so Cassie and I found extra blankets and set up vigil in the sitting room. The crunch of gravel outside, in the wee hours of Friday morning, indicated the group had returned from the hospital. Roger did not look well. He had a large lump on his head and a severely sprained ankle, as Alex had predicted. But what was more disturbing than his bandages and crutches was his behavior. He acted like a man in shock. Mute, wide staring eyes, only exhibiting emotion when Alex started to help him toward the back master bedroom. "I want to stay out here." He murmured.

"Honey, you have to rest, in bed. We need to elevate your leg, and you need quiet so you can sleep." Gretchen reasoned. "Let's go."

"I want to stay out here." Roger reiterated through gritted teeth. He shot me a glance and his meaning was not lost on me…having already seen the recording…even though he didn't know the tape existed. Roger simply seemed to find me a comrade now that we had both been spiritually attacked. I felt a pang of sympathy and rushed to his rescue.

"Uh…I think Roger just wants his own space to stretch out and recuperate, Gretch. Cassie and I were wondering if you didn't want to sleep upstairs with her while I bunk with Mom tonight."

"That's ridiculous…," Gretchen began, and fell short when she caught the grateful expression on Roger's face. Hurt, her eyes became misty. She sniffed and turned coolly toward Roger, "Whatever you would like." Then, bursting into tears, Gretchen sprinted up the stairs.

Helen sighed and shook her head. She followed Alex as he assisted Roger down the hall toward the first floor bedroom.

Petey clamored behind Cassie and me as we mounted the steps. We found Gretchen sprawled on the bed in the third bedroom bawling her eyes out.

"This is a disaster." She sobbed as Cassie sat next to her and softly began to stroke her back. "I don't know how we'll ever get past it."

"Gretch…you need to chill out. We have some things to discuss." I looked around for an electrical outlet. Cassie and I had gone over the film so many times we had run the camera battery low.

"Yeah, like how my marriage is over before it even began." Gretchen's voice was muffled as she spoke into her crossed arms. "Like how I'm completely financially entangled with a man who looks like he'd rather jump out a window than come within two feet of me."

"Sit up and look at this. I think you'll understand how he feels."

Gretchen raised her head doubtfully, and then she saw the camera. "What's that? Where did you have that one?"

"In the foyer. Pointed up the stairs." The old camcorder whirred as I rewound the tape. Gretchen sat up on the edge of the bed and I settled next to her. She was sandwiched between Cassie and me. Cassie put a supportive arm around her shoulders. "Watch this."

I fast forwarded past the first ten minutes or so of tape where the camera revealed nothing but the stairs, then I let it run. After a few seconds, the black and white image of Gretchen in her nightgown drifted into view, coming down the hall from the master bedroom. She floated, rather than stepped. It appeared that she was entranced, or sleepwalking. Gretchen let out a sharp breath and began to tremor. "Look at how weird I look. I'm sleepwalking just like Roger said."

Cassie and I remained quiet. We watched the little screen as the image of Gretchen made her way up the stairs and out of sight to the darkened second floor. A thin white mist about the size and shape of a basketball swirled behind her and ascended as well. Less than five minutes later, Roger, still dressed, came up the hall and headed up the steps, undoubtedly to visit with his mother. Gretchen never reappeared. She must have been crouched, hidden somewhere up on the landing.

I fast forwarded the tape for approximately ten minutes of footage and we waited several seconds until just barely there was a flicker of movement that occurred toward the top of the darkened staircase. Suddenly, Roger's feet appeared. He had made it about a third of the way down on the stairs that we could see when he suddenly looked to the right over his shoulder, then appeared to fly off the staircase as if pushed. He groped unsuccessfully for the rail or the wall, and came down clumsily on a step about one fourth from the bottom, his feet in every which direction. This was where he sprained his ankle. Then Roger tumbled the last three or four steps before striking his head on the railing post. He ended his descent sprawled unconscious on the floor.

Gretchen gasped and covered her mouth. "Poor, Roger!" She moaned.

"Hang on." Cassie said glumly.

Roger lay unmoving as the form of Gretchen glided back onto the screen. She drifted down the stairs, past Roger's body as if he weren't even there, and then headed down the hall, back to bed. The misty ball that had been following Gretchen stopped and hovered low over Roger for a moment, like an animal sniffing dead prey, then, satisfied; it followed Gretchen and disappeared out of sight.

About two minutes later, the sound of the front door opening could be heard. Alex ran to stoop over Roger's unconscious form, checking for a pulse, and then he headed into the hall to the clerk's desk under the stairs. His voice could be heard calling 911.

Gretchen was speechless. I took the opportunity to back the film up and play Roger's fall in slow motion. Right after he turned his head to the right to look behind him, you could clearly make out Gretchen's foot on a step, and the hem of her nightgown. In a swift motion, her hand rose quickly to his back. A fuzz of what might have been the mist ball was in the upper left corner of the screen. It was fast, but Gretchen appeared to have pushed Roger...then stayed on the staircase out of sight to watch him fall before she finally descended herself.

While all of this was going on in the house, I was having my little incident outside with the scarecrow. After explaining everything to Gretchen she was convinced that a séance was absolutely necessary. She was desperate to uncover whatever possessed her and seemed intent on destroying the life she and Roger meant to have together in Spring Valley.

I consulted with Alex after he had situated Roger, then we showed the tape to everyone else as they awoke that next day. Everyone was in agreement, even the once reluctant Roger; a séance had to be the next step. According to Prudence, Ms. Shine would arrive at 10 p.m.

We spent the daylight hours of Friday catching up on sleep, and taking care to stick closely to one another. Alex left the house once that morning, taking a quick walk up the hill to confirm the scarecrow's whereabouts for me. He hung exactly where he had before, pole up his ass, floppy felt hat pulled low over who knows what kind of face, and dried arms and legs listless in the breeze.

It was only after lunch when Alex was scrolling through the digital pictures he had taken since he arrived that we were shocked to discover the hideous purple face of the demon superimposed on the scarecrow. Head lifted, those black eyes stared right into the camera lens from beneath the disintegrating hat. It was a shot Alex had taken in the morning before the crow attacked and all the other pictures around it were clear and normal.

As time ticked agonizingly by I found myself peeking frequently out the kitchen window toward the overgrown garden with a sick heart. Fall had once been my favorite season, October my favorite month, and Halloween a source of delight. Somehow I knew I would never enjoy autumn again.

Chapter 26

Edna Shine arrived with her niece, Amber, promptly at 10 p.m. as promised. Dainty and fragile, she was carefully assisted from the car and cautiously aided up the porch steps by the pretty young, blonde woman. Once Edna crossed the threshold of the house it was obvious that her age, size and blindness were not obstacles for her hardy spirit.

Edna's skin was transparent and paper thin. Purple veins stood out on pale arthritic hands, a sharp contrast to her severe, lacy, black dress. Her stockings were also black and her shoes square heeled and practical. It was not hard to imagine her sternly heading up a classroom, and yet, she also exuded a kind, wise essence. Her wispy grey hair was pulled back in a bun, and her only jewelry was a large ring with a strange purple stone on her left hand. Her unseeing eyes were light blue and milky like marbles.

Though it was obvious she had lost her physical gift of sight, Ms. Shine honed right in on Gretchen, who was wearily lingering in the back of the crowd in the foyer. Edna's head swiveled in Gretchen's direction and she tottered purposefully forward with her niece at her elbow. It seemed Amber was only necessary to maintain balance, rather than serve as Edna's navigation. We all parted as she made a beeline for Gretchen. "Hello, dear," she patted

Gretchen's arm comfortingly. "Where would you like me to sit so we can get this all sorted out?"

Gretchen hesitated and her eyes grew cloudy with tears. She swallowed a lump in her throat. I could tell Edna's kindness and words of hope, no matter how minor, had touched a nerve. "I…I'm not sure. What would be best?"

"How many are here?" Edna turned her tiny frame slightly as if she were counting. Just then Prudence clattered up the porch steps in her clunky black boots.

"Ten total, Auntie." Amber piped up. "Including us."

"A table would be best." Edna's feet began to shuffle as she steered herself toward the dining room. Alex and I exchanged a glance. Weird. Impressive, but weird.

Helen was extremely pale and I noticed her hands were shaking. "Would anyone like a beverage?" Everyone just looked at her quietly. She was trying to be polite, of use. It wasn't necessary…we were all so nervous and anxious to get started.

"No, dear. Just a chair." Edna smiled wanly as her niece led her to the head of the long antique table. "Now, everyone grab a seat and settle down. Roger?"

"Yes, ma'am?" He was moving slowly around the table on his crutches.

"You to my left…Gretchen to my right. Naturally I feel the energy is centered on the two of you."

"Should we dim the lights?" I asked.

Edna smiled. "That's only for effect, but sure, if you'd like. It doesn't matter to me, of course."

I hesitated by the switch feeling stupid for having asked, but Amber suggested that we might go ahead and turn off the electric lights and light the candles on the table centerpiece. She explained that it truly was only for effect as far as Edna was concerned, but sometimes it got everyone else in the mood and improved concentration.

Under Gretchen's direction, Helen retrieved a book of matches from an ornate buffet against the wall in the corner by the window and painstakingly lit the six candles in the middle of the table's brass centerpiece. I doused the overhead lights and took a seat between Cassie and my mom.

Satisfied that her Aunt Edna was situated and comfortable, Amber left the room and went outside for a moment. I heard the screen door slam, and then she returned; extinguishing the foyer lights behind her. A faint yellow glow from a lamp left on in the sitting room filtered into the dining room through the foyer, as pale moon rays crept through the windows. Other than that, the candles were burning brightly and were our main illumination.

Amber carefully laid a wooden case of some sort on the table and flipped the latches. She gingerly lifted another piece of wood that unfolded. Right away we all knew it was a spirit board...but nothing you would buy in a game store. The polished wood was shiny and worn from use. The numbers, letters and symbols were hand painted. It was obviously ancient and homemade.

Edna's craggy fingers extended and rested tenderly on the crude pointer as soon as Amber placed it in front of her. Gretchen and Roger eyed the board skeptically. Alex and Pru were seated across from me on Roger's side of the table. The three of us exchanged a glance. Helen had taken a chair between Roger and Alex as Amber made her way to sit at the other end of the table. Cassie, me and Mom made up Gretchen's side of the room.

Edna was quiet, slowing moving the pointer around until she had positioned it on the board to her satisfaction. I had seen a spirit board before, but had never used one. The movies had knocked a degree of respect for the device into me and I had always been afraid to mess with one. I wished I was sitting closer to Edna, as I could barely make out the painted figures on the wood in the darkness with my old glasses.

"Now, let's get started." Edna reached over and patted Gretchen's arm reassuringly again. This woman must have been part bat. She was right on target every time. "Everyone, rest your hands gently on the table in front of you. Both hands. No matter what happens, remain calm and try to concentrate on centering your energy here in this room. We'll need all of it if we are to harness any spirits and get to the bottom of this poor couple's problem."

Helen looked like she wanted to throw up and/or bolt from the table. We all followed Amber's example and relaxed our hands in front of us. Amber closed her eyes, but the rest of the group focused their attention on Edna Shine whose presence seemed transformed in the flickering candlelight. Her face was serene and her posture rigid. She seemed larger than she had when she first sat in the chair. Younger. Stronger. Only her hands were moving, caressing the pointer, and then slowly moving it in little circles.

Other than the slight scrape of wood against wood, and the tick tock of the hall clock, the room was silent for several minutes. A couple of us cleared our throats, but Edna didn't move, she just kept pushing the small piece of timber in little circles before her. Finally she spoke and her voice resonated with strength and purpose.

"We ask God for protection as we seek to solve this problem for Gretchen and Roger. Surround us, oh Lord, with your white light of love and security. Keep us safe from harm."

Again, Edna was silent and continued the slight movement of her hands. Scrape, scrape. Tick, tock. The poison ivy was itching between my shoulder blades, but I didn't want to move my hands from the table and disrupt any cosmic energy we might…I said *might*…be generating. I snuck a glance out of the corner of my eye at my mother. She had her eyes closed, but must have felt my stare. She snuck a peek back at me and the corners of her mouth turned up slightly.

Soon, I caught my mind drifting. I wondered if I'd left my curling iron on upstairs. Then I wondered where my set of the van keys were, and if the windows were rolled up. Cassie would kill me if I lost the van keys. Was it supposed to rain? My eyes swept the table. Everyone else appeared to be concentrating. Maybe I had ADHD. The thought was alarming to me. Would I need medication? Would it mix with my anxiety drugs? When was the last time I balanced my checkbook?

The flickering candle light sort of bothered my eyes, and sometimes weird lighting threw me into a migraine. I wasn't having trouble seeing was I? My stomach hurt and I felt a little sweaty. I swallowed my panic and focused on a spot on the wall beyond Alex and closed first one eye, and then the other. I thought I was okay. My pack was right upstairs anyway. Wasn't it? It was. I remembered putting it on Mom's dresser after I gave her evening pills to her. Feeling relieved I noticed Alex was winking at me. Had he thought I was winking at him? I felt his foot nudge me under the table and I shot him a dirty glare. Then his nose wrinkled and he coughed. Soon I smelled it too. Everyone but Edna gagged and shifted in their chairs. A noxious odor permeated the room. Pru's cheeks ballooned as she held her breath. Amber maintained her composure, though I could see her eyes were watering beneath her lashes. She opened one eye and peeked at her aunt.

"Be calm," Edna whispered, the rhythm of her hands never ceasing. "Sometimes the spirit world communicates with us through scent." Then Edna's head turned and her unseeing eyes seemed to look right at me. "And sometimes, somebody shares a grilled cheese sandwich with their dog at lunch." My gaze darted around the room and sure enough, Petey's dark, buggy eyes glimmered accusingly at me from beneath the buffet in the corner. I shot Alex a glare and mouthed 'I thought you put him up.' He looked incredulous and shrugged. Then, within seconds, the full meaning of what Edna had just said dawned on us both. How'd she know what we'd had for lunch? Or that a dog was in the room, for that matter?"

Alex turned briskly around to open the window behind him, and then placed his hands back on the table. A slight breeze affected the candles for a moment then Petey's fumes began to fade. I saw him scoot a little further beneath the buffet.

Everyone resumed their positions of concentration and several minutes later Edna spoke again. "If there is a spirit person in this room with us, please make yourself known." All was quiet, but I thought the air felt a little thicker and the walls a little closer. I was probably imagining it. The clock in the hall struck eleven p.m. Edna seemed to have an uncanny sense of direction, but I was starting to question her actual ability to conjure up spirits. It had been almost an hour. "I repeat. If there is a spirit person in this room, please make yourself known to us."

Silence. Monotony. Cassie had her eyes closed and by the deepening of her breathing I thought she might be falling asleep sitting up. I nudged her with my elbow and she nudged me back. Just then, something hit the screen of the open window...hard. Everyone but Edna and Amber gasped and jumped in their chairs.

"Steady. Be calm." Edna whispered. An unearthly wail filled the room and the candles flickered as the breeze outside picked up.

"Caramel!" Gretchen started to get up. Roger sneezed, and then Petey let out a little groan and echoed Roger. "Ahhh...pooo!"

"Stay seated, Gretchen." Edna commanded with authority. Gretchen looked a little dazed but followed her command.

The cat mewed sweetly, patting at the screen with her paw a few times. She then began to stalk angrily back and forth on the window sill, her tail thrashing. A growl from deep within her raised goose bumps on my arms. It was like she was trying to entice us to the window and was livid when no one responded. With a yowl and a hiss she swiped at the screen and jumped down, running off into the night, her enraged cries growing fainter.

"Ahhh...pooo!" Petey sneezed and was but a shadow beneath the buffet as he tried to wedge himself even further into the corner. The candles flickered as if they might go out, and then the flames seemed to gain strength and stretch higher.

We were all so distracted by the cat that we hadn't noticed the furious circling of Edna's hands. Her brow was furrowed with concentration and the sheen of sweat dotted her forehead as she swayed and her hands moved around and around. A couple of the piano keys tinkled softly behind us...so softly, it was barely audible.

"Someone is with us." Amber whispered. "Whatever you do, keep your hands on the table. Cassie, can you read out whatever the pointer shows, please. Roger and Gretchen, be still. Be very, very still."

Edna continued her cycle for a couple more minutes, and then the pointer began to move purposefully to the symbols on the board. "H. E. I." Cassie craned her neck and said each letter individually. "S. M. I. N. E."

"He is mine." Edna echoed, translating in a hollow voice that was not her own. It almost wasn't human. We were frozen to our seats. I was paralyzed with fascination and couldn't have moved my hands off the table if I tried.

"Who are you?" Amber asked into thin air. The pointer moved again.

'H. E. I. S. M. I. N. E." Cassie watched the board and repeated.

"He is mine." Edna said again.

"Who are you, and who is he?" Amber inquired patiently.

"R. O. G. E. R." Cassie said each letter individually again. Roger looked horrified and Helen gasped. I didn't know what to make of Gretchen's numb expression.

"Roger." Helen uttered with panic.

"Shhhh." Amber said gently. "We're just gathering information. It's alright." To the air in the room in general she said again. "Who are you?"

"W. H. O. A. R. E. Y. O. U."

"Who are you?" Edna's voice seemed to take on a combative tone.

"You know who I am. You know who we all are." Amber shot back. "Who are you? Are you a Powell?"

Edna's hands began to circle again. There was no response for several seconds and then, "I. W. A. S." Cassie spelled out.

"I was." Edna almost spat the words.

"Are you male or female?" Amber inquired.

Edna laughed a chilling, wicked laugh.

"Are you male or female?" Amber persisted.

This time Edna only moaned, sounding unearthly and sad.

"Why are you here?" Amber asked forcefully.

There was no reply. Edna's circling had slowed until her hands finally fell into her lap.

"Why are you here?" Amber persisted.

Edna's head tilted back and the whites of her eyes glowed beneath half closed lids. It occurred to me that she was in the exact same chair Gretchen had occupied when she was possessed at the engagement party. I glanced to Gretchen to see if she had all of her faculties. She appeared to be in awe of Edna, but not out of her own head. Then, the candles went out, not by a breeze, but as if someone snuffed them all one by one.

"I… am…here," Edna croaked as if her vocal cords were made of rusty pipes. The raspy sound ground painfully out of her throat and reverberated in the near darkness; her voice slow and broken as if she was not used to speaking. "I am here…because…I can't be there."

"Be where? The other side?" Amber inquired.

My throat felt tight. The air in the room felt closer and closer. Edna cackled with evil glee again then continued on. "I am here…for him." Her head lolled unnaturally toward Roger. "For her." It lolled toward Gretchen. In the scant light from the foyer and the moon outside I could see the glint of tears rolling down Helen's face. Her fist was practically stuffed in her mouth to keep from crying aloud. "I am here…to take the Powells." Edna continued.

"The Powells are gone," Amber said. "You must leave this place. We can help you go."

"Poison, burning, drowning, stabbing…" Edna began to rattle off various violent methods of dying in the disturbing unearthly voice.

"Did you do these things?" Amber asked.

"Choking, shooting, hanging..." Edna continued.

"Did *you* do these things?"

"He is mine. She will do my bidding until he is mine. They all do my bidding."

"He's not yours. The Powell's are gone." Amber repeated forcefully.

"They're all mine." Edna said weakly, and then slumped in her chair.

Amber waited for a beat or two. Helen was sniffling into her hands. "It's over. It's gone." Amber said. "Someone get the lights please." She rose from her chair to go to her aunt as I limped to the switch by the door. She was right, the atmosphere of the room felt lighter and brighter than it had just seconds before. The entity that had been with us was gone, or had at least receded a safe distance to observe us. Edna was coming out of her trance looking grey and drawn. "Would someone bring her some water please?" I left the room and motioned for Alex to follow me, mainly because I didn't want to go to the kitchen alone, but also to get his impression of the séance.

"Well, what did you think? Authentic?" I whispered.

"I think so, although, she is from around here. Maybe she just knows something of the family history."

We got the water quickly and returned to the dining room. Edna had a little more color in her cheeks, but the focus now seemed to be centered on Helen who was holding Roger and sobbing inconsolably. Everyone looked confused and uncomfortable, especially Roger. Everyone that is, but Edna.

Edna accepted the water from me and took a sip with a shaky hand. Amber took the glass from her and set it on the table, and then she began to dismantle the spirit board.

"It's time to tell the truth, my dear." Edna said in a weak voice that was at least her own. I wasn't sure who she was talking to.

To my surprise Helen sighed and released Roger. "I know. I know."

"What does she mean? Mom?" Roger was completely bewildered.

"Whew. Could someone get *me* a glass of water, please?" Helen's face was flushed and red from crying. She was clearly miserable about something and I felt my heart tug for the gentle woman in deep distress.

Gretchen left and came back in moments with another glass of water.

"Okay. Okay." Helen breathed deeply and seemed to be steeling herself for something. "God, I prayed I'd never have to admit this."

"What in the hell is going on?" Roger's eyes were wide with concern, and a liberal amount of fear. "Would somebody please tell me?"

"Roger," Helen took his hand and traced the lines of his palm with her forefinger. "Oh hell, I'm stalling. I'll just spit it out. You're a Powell."

"A what?!" Roger yelped. The rest of us were dismayed.

"You're a Powell, honey." We all stared at Helen in disbelief. Only Edna looked unsurprised. She just took another dainty sip of water.

"Who? How? A Powell?" Taken aback, Roger looked around the room until his eyes fixed helplessly on Gretchen.

She remained at a distance. "But my father died, before I was born. You said yourself he was…"

"I know what I said. It was just to protect you. That's why we moved away from Spring Valley when you were little. I hated even coming for a few visits, but I wanted you to at least know my family a little bit. The curse. I was afraid of the curse."

"My dad, father…who was he?"

"Lillian's brother. Kenneth Powell." Helen said guiltily. "I met him when I was working at the Elderberry Inn years ago. He was often there because they owned the restaurant. The Powell's owned a little bit of everything back then. He was older than me…but unmarried. So charming. I don't know what I was thinking. Every one knows a relationship with a Powell is doomed, but, when you're in love, at least I thought I was in love, you never think it could happen to you. We were together just a few months. Then, one day, his fiancé arrived from the Northeast. Fiancé? I didn't even know he was engaged. He broke the news that he was to marry June that spring. I was so humiliated I quit my job and left town, and found out I was expecting you a few weeks later. I thought that if I stayed away none of this Powell business would affect you. Of course, I'm a fool. No one else could escape it, how could we?"

"I…I don't know what to say."

"Neither do I. I'm so, so very sorry."

"So, basically, you just made up my father…the father I thought was dead?"

Helen hesitated, looking ashamed and heartsick. "I did. I'm sorry."

"Did he know? Did Kenneth Powell know…about me?" Roger's expression was pitiful.

Helen shook her head. "No one knew. No one but me. We came back when you were little, as I said, to visit relatives, but not long after you started school I decided to stay away for good. It was hard to see Kenneth around town. I'm not one for keeping secrets and I felt guilty. He had red hair too you know." Helen smiled ruefully, but when Roger reached tentatively, thoughtfully to touch the crown of his own copper head, she wilted. "He and June had no children. I heard about his death, supposedly an accidental drowning, some years later."

"So, the curse…it's true. Something haunts the family…not necessarily the land?" Gretchen had finally spoken and looked like she was slipping into shock. Cassie pulled out a chair and sat her in it.

"The curse is true." Edna said matter of factly. "And you're right; it appears it is the blood, not the land. The spirit is strong. She's had a lot of years to gather her strength. She can move objects…change shapes"

"The cat," I whispered to no one in particular as the pieces started to fall into place. I thought of the bird that attacked Alex and I, as well as the scarecrow.

"The same cat…all along…all these years I'm sure," Edna confirmed and nodded.

I thought about the pictures containing a cat in the museum and of the portrait of the animal perched on Lillian's lap. Did the cat draw its energy from the family members? Particularly the women? Why would Lillian choose to pose with it? Unless, of course, Lillian's resolve to remain unmarried and childless had been far stronger than the spirit's desire to kill and they had come to some kind of truce in later years. The spirit probably knew of Roger and could foretell his eventual ownership of the house anyway, so she was less concerned with Lillian as time wore on.

"Can you tell us anything other than what she said directly to us?" My mom inquired. "Did you gather any other impressions of her?"

"Her appearance to me, in my mind's eye, is ghastly. Repulsive. A reflection of her death. She likes to appear that way to shock anyone who sees her. In a sense it's to show the mortal realm what became of her." I listened to Edna and thought back to the apparition in the cottage bathroom, and Mom and Alex's pictures, shuddering involuntarily. I felt Alex's warm arm slip around me and I leaned against him gratefully while Edna continued.

"She's angry and has been bent on revenge. I couldn't get a name, though that would be helpful in confronting her directly. I do sense that she uses the women to punish the men. I've always wondered about the involvement of an earthbound spirit," Edna said thoughtfully. "But, I've never actually been here to feel it for myself. I asked to come here once. Years ago I offered my services. The family declined. The Powells tended to keep to themselves. Now it appears that the wives have been her tools and I've no doubt, after feeling her fury, that many of the women were guilty of the murder of their husbands, at least physically. Mentally they had no idea what they had done, except maybe Blanche. I knew her you know. A lovely woman. A pure soul. Came to church when I was a child. No doubt at some deep level she knew what had happened to her husband, that's why she went mad. After the death of Jack, after the fire she set and her stay at the asylum, she came back and the family tried to seclude her. Protect her. She killed herself in this house. The family kept it a secret, but she hung herself in a closet upstairs. I felt her lingering in the foyer when I came in."

I was looking at Alex and trying to grasp the horror of having the person you loved and trusted most in the world suddenly turn on you and take your life.

"So, they all took a chance on love and met certain doom," Roger said under his breath, trying to get a grasp on the situation himself.

"There's no hope. He's a Powell, I'm destined to kill him, and we're doomed too." Gretchen's eyes were wild and her voice had reached a hysterical pitch as she ran her fingers through her hair. She stood up and paced in a little square at the edge of the dining room rug. "I don't believe this is happening."

Edna regarded her calmly with her filmy, sightless eyes. The rest of us felt helpless to console her, obviously the curse held some bearing. "Unless we know something about her, or have something we can use to take power over her, I'm afraid there's not much else I can offer. Without a name…or even a belonging, I can only try to connect with the ghost…and she doesn't want to leave or tell me any more that can help us."

Everyone looked dejectedly at one another when suddenly a thought occurred to me.

"The book," I blurted. "We have a book …from the Powell family. Would you look at it? Maybe you could draw some clues as to her identity from the items in it." I avoided looking at Prudence. Soon enough she would see that I had stolen the book she had shown me at the library.

Amber looked at her watch and started to protest but Edna waved a hand in her direction with a small, tired smile. "I'll give it a try."

"What book?" Roger and Helen looked confused. I had shown it to Alex, but no one had filled Roger in at all. As I did so, Cassie retrieved the volume from the sitting room bookshelf where it had been stowed before the engagement party began. I shot Prudence an apologetic glance, but as Cassie placed the book in front of Edna, she looked intrigued rather then angry. I suspected she would have done the exact same thing if she were in my position.

Edna placed her hand over the worn, black cover and closed her eyes. We waited quietly, expectantly as she opened the book and began to finger the items inside carefully, one by one. I was losing hope, page by page, but as Edna approached the back of the book she skipped over several sections and withdrew the satin pouch. She held it to her chest. "This is it," she whispered. The lights in the room flickered. "This was hers."

"You're kidding," Gretchen breathed. "Can you tell who she was? Can you tell what she wants so we can stop all of this?"

Edna was silent, pulling out the tiny piece of old jewelry and holding it in her palm. "This was once a brooch...a locket with a pin...but the pin was separated from the back, many, many years ago. Someone put it in this purse, perhaps an attempt to contain the spirit, but over time no one remembered that it was hers." She slipped the locket back into the pouch and shook her head with frustration. "I still can't get a name. She wouldn't like that you've found it." Her brow wrinkled deeply with concentration. "I can't get anything else. It's been so long since she physically touched it that it's quite easy to block me out. Since I can't get a name, might I make a suggestion?"

"Please." Roger piped up.

"We could spend all our time trying to figure out who the spirit is and the origin of the haunt, but that information might also remain a mystery forever. In the absence of more ammunition so that we might be able to bind the spirit from doing harm, I recommend an exorcism. Exorcise the house. Exorcise the grounds."

"But you said it was the family…the blood. Not the property." Roger hobbled to the chair next to where Gretchen stood. He lowered himself slowly and rested the crutches against the wall. He and Gretchen considered each other briefly but made no move to touch.

"Then exorcise yourselves."

"Can't *you* help us, Ms. Shine?" Gretchen begged.

Edna slowly shook her head. "I can show you things, child. I can even tell you things, but I can't help you or the spirit unless she wants to cross, or unless we have the tools to force her through. Trust me, right now she won't go on her own. I feel she's not done with the family yet. There will have to be a show of force. She must be made to cross."

"How much time do we have?" Gretchen inquired.

"That's hard to tell. I'm afraid to say that you are really at her mercy. I would move quickly. As I said, she's very powerful. It feels as if she's had centuries to gain momentum."

"Well, hmmm." Helen looked at Roger and Gretchen, "We're not Catholic, but I think Father Ryan is still the parish priest in town. I suppose we could contact him."

"Father Ryan is actually in Rome," Prudence piped up. "He's not due back until next month."

"Oh." Helen looked lost. Defeated.

"Might *I* make a suggestion?" Amber took the group's silence as her answer. "Reverend Pulpit."

Edna nimbly snapped her arthritic fingers and startled everyone. "An excellent idea! Reverend Pulpit."

"Justice Moses Pulpit?" Helen inquired, while everyone else looked puzzled.

"Can you think of anyone more faithful? Or, more able?" Edna smiled and tilted her head toward Gretchen and Roger. "He's your only hope on such short notice. I'm sure he would be relentless."

"I remember Justice Moses Pulpit," Roger looked thoughtful and seemed to come alive a little. "That's right. He's a Reverend now. I've seen his name in the local papers for Sunday morning service ads."

"Yes. Yes, I'd forgotten." Helen looked a little hopeful. "He has a church over in Stanley now. His mother and I worked together at the Elderberry Inn years ago. She was in housekeeping." Helen smiled. "We exchanged Christmas cards for the longest time."

"I remember playing with Justice a couple of times. We were really, really little." Roger said. "Of course, I haven't seen him since then. Do you really think he could help?"

"Divine intervention and Reverend Pulpit are your only hope." Edna motioned toward Amber. "Well, I'm an old lady and it's far past my bed time." She rose stiffly from her chair, accepted Amber's arm, and immediately began shuffling around the dining room table toward the foyer. "Please contact me once you've spoken to Justice. I had him in my class you know and I would love to see him again. I might be of some help as well. In the meantime, I'll try to concentrate on a name and I'll contact you if I come up with anything else."

After Edna left, Prudence got out the local phone book and we looked up the address and phone number to the church in Stanley, a little town 15 miles north. We found Justice Moses Pulpit's home number as well, just in case we couldn't get ahold of him at the church.

There was little discussion of the séance after Prudence headed for home. Everyone was drained of energy as they retreated to their various corners of the house. I got Mom settled in for the night, then Cassie, Alex and I took it upon ourselves to stay up and start cleaning and decorating the house on Gretchen's behalf...should there actually be a wedding on Sunday. The professional party planners in us could not stand to be unprepared, even if there was the remotest possibility that the show might not go on.

Chapter 27

Saturday

I awoke, uncomfortably curled up on the sitting room floor, surrounded by tulle and ribbon, when Cassie stumbled in from the kitchen, the front of her apron covered with flour and sugar.

"The wedding cakes are cooling," she reported, flopping down in one of the chairs by the fireplace. Her face was puffy and she yawned widely. "Your boyfriend ran into town for milk and butter, and a measuring cup. For some reason it wasn't in the sink or the dish washer this morning. Oh yeah, and, the oven turned 'itself' off around 3 a.m. or I would have been done sooner. Alex thought he might try to check for Reverend Pulpit at the church on the way home."

"What time is it?" I stretched out flat on the floor, trying to un-wrench my aching back.

"Early. Just after eight."

"Have you even been to bed yet at all?"

"Nope," Cassie replied and heaved herself up from the chair. "But, I'm headed that way now. You're on ghost watch. Roger is still asleep, or at least pretending to be. I just looked in on him. I haven't heard anything from Helen, Gretchen, your mom or psycho pup."

As if on cue Petey skittered down the stairs. Unable to stop on the polished wood floor of the foyer, he slid head first into the front door and rocked back on his haunches, the one ear bent further than usual, and his dark eyes rolling around in his head.

"Looks like Mom's up." I observed. Cassie grimaced at the dizzy Pug and trudged upstairs. I let Petey out into the brittle, autumn morning, abundant with frost and brilliant sunshine and watched from the porch while he did his business. It was going to be one of those days where Mother Nature couldn't decide which way she wanted to go, vacillating between the sure promise of winter and a last stab at summer warmth.

I followed Petey slowly as he headed back upstairs to the comfortable warmth of my mother's bed. My foot was still tender and I was distracted, a to-do list running through my head of things yet to be done. There might not be a wedding...but what if there was?

Hopefully this Reverend Pulpit could save the day. Roger was of no use for decorating with his bad leg. Nor would he be in the mood. Besides, I was sure he and Gretchen would avoid one another at all costs today. In fact, I could predict exactly what was going to happen. Feeling guilty that he was a Powell and had unwittingly brought all this misery upon Gretchen, Roger would keep to the downstairs bedroom, while Gretchen, questioning her own sanity and afraid she might accidentally kill Roger, and most definitely lose her mind, would stay upstairs and visit with my mom, or read in the double bedroom. Helen would likely rattle about nervously, either moping around Roger's or Gretchen's door, or assisting one of us. I almost felt sorriest for her. She was completely depressed.

Of course, until some resolution could be found none of us would be acting like ourselves. Cassie and I would attempt to perform normal tasks, but would surely be jumpy, edgy, and preoccupied, watching the clock and tensely trying to get through the day. Alex, the diplomatic healer, would try to hold us all together.

All of these thoughts were zipping through my head and just as I felt I couldn't handle one more thing, I reached my mother's door. Finding it cracked, I pushed it open without knocking. Mom was standing at the dresser brushing her hair. Hearing me enter she spoke without turning around and clearly said, "Caroline, wake your brother. We'll be late for church."

I could not have been more horrified if I had found the violet apparition lounging on the four post bed with the devil himself. Something deep within my chest actually moved, uncoupled. The pain that followed was surely my heart breaking. Breathing was impossible and tears immediately spilt down my cheeks. Instantly, Mom's shoulders stiffened. I could tell she was grappling for composure. For almost a full minute we simply regarded each other, wide eyed, in the reflection of the mirror, absorbing the moment and the gravity of the situation. My sister Caroline and my brother Brian hadn't lived with Mom since before I was born. Petey leapt up onto the bed with a snort and considered each of us, his head cocked with a concerned expression on his scrunched up little face.

Slowly, Mom lowered her arm, laid the hairbrush on the dresser and turned. I couldn't move, my hand was still glued to the door knob. She closed the space between us quickly and took my hot, wet face in her cool, dry hands. I was a bit taller than her and she looked intently up into my eyes with a small reassuring smile and a lovely, soft stare. "Deloris

Eugenia Gladiola Marche," she said evenly, with grace and purpose. "I love you. My precious, baby girl. I love you and I know who you are."

All I could do was sob and fall into her arms. "I love you too, Mom." The fact that it was she who was becoming more ill, and it was she who was comforting *me*, made me cry all the harder. I was losing her and she would prepare me for it. Prepare me and protect me as she had her entire selfless life, doing her best to make my hardship easier. Without a choice I would allow it, because the easier she could make things for me, the easier it would ultimately be for her. This awful cycle...this thing of strength would be our last gift to one another and I simply was not ready.

"I don't want you to disappear," I choked. I had never in my life voiced my fears out loud so succinctly.

"Disappear," she murmured calmly into my hair as if she were trying the word on for size. "I suppose that is what this seems like to you. I'm so caught up in the daily struggle I never thought of it that way." Then Mom held me at arms length and said forcefully. "You'll never be without me. Never. Deloris, do you hear? Look at me." It hurt to look at her. She took my limp hand in hers and moved it over my heart. "I'll always be here." She moved my hand to touch my head. "And here." We both smiled through our tears and she held my face again. "You know everything I would say, or think, or do, so...you'll *never* be without me." I hugged her fiercely again.

Mom let me have my time. For several moments she held me against her frail frame, stroking my hair and back, then, unable to bear my pain any longer and proficient in the art of distraction, as all good mothers are, she asked coyly, "Want to see something interesting?"

I sniffed. My curious 'What?' was muffled in her soft hair against the curve of her neck.

Mom held me at arms length again and a mysterious sparkle lit her eyes. "I finished the book last night." I looked confused. "Lillian's poetry book."

"So?" The headache I had been anticipating was finally emerging due to stress, lack of sleep and hard crying. I knew I needed some breakfast and quiet before I was in bed with a migraine for the rest of the day. I wiped my cheeks with my t-shirt sleeve.

"So," Mom crossed to the nightstand and picked up the little purple paperback. "What if she mentions our spirit friend?"

Now she had my attention. "In what way? The lady at the museum didn't say anything out of the ordinary, just that the poetry was over most folks heads. But you, being a literature professor, probably didn't have that problem."

Mom sat down on the edge of the bed and patted the spot next to her. I sat down too, and Petey, not to be left out, squeezed between us, coating the side of my arm with his slobber. Mom turned to a dog eared page near the end of the book.

"All of it is very basic poetry. Nature subjects, observations about growing older, etcetera. She wasn't half bad, but, listen to this one…" Mom began to read a very small untitled poem that might not mean anything to anyone else, if they had not been studying the history of the family and if they had not been enlightened by last night's séance.

> *I am the link that breaks the chain*
> *The sacrifice that must remain*
> *Solitary and alone*
> *Until my soul has shed the bone.*

I am the link that breaks the chain
Wracked with woe and bathed in shame
Though Rachel hounds me night and day
Without our name she cannot stay.

Mom finished reading those eight simple lines and we were both quiet, thoughtful for a moment. "Rachel. So the spirit's name is Rachel?"

"I think so. And apparently, Lillian remained single and childless purposefully to end the bloodline." Mom replied.

"She really thought she sacrificed herself," I said softly. "Only Helen knew about Roger. I wonder if the spirit had communicated its name to Lillian somehow, or if the family knew it all along. We've got to tell Edna." Abruptly, the bedroom door slammed shut. Petey whimpered and dove behind the bed pillows. Mom and I jumped, and stayed immobile for several seconds. When nothing out of the ordinary materialized in the room we scrambled to our feet.

"Breakfast?" I inquired.

"Breakfast." Mom nervously agreed. I reached for the door handle and cringed, half expecting some invisible entity to be holding the door closed from the other side. It swung open easily when I twisted the knob and we scurried behind Petey down the stairs.

Alex arrived an hour later as Mom and I were having coffee with Helen and making small talk about the sudden cloudiness outside. Unable to get any rest after all, Cassie had staggered downstairs for some orange juice only a few moments before.

Alex deposited three paper bags of groceries on the counter, and bestowed a new glass measuring cup upon

Cassie, who held up the old one that she had just found in the back of the freezer while getting ice. Another article misplaced to further annoy us.

Alex only laughed, and by the smile on his face I could tell the trip to town and beyond had been successful. He had not met Reverend Pulpit, but he had stopped in the little church and caught the preacher's secretary working feverishly on the weekly service handout. Because the situation was desperate, Alex went ahead and told her everything. She, in turn, called Justice Moses Pulpit at home and woke him up. After relaying the story, she told Alex that the Reverend and select delegates from his congregation were eager to arrive at Roger and Gretchen's at dusk and do all they could to help. We had several tense hours ahead of us.

Chapter 28

The rest of the day went pretty much as the day of the séance had. Everyone stuck close to someone while managing to avoid certain others. Roger was in bed staying off his feet, gathering strength for the evening ahead, while Gretchen hung out in the sitting room with Mom and Helen. Cassie, Alex and I stuck to the kitchen, trying to be productive. I was a nervous wreck, especially after what had happened with Mom that morning. I almost, I repeat, almost, considered taking some of the anxiety meds the ER doc had given me, but my fear of pills outweighed my fear of…well, fear.

We had a very late lunch and just before dusk Cassie found me slamming around the bedroom we had been sharing next to Helen's upstairs. "Damn, blueberry faced bitch!" I was chewing an antacid and throwing cushions off a little love seat in the corner.

"What are you doing?"

"My pack!" I exclaimed. "My waist pack was right there!" I pointed to an empty spot on the dresser. "It was right there earlier today!" I bellowed.

"What do you need it for?"

"Mom's meds are in it and I want her to have everything she needs before we get started tonight. We need to get this wedding over with and get the hell home."

Cassie was pulling open the dresser drawers.

"I already did that!" I snapped and started stripping the bed.

"I didn't know!" She snapped back.

"Sorry." I collapsed on the edge of the mattress and buried my face in my hands. Cassie continued to open and slam dresser draws anyway. I looked up into thin air and shouted at the top of my lungs, "YOU CAN SCREW WITH ME BUT DO NOT MESS WITH MY MOTHER!!!"

"Jeez, Al!" Alex hollered from the doorway. "What's going on in here?"

"Her pack is gone." Cassie was now crawling around on the floor much as my mother had done the day she was looking for her shoes. Petey ran in and attached himself to the ample calf of Cassie's leg. "Get off me!" she growled.

Alex looked puzzled and reached to open a dresser drawer.

"We already did that!" Cassie and I yelled simultaneously.

"I didn't know!" He yelled back at us. "Do you want me to call the pharmacy in town? I don't think they're closed yet. We could try to get more medication."

"What's all the shouting about?" Helen peeked around the corner of the doorjamb. "Al? Isn't this yours?" She extended her arm and laid my waist pack on the corner of the dresser, exactly where it had been the last time I had seen it.

I rushed over to check the contents, mercifully finding everything just as it should be. I hastily took out Mom's pills and collected what I needed. "Where did you find it?"

"Gretchen found it on the mantle in her bedroom."

"I haven't been in there since yesterday." I gasped. "And, I gave Mom her meds this morning right here in this room."

Just then the door bell rang. We all hesitated, looking solemnly from one to the other. It was time. Alex scooped Petey up and put him in his kennel in the corner. "It's okay, little buddy," he said softly in response to Petey's sad eyes. "You're not in trouble. You'll just be safer up here."

Helen heaved a heavy sigh. "I hope this works," she whispered. We trudged down the darkened hall to the steps and descended to the foyer where Gretchen and Mom had collected behind Roger, who was leaning on one crutch to open the door. I slipped Mom her meds and she hastily swallowed them without water. Prudence stepped into the house and we heard Amber speaking to Edna Shine as she assisted her up the porch steps.

"Reverend Pulpit should be right behind us," Prudence informed us as she took off her oversized black jacket and hung it on the hall coat rack.

"Hello everyone," Edna stepped over the threshold and made a beeline for Gretchen. "Hello dear." The blind woman's radar never ceased to amaze me. Amber relieved Edna of her coat, hanging it on the rack as well, and then she took her aunt's fragile elbow and hung on as Edna took off. As they passed me Edna briefly paused and took my hand. Her skin was cold. "A veil will lift tonight. Do not be afraid. You are stronger than you know," she whispered cryptically. What did she know about me? I swallowed hard and Amber smiled reassuringly as they moved toward one of the chairs near the hearth in the sitting room. Mom followed with Lillian's book of poetry.

The rest of us crowded inside around the open front door and watched as a large black sedan with tinted windows slid to a stop behind Pru's little old compact car. Before the engine shut off the back doors opened and two large African American women stepped out of either side, then, momentarily, another thinner woman wriggled from the middle of the back seat and emerged. The front passenger door swung open and I was surprised to see Flossie, the woman from the museum, step onto the gravel, a weathered Bible in her hand. The ladies were dressed to the nines and huddled beside the car chatting and brushing the wrinkles from their skirts while they waited for Reverend Pulpit, who, at last, emerged himself. He walked slowly around the front of the car and Flossie handed him the worn Bible. Then, straightening his collar, he ascended the porch steps purposefully. His assemblage was close behind.

Roger swung the door open and we all stepped back as Justice Moses Pulpit entered the foyer. Reverend Pulpit was slim in his dark three piece suit. He exuded intensity and Godliness. He had a serious presence, and with a name like Pulpit, how could he not have become a man of the church? He had the darkest skin I had ever seen. He was handsome, confident, and though he could barely be thirty years old, I detected the slightest hint of gray at his temples. His intelligent brown eyes washed over each of us in turn and I felt a sense of power and peace from the moment he entered the foyer.

"Roger, it's been a very long time. So good to see you again." He was soft spoken and greeted Roger solemnly, clasping Roger's hand in both of his. He took Gretchen's hand in the same manner as Roger introduced her next. Reverend Pulpit nodded to each of us, bestowing a slight reassuring smile and a wink on Helen in particular. He introduced the women who accompanied him. Apparently, Flossie had been the church secretary for many, many years, even before Reverend Pulpit had become the current minister. The other women, Grace, Marjorie and Felicity, were Sunday school teachers and choir members. The

Reverend referred to them all as "worthy soldiers in God's army."

Introductions made, we joined Edna, Amber and Mom in the sitting room where the events of the evening would begin. The Reverend and Edna had spoken previously on the phone but he took a moment to greet her and Amber individually in hushed tones before seating himself on the sofa near the window. I had heard Edna murmur the name 'Rachel' and Reverend Pulpit nodded solemnly. Now he placed his worn Bible on the coffee table and sat back self-assuredly.

"Our aim," he began quietly, "is to cleanse this home of evil and invite the goodness of God to dwell here forevermore. I'm going to ask each of you to concentrate on that purpose as the cleansing progresses." We all nodded obediently.

Amber reached into her purse and pulled a small metal box from the bottom. She sat it on the coffee table next to the Reverend's Bible.

"What's that?" Cassie inquired.

"It's a mirror box," Amber replied.

"I don't see any mirrors." We all leaned closer as Amber opened the lid and revealed that the entire inside was comprised of mirrors; top, bottom, and all four walls.

"Could someone get some paper and a pen?" Edna asked.

Gretchen retrieved the objects from a drawer under one of the gaming tables and handed them to Amber.

"Now the locket," Edna commanded.

Alex went to the dining room where the old book had been left on the buffet after the séance. Part of me expected the piece of jewelry to be missing, but when the pouch was opened and turned over Amber's hand, amazingly it slid out. Perhaps the spirit was that confident of her powers.

"Now we have two major tools...a personal possession *and* a name. So, we're going to try and bind the spirit from doing us harm." Amber tore a small slip from the paper and wrote the name of 'Rachel' on it as Edna spoke. Then Amber placed the paper and the locket containing the scrap of cloth into the box and snapped the lid shut, fastening a tiny clasp. "It is our hope that the mirror box will contain the spirit's powers as the glass reflects the artifacts from all sides and traps their images within."

Amber held the box out to Edna who placed her hand upon it. "We bind you Rachel from doing harm in the name of God the Almighty and all that is righteous. Amen." Amber placed the box back on the table.

"Now," the Reverend stood. "I am going to bless the house, from room to room. You may follow, or you may remain here, but I ask if you remain that you clasp hands and create a prayer circle. Sisters Grace and Flossie will stay and lead the prayer. You must stay mindful and concentrate on the power of God's word, no matter what occurs. Our goal is to wear the spirit down. Agreed?"

"I'll stay," Cassie blurted first, followed by Mom, much to my relief, and finally Helen, Edna and Amber.

"I'll stay too." Gretchen stated with a glance toward Roger who only nodded. Then she clasped her shaky hands in her lap and cast her darkly circled eyes to the floor.

"Good," Reverend Pulpit said with approval. "The rest of you can assist me. It is very important that we stay together as we move from room to room. If this spirit is as strong as Ms. Shine believes it to be she may try to separate us. We have to exhibit a united front in combat. As sure as there is ample evil in this world, God has given us ample good to confront it. Is everyone ready to begin?" We nodded, remaining silent and in place as he took two bottles of holy water from his pocket, and three small pen flashlights. He placed them on the table next to the Bible and removed his coat, suit vest and tie, draping them over the back of the sofa. Next he rolled up the sleeves of his white dress shirt and unbuttoned the top button. He handed the Bible to Felicity with a flashlight, and one of the bottles of water to Marjorie, with a flashlight. The other water and penlight he kept in his palm.

Alex reached to grasp my hand. This was it. Our first exorcism. My mouth was dry and I sort of felt like I might throw up.

"Let us pray." The Reverend bowed his head and we all followed suit. "Lord, fill us with the light of your love. Protect each and every good soul in this home tonight." Reverend Pulpit's voice was warm and soothing. I felt a blanket of calm settle over the room. Though he spoke gently, the strength of his faith was unmistakable. There was a power in his words and his manner that could not be denied. My hopes of success grew with his every breath. "Bless Roger and Gretchen. Give us the might to rid this dwelling of evil, Lord. Deliver us from harm as we do your bidding and enforce your law of heavenly peace. Oh God, enfold us in your love and protection. In the name of your son, Jesus Christ, we pray. Amen."

'Amen' echoed around the room.

"Let's get started." Reverend Pulpit said firmly, and headed purposefully through the archway to the foyer.

I could hear Grace directing everyone who stayed behind to move the furniture into a circle as Flossie lit white candles on the coffee table in the center of the circle. Alex, Roger, Prudence and I collected behind Marjorie and

Felicity. The Reverend turned to face us. "Is there an attic?" Roger nodded. "I'd like to start upstairs and work my way down." Roger pointed up the stairs and we flipped on lights as we went. We could hear the prayers begin in the sitting room as our own troop headed to the second floor where Roger indicated a folding stairway in the ceiling outside of the bedroom Helen was staying in.

Though it was obvious he was in great pain, Roger was determined to climb the steps first, in spite of his throbbing ankle. He was taking his position of man of the house seriously, and the fact that Powell blood ran in his veins, and his veins alone, he likely felt responsible for the entire situation. He wanted to ensure the exorcism was a success and since his entire future relied upon it, no one argued with him.

Alex held the crutches as Roger painstakingly mounted the wood ladder. The Reverend patiently allowed him a fair head start then began to follow up the stairs. "You can wait here for now," he said to his parishioners and the rest of us. A soft yellow light suddenly streamed down from the attic as Roger pulled a cord. "This won't take long. Sister Felicity, please begin where we agreed." He turned and climbed until his shiny dress shoes disappeared into the opening at the top of the stairs.

Felicity nodded and flipped to a page marked in the Bible. She began to read scripture and Marjorie joined in, their voices gaining momentum. I heard the Reverend join in from upstairs and the floors creaked above us as he performed his task, which I knew would entail drawing a cross of holy water on each window pane and doorway as he blessed the home.

Before long Roger and Reverend Pulpit were descending and we began a slow procession from bedroom and bathroom, to bedroom and bathroom. We were praying and chanting all the way, sometimes such simple verses that Pru, Alex and I were able to join in by heart. Petey sat wide eyed but quietly in his little kennel in my bedroom, as if he understood the seriousness of what we were doing.

When we descended and reached the foyer again we turned left and started toward the back of the house. Those in the sitting room were singing a hymn. Our group headed out onto the screened in porch, then into the yard, blessing the back door, reentering and heading toward the kitchen, and then through the butler's pantry to Roger and Gretchen's private rooms. It was there that I first noticed that tightness around my throat and some disturbance began. As Reverend Pulpit crossed from window to window I felt something brush my leg and thought I saw a scrap of tan fluff run out into the hall. Everyone else was intent on the blessings. "Did you see that?" I whispered to Alex and Pru.

"See what?" Pru asked.

"I think that cat was in here."

Alex looked around and shrugged. "I didn't see anything," he whispered and chimed in when Marjorie and Felicity began the Lord's Prayer. As each of us began to pray the familiar words the overhead light of Gretchen and Roger's bedroom began to flicker. Several of our voices wavered but the Reverend raised the volume of his and rolled his hand in our direction, encouraging us to continue.

The adjoining bathroom door slammed shut, then opened, then slammed shut again. Alex and Reverend Pulpit shoved against it with their shoulders until they had forced it open. Roger and Alex stayed by the door to ensure it stayed that way as the Reverend climbed into the tub to draw a cross on the little stained glass window panes above. Marjorie had her own vial of holy water and was finishing the bedroom windows as Felicity selected another scripture. Suddenly all of the window shades that had just been pulled down after the blessing snapped up and fluttered violently.

We huddled closer and squeezed through the bedroom door back out into the hall, the lights still flickering behind us, the bedroom door slamming with finality as soon as the last of us left the room. In the hall the foyer ahead was dark but the lamp on the check-in counter under the stairs seemed to throb brighter than ever before. When the bulb burst Prudence and I shrieked, but the ladies of the church never broke stride.

"Continue! Continue! Lord Jesus, hear our prayers!" Reverend Pulpit beseeched from the interior of the corridor restroom, where he made the sign of the cross over the door jamb. In the shadows of the darkened hall I thought I saw the form of a nun round the corner in the foyer to scurry up the stairs. I froze and Alex nudged me on.

"Did you just see her?" I inquired, blinking rapidly.

"Shhh," Prudence hissed as Reverend Pulpit directed us into the dining room from the doors closest to the kitchen and then on toward the nook with the winding stairs that led to the old servant's quarters.

Incredulously I brought up the rear of the crowd, Alex dragging me by my cold hand as the keys of the old piano tinkled and the chandelier swayed. When the lights in the dining room and the tight staircase went out we all stopped, waiting for Marjorie, Felicity and the Reverend to switch on their tiny, but powerful penlights. Ascension was slow as the staircase was tight and Roger was losing steam in the lead. My own foot was throbbing painfully and I could only imagine what his ankle must feel like. Occasionally we stalled, jammed together in the cramped space so Roger could catch his breath or adjust his crutches on the steps;

however, Reverend Pulpit never ceased his prayers. They flowed so naturally from his lips that I was sure he never seemed to repeat the same mantra as he called for God's mercy and healing light.

Everyone was sweating by the time we reached the little room at the top. In the darkness of the storage area I held the Reverend's penlight while Prudence and Alex helped move boxes so he could get over to the single window. Roger's face was drawn and he leaned heavily on his crutches, but his words were strong as he prayed along.

Did no one see the bed in the corner, and the old woman sitting up on the sagging mattress, huddled beneath the covers, watching us? She wore a white sleeping cap and her eyes were sunken in the dark sockets of her withered face. She appeared as surprised and frightened to see us as I was to see her. I rubbed my forehead and pinched the bridge of my nose as the image dissolved before my very eyes, bed and all. I tugged at the sleeve of Pru's black sweater. "Did you see…?" my voice trailed off as she looked questioningly at me…perhaps a little annoyed at my constant interruptions. "Never mind," I whispered and swallowed hard, the lump tightening my throat growing ever larger.

We filed from the room and I struggled now to stay in the middle of the pack, casting a look back at the empty corner of the room before it fell into complete blackness behind us. The descent was also slow.

In the dining room, the piano had stilled, but the chandelier still swung and began to blink off and on. We could hear everyone singing from the other room and joined in. When the front door in the foyer started to open and slam on its own everyone raised their voices over the din, everyone but me that is. In my panic I barely found the air to squeak a word. They died in my throat completely as a fat balding man in a stained nightshirt approached everyone in our group one by one. He was exasperated when no one in front of me acknowledged him, and started whining like a child and stomping his feet, which were encased in black socks. His big toe stuck out of a hole in the right one and his yellowed toenail looked sharp enough to commit a murder. The man's legs were bare and mottled with red sores. I felt myself grow ill and shrank back against the wall as he caught my eye and walked right through Alex to get to me.

"I was told I would have pudding with every meal! Sister Amelia told me I could have some pudding!" His eyes blazed and he pressed his bulbous nose close to mine. The veins stood out on his sweaty head as he screamed in my face. "I want my pudding!"

I felt like my heart was going to stop and stared dumbly at him, silently willing him to go away. Finally, in a frenzy, he turned and stomped right through the side of the piano, and then through Marjorie, who seemed to shiver but continued walking. With a single angry glare back at me, he trudged through the middle of the dining room table and exited via the wall by the window, shouting for Amelia, the nun, the entire way.

"Al? My God, you're shaking like a leaf." Alex pulled me close and guided us around the long table behind the rest of the group who headed through the archway into the foyer. I leaned heavily against Alex, almost pushing him into the wall to avoid the shadow of a body hanging from the dining room archway. Then, mindlessly I broke free of my boyfriend's comfort when I heard poor Petey yowling upstairs. What must he be seeing? Reverend Pulpit had to pull me away from the staircase as I instinctively headed that way. He shook his head at me and gestured toward the sitting room, which was the last of the ground floor rooms to be blessed before we proceeded outside to access the cellar.

In the upper corner of the foyer near the sitting room archway a collection of children of all ages perched on an invisible ledge by the ceiling. They were watching us curiously, their chubby, bare feet dangling. They giggled and whispered behind their hands to one another when they realized I could see them. When I pointed dumbly upward one waved to me. Alex glanced heavenward and, seeing nothing, lowered my arm to hold my trembling hand again.

The folks in the parlor looked up but did not cease their prayers as Reverend Pulpit and Marjorie advanced toward the windows. We all joined the circle and a chair was pulled up for Roger who practically collapsed into it. My mouth gaped at the sight of Lillian Powell, as I had seen her in the portrait at the museum, leaning against the fireplace behind Edna, her arms crossed, a small smile on her face. Edna seemed to be staring right at me as if she could easily see everything with her pale, sightless eyes. She turned and exchanged a knowing glance with Lillian before looking intently back at me. This was crazy. I blinked and shook my head, clutching Alex's hand tighter as Lillian faded away and the rest of room seemed to become blurry.

A familiar prayer began again and Reverend Pulpit became more fervent in his pleadings with Jesus and the Father above as Flossie, Marjorie, Grace and Felicity interjected 'Amen' accordingly. He had climbed onto the couch and was pulling back the curtains to draw a cross of holy water on the front windows.

Suddenly, the little mirror box rose into the air from the coffee table top. It lifted slowly and hung, suspended for a moment, catching everyone's attention before it spun about and crashed back down onto the table. The lid popped open and the locket and slip of paper slid out in a pile of shattered glass. Well, so much for that concept. That's when all hell broke loose.

Chapter 29

When the mirror box broke the atmosphere of the entire room changed. Earlier I thought my vision was blurring, but soon I realized that a frigid mist actually seemed to be seeping from out of the fireplace, crawling over the hearth to lick around the furniture and legs of the group before drifting up to form a cloud near the ceiling. From their reactions I knew that everyone not only saw what I could, but heard it as well. The familiar yowling of the big tan cat resounded from the four corners of the room though the creature could not be seen.

Our chanting quickened and Reverend Pulpit took the Bible from Felicity, thumbing rapidly through it for more ammunition against the demon that surrounded and hovered above us. The door in the foyer slammed madly, open and closed, the penlights blinked out one by one as their batteries drained, and the candles flickered until they extinguished. It was dark inside and out.

The iridescent mist stretched and twisted above us. Occasionally, a long finger of it would dwindle down, nearly touching one of us on the head, before being reabsorbed into the rest of the matter. Thunder and lightening cracked and blazed and a violent burst of rain hit the windows. Grace and Flossie began a rousing chorus of a well-known hymn and we all followed their lead as Reverend Pulpit stood upon the sofa clutching the Bible to his chest and shaking his fist at the gathering vapor. He began to recite scripture by heart in the darkness as he cast holy water toward the ceiling.

Gradually, a bright blue light began to emanate from the core of the wisp above us and when the Reverend shouted the name of Rachel for the first time the yowling of the cat became the eerie scream of a woman. Gretchen fainted on the floor and though Roger, Helen and my mother knelt next to her, they never stopped singing.

Edna's little body drew our attention next. She rose from her chair and her dainty bent form straightened to full height. Her eyes closed, and she stiffened, lifting several inches from the ground. I had never been more horrified. Even my experience in the bathroom and with the scarecrow paled in comparison to what I saw happening to Edna. Cassie and I shot each other a terrified glance that intensified when we realized Amber was starting to panic as her aunt levitated even higher. Obviously, this was something new.

Reverend Pulpit jumped from the couch and stood before Edna whose pleasant face was now a demonic sneer. He splashed her with holy water and her head snapped to and fro as she growled and writhed in mid air.

"In the name of Christ and our heavenly Father...I drive you out of this body and out of this home!" Edna's form started to convulse with laughter and she spat in his face. He merely wiped her spittle from his cheek and continued praying and splashing her form. I wondered how Edna's frail body could survive this intense possession. Amber stood helplessly by, praying and wringing her hands.

"We will not fail! We will not fail!" Reverend Pulpit bellowed and Edna suddenly wilted before him. The Reverend and Amber caught her and lowered her into the chair. She seemed disoriented momentarily, and then her lips began to move slightly as she joined in the singing and praying again.

The blue mist brightened and collected into a violet orb that abruptly shot from the room, through the foyer, and out the front door, which was being held open by unseen hands. We pursued, some quicker than others, with Reverend Pulpit in the lead.

The light was shooting around in the branches of the great oak tree in front of the house like a comet, jumping and twisting. The Reverend and the ladies from the church rushed out into the rain, followed by me and Alex. Everyone else hovered under the overhang of the porch, although I spied Roger trying to hobble down a step or two. Helen appeared to have remained in the house, I assumed with Gretchen who was probably still unconscious.

The wind was tornadic and the rain drops blew with such force that they stung the skin.

"Demon! Show yourself!" Reverend Pulpit bellowed.

The orb froze high in the leaves then bounced down from branch to branch to spin around the tree trunk, growing longer with each rotation until it resembled the form of a human. It hovered and glowed beneath the lowest, strongest branches, pulsing with energy.

"I call on the power of Jesus Christ to banish this specter named Rachel. Deliver this home and these people from this spirit called Rachel who can no longer control this property or its owners."

Each time Reverend Pulpit said the spirit's name it became a little clearer, changing from violet blue to deep purple until I could clearly see a woman take shape. It was the woman in the mirror, dressed in a long, heavy dress, deep red marks visible around her neck. A phantom noose, which was attached to the branch above, was looped beneath her chin. The vision of a ghostly horse slowly developed as well, frothing and stamping between her legs. Rachel's face was twisted in fury, but then she smiled beguilingly as she raised an arm to beckon Roger who tripped and fell backwards on the stairs, his crutches clattering down the steps into the mud.

Thunder cracked and a deafening shriek issued from the demon's gaping mouth. The Reverend was relentless, stepping closer, flinging holy water in her direction, in spite of the blowing rain. When he ran out of his water Marjorie thrust her bottle into his hand.

The form known as Rachel looked me square in the eye and I felt the tightness in my neck become unbearable. Part of me felt sadness for her, for when she was not shrieking you could now see that she had once been a beautiful woman. I wondered what had driven her to such evil and ugliness as I reflexively reached to see if I could physically remove any restrictions from my throat. I tugged at my sweatshirt collar and started to gag as the specter laughed hysterically.

Rachel smiled seductively, evilly, and beckoned again to Roger who remained down on the rain-slicken steps in shock. Alex slipped in the mud trying to get to him and I looked back to see Helen helping Gretchen through the front door.

"Come." I heard a soft, tempting whisper demand, blending with the howling wind. "Come, Powell. Come to me." Roger heard it too and was horrified, clambering backwards like a crab to fully join the others under the overhang of the house.

"Leave us alone!" Roger yelled. "You're not welcome here!"

Reverend Pulpit was becoming hoarse but still he shouted at Rachel to leave. It was then that I noticed the other bodies in the yard, dozens and dozens of them. I glanced at Alex but he seemed oblivious, mesmerized by Rachel's flickering shape. The Reverend, Flossie and the other ladies were intent upon their incantations. The veil that Edna had referred to was definitely raised and my little gift of sensitivity had sharpened tonight. I wiped the rain drops from my eyes and glasses and spun in a circle, not knowing how to feel.

Ghosts stood all around, from every era. Too many of them to count. Men, women and children. Nuns and settlers. Indians, soldiers and hospice patients. Some appeared healthy, but others appeared in the condition of their passing.

The handsome man next to me had a blackened bullet hole in the center of his forehead. A docile looking woman clung to his elbow with one hand and gripped a smoking pistol with her other.

Reverend Pulpit was oblivious to the couple near him but I saw them clearly. Both were covered in blood, he was missing an arm, his head holding on by a thread of flesh; while she clutched a hatchet.

Next, I assumed I spied the famed Blanche in the crowd; a pretty blonde in clothing about right for her time. She sported a noose that appeared to have been woven from bathrobe belts around her mottled neck; her arm was wrapped around a dark, crispy form that had once been her Jack, no doubt, before she set him aflame.

It seemed that each soul who had ever trod on the grounds had appeared and no one but me, and assuredly Edna, could see them. Right now the ghosts were all focused on Rachel's purple light.

When Rachel noticed the other phantoms she started shrieking obscenities. I pressed my hands against my ears as the spirits began to advance forward. The specter of the horse disappeared and Rachel clutched at the rope around her neck. Now she dangled, sneering and growling at the ghastly crowd who began to chant her name. The closer they edged the louder she became. Soon she was convulsing and spitting curses from her swollen face as the noose tightened.

When the first of the ring of spirits reached her a single man advanced. He was large and burly, his skull caved in on one side. He began to pull and tear at her figure and then the rest of the apparitions followed suit. Rachel began to spin by her neck, slowly, then faster…like a whirling dervish, as if she were trying to ward them off.

"She's weakening!" I heard Edna cry over the thunder and lightening, over the praying and chanting.

I glanced back through the throngs of spirits pushing past me from the house toward the tree. When lightening lit up the sky I glimpsed a familiar face on the porch next to my mother. The image of my father beamed back at me and placed a protective hand on her shoulder. She appeared calm, unaware of his presence as she watched the display of light that we now knew as Rachel spin on the tree branch; however, I noticed Mom tilted her head ever so slightly in his direction when he touched her, as if she could sense something there.

I was mesmerized, beyond numb, but forced to tear my eyes away when a deafening crash sounded behind me. Another bolt of lightening split the mighty oak tree in two. Alex hit me hard and we went down in the muddy yard. Half of the tree fell where I had been standing, the other half smashed into the side of Prudence's nearby car.

From the ground I watched Rachel split into thousands of fragments of light that ricocheted into the darkness of the sky. When she had completely disappeared, the other spirits seemed to burst like bubbles, one by one, vanishing with satisfaction as their part in banishing Rachel was complete.

The abrupt thunderstorm ceased, almost instantaneously. As I noted the immediate change in the atmosphere I looked toward my mother and was disappointed to find her standing alone. My father was gone.

Everyone looked from one to the other in disbelief and then a cheer went up all around. It was unquestionable, Rachel was gone. In less than two hours, the evil that had plagued the Powell's for centuries had been defeated.

Roger and Gretchen hung heavily onto Reverend Pulpit hugging him in relief, as Flossie, Marjorie, Grace and Felicity joined hands, and continued to praise God.

Chapter 30

Saturday - One Week Later

By ten a.m. the following Saturday I was on my second pot of coffee. Gretchen's wedding had gone off without a hitch the prior Sunday. After the cleansing of the house it was as if a black cloud had been lifted from the entire property and all was well.

We had been home since Monday evening and it had been a crazy week. The state sheriff's banquet was that night and we had to leave by three to set up. This was one of our biggest events ever, a guarantee of over four hundred people, and a round of thunderstorms had put the electricity out at the Delectable Dish mid-week. They were still working on restoring power to most of that end of town, so the base of operation had been moved to my home kitchen Thursday afternoon.

Not being in our usual surroundings, and, short our best food processor, which I broke when I dropped it on my *good* foot the night before, things were running a bit behind. My face was healing nicely, which was great for business, except between both my injured feet I walked like a drunken penguin.

Personally, I had been up since four a.m., woken by a hysterical phone call from the local sheriffs' secretary. She needed to add some menu items, report a shrimp allergy, and increase the count of canapés and crudités. Apparently, a group of officials had determined they could make it at the last minute and a couple of speakers had been added to the list. I called Cass and she was over by six a.m. We were nursing blisters by eight o'clock from frantically chopping and dicing by hand. Exhausted, but hopeful that everything else would soon fall into place, we barely had time for a breather when Alex came to help out.

Food, in various stages of preparation, was strewn on every open surface in the farmhouse kitchen. Bleary eyed, and still in my pajama pants and a coffee stained t-shirt, I had my hair pulled back into a sloppy pony tail. I was on one side of our kitchen island wrapping what was literally my thousandth little tiny sausage, in little tiny bits of pastry dough, while waiting on the ham to come out of the oven. Petey snoozed under the table behind Alex, who was on the other side of the island counter, carefully arranging the three tiered cake onto its plastic columns to see how it would look. Cassie planned to ice it and box it up while I ran my Mom to a last minute doctor's appointment.

Mom seemed rested up physically, but the stress of the last weekend had taken a noticeable toll on her mentally and she really needed an evaluation. Thank God her specialist had Saturday morning hours and was able to squeeze her in, at least to see the nurse practitioner and get some lab work started.

At the moment I was pretty upset because Mom had waltzed into the kitchen earlier and announced she was ready to go. Unfortunately, she was lacking one crucial element of attire…her slacks. Luckily Alex had not yet arrived. Poor

Mom would have been mortified. I just felt really, really tired and depressed.

The front doorbell rang and Cassie took off to answer it as Alex stood back to survey his work. The cake was nicely assembled. "I really think I'm getting the hang of this cooking stuff," he smiled.

"Yep, you're my favorite helper." I humored him. Sometimes it wasn't just the help that I appreciated about Alex. He also gave me something nice to look at while I did my own work. Tipping the coffee carafe over my cup, only a single drop came out. Damn. Oh well, I needed to throw some clothes on and get out of here anyway.

Cassie huffed back into the kitchen carrying a good sized box. From the sheen of sweat dotting her upper lip I noted that it must be heavy.

"What in the world is that?"

"I don't know," Cassie wheezed, trying to catch her breath while fishing scissors out of the junk drawer. "But it weighs a ton. Here, you open it."

"I need to get changed," I protested.

"It's addressed to Petey," Alex observed curiously. "And there's no return address."

That captured my attention. "Petey?" I wrinkled my brow and glanced at him. He was still under the table, but at the sound of his name he stretched his corkscrewed butt into the air and opened one buggy eye and yawned carelessly. "Do you have a secret admirer, Petey? Hmmm?" I hacked through an abundance of tape and lifted the lid. The box was full of foam peanuts and a large manila envelope rested on top of them. I pushed aside a couple of my sausage pans so they wouldn't get packing materials on them, and handed Cassie the envelope. She started to open it while I scooped some peanuts into the upturned lid, unearthing the contents of the box. My hands touched the top of something gray and hard, and then, simultaneously, Cassie and I moaned. "Oh my God! Look!"

I lifted the concrete squirrel from Spring Valley out of the box as Cassie shoved a photo under my nose. There was Gretchen, serene and lovely in her wedding gown; stress from the prior weeks erased from her beaming face. All of the onlookers at her small wedding smiling from either side of the red carpet rolled across the backyard lawn to form an aisle as she headed toward the camera, and ultimately, her happy bridegroom, Roger.

"Awwww..." It was so sweet. "Awwww...No!"

"Let me see! Let me see!" Alex leaned anxiously over the island counter as Cass and I stared in horror at the sight in the background of Gretchen's photo. Was it a purple specter? No. The frightening caramel cat? No. Worse yet. It was Petey, atop the cement squirrel just beyond the lacy train of Gretchen's beautiful gown, his mouth frothy, and tongue lolling, eyes about to pop from his head with exertion. Cassie swapped the top photograph for the one beneath it which was another 8 x 10, this time of Gretchen and Roger exchanging their rings, Petey was unconscious in the landscaping.

"I thought you put him up!" I shouted at Alex.

"Cass said she was gonna do it!"

"I was *in* the wedding!" Cassie shrieked. "Why would I be watching the dog?"

"They can edit him out, can't they?"

We were all shouting and pointing fingers when the inner screen door of the kitchen slammed open and closed with a "thwack!" An enormous bird flew into the room and perched on the top of a parted cupboard door. Incredulous, it took me a moment before I realized it was Betty Jane, and there stood Aunt Rose beyond Cassie and Alex. Rose didn't bother to close the heavy outer door and the morning sunlight pouring through the screen silhouetted her. She sported purple spandex exercise pants, beneath an oversized bright red hooded sweatshirt with a Christmas tree drawn in green glitter on the front. Her hair was monumental, and a cigarette clung to her dry bottom lip. Her arms hung at her sides and she dropped a suitcase from each bejeweled hand. Thud. Thud. We had stopped bickering and stared at her in shock.

Rose slowly raised a hand, drew a long puff on her cigarette and contorted her wrinkled face, blowing the smoke toward the ceiling. One ring…two rings…her gaze was serious and angry. I shook my head and suppressed a sudden urge to slap myself, hard, across the face. This day was not shaping up well.

"I've left Barney." She announced gravelly, with the intensity of a war proclamation.

"Aunt Rose? What?"

"I said, I've left Barney." She emitted a croupy cough.

"Left Barney!" Betty Jane echoed and paced atop the cabinet door.

"But…but, Aunt Rose…it's *your* trailer."

"It's a long story." About that time Rose's cell phone rang a zippy little rap beat. She put the cigarette back in her mouth and retrieved the phone from the pouch of her sweatshirt. "There's the little bastard now." Flipping open the phone, she marched her hot pink walking shoes toward the back door. "Something's burning," Rose croaked over her shoulder. Thwack! went the screen.

"Huh?" was all I could manage before Cassie started screaming.

"The ham!" Cassie opened the oven door and smoke rolled out. "The aluminum pan has split!" The oven sizzled and hissed. Little flames began to roll beneath the bottom rack where the grease and juices pooled.

As Alex sprang into action; this was his specialty after all, Betty Jane leapt from the cabinet to make a low pass across the room. Petey, wide awake from all the screaming, spied the bird, let out a determined snort and, considering his size and the fact that he had no wings, took a pretty fantastic leap from the under the table. Unfortunately, he missed Betty Jane completely and crashed face first into the side of the island counter, where he slid to the floor in a heap. To avoid the dog, Betty Jane swooped up and hit the cake, knocking layers every which way. Plastic columns bounced onto the floor.

Stunned, I watched Alex run back to catch one of the layers, and grapple for another, as Betty Jane perched upon his head and took an enormous crap on his shoulder. He froze in horror and dropped everything he had just managed to salvage.

I was stupefied. Mortified. Go ahead…think of another 'fied'. I dare you. That one would surely describe me as well. I took a mental inventory of the madness surrounding me. This was my life. Ghosts. Crazy relatives. I had just survived the week from hell…quite literally. Now, in less than five minutes my kitchen had become an insane asylum. I could not catch a break.

Through the smoky room and out the little window over the sink I glimpsed the top of Aunt Rose's hair swaying in the breeze as one entity. She stalked angrily outside. I was exhausted. My head throbbed, my feet throbbed, my eyes and blisters burned. I was encircled by trays of hundreds of tiny weenies, due for the oven that my best friend was filling with fire extinguisher foam. I had a business to run and hundreds of people to feed in approximately six hours. This morning I had to remind my mother to put on her pants. My dog was unconscious on the floor, while his concrete squirrel lover leered upon him from the counter, right next to photos of Gretchen. Dear, sweet Gretchen, blissfully unaware of the indecency occurring just beyond the train of her lovely wedding dress. Puppy porn immortalized in her photo album for eternity.

And last, but not least, in all his glory, stood my boyfriend, hotter than hell with a goofy, crooked grin on his handsome face. He clutched clumps of cake in his meaty fists, while Betty Jane walked in little circles on his head, kneading his hair with her big, ugly bird feet. Doody ran down the front of his t-shirt and dotted the floor.

What a disaster! Suddenly the sadness and stupidity of it all came crashing down upon me, and logically, my only option was to have a complete meltdown.

"And you date *me* because…?" I threw my hands in the air and burst into tears. I wasn't even sure Alex could hear me over the creative string of obscenities spewing out of Cassie. She was wrestling the foamy, charred ham over to the kitchen sink.

Alex just rolled his gorgeous, puppy dog eyes as if I had said the craziest thing he had heard (or seen) all morning. "Oh Al, honey," his face grew grave and I braced myself for one of his profound declarations of deep, true love, perhaps as heartfelt as the one in the hospital parking lot the week before. "I date *you* because I don't want to miss what happens next."

"Good gravy!"

The End

About the Author

Susan Ronayne is an ardent reader, writer and student of psychology. Susan has two grown children and she and her husband live in rural Kansas. Susan's fascination with the supernatural developed as a result of childhood paranormal experiences. Susan also takes great interest in tales of hauntings reported to surround historical events and places. These personal interests were the inspiration for *Marche's Madness*.

For more information about the author, or to sneak a peek at the next Al Marche adventure, please visit our website at **www.bullybookspublishing.com**.

Ordering Information

If you enjoyed this novel and would like to purchase additional signed copies, please access our website at:

www.bullybookspublishing.com

Signed copies of this novel can also be requested via regular mail. Send your request, with check or money order payment of $12.95 + $2.50 shipping and handling (total of $15.45 per book) to:

Bully Books
P.O. Box 195
Paola, KS 66071